"In this book, the authors delve deep into the affective vibrancies and forces of digital life. As they show, feelings are the foundation of many online interactions and content. Feelings are aroused with and through the internet and compel us to want to stay engaged online - to upload, like, comment, share and post photos, videos, emojis, GIFs and memes. This book provides important insights into these processes."

Prof. Deborah Lupton, author of *Data Selves:*
***More-than-Human Perspectives* (Polity) and**
***Digital Food Cultures* (Routledge)**

"From affective atmospheres to woebots, from artificial intelligence to the emojification of the everyday, Darren Ellis and Ian Tucker pursue how bodies, collective and individual, are continually shifting in conjunction with technological and digital processes. Always empirically situated, Ellis and Tucker's nuanced psycho-social approach to affect and emotion reveals possibilities for critical intervention into our contemporary moment, while simultaneously opening pathways for future-oriented analyses to undertake."

Prof. Gregory J. Seigworth, co-editor of *The*
***Affect Theory Reader* (Duke University Press,**
2010) and co-editor of *Capacious: Journal for*
Emerging Affect Inquiry

Emotion in the Digital Age

Emotion in the Digital Age examines how emotion is understood, researched and experienced in relation to practices of digitisation and datafication said to constitute a *digital age*. The overarching concern of the book is with how emotion operates in, through, and with digital technologies. The digital landscape is vast, and as such, the authors focus on four key areas of digital practice: artificial intelligence, social media, mental health, and surveillance. Interrogating each area shows how emotion is commodified, symbolised, shared, and experienced, and as such, operates in multiple dimensions. This includes tracing the emotional impact of early mass media (e.g. cinema) through to efforts to programme AI agents with skills in emotional communication (e.g. mental health chatbots). This timely study offers theoretical, empirical and practical insight regarding the ways that digitisation is changing knowledge and experience of emotion and affective life. Crucially, this involves both the multiple versions of digital technologies designed to engage with emotion (e.g. *emotional-AI*) through to the broader emotional impact of living in digitally saturated environments. The authors argue that this constitutes a psycho-social way of being in which digital technologies and emotion operate as key dimensions of the ways we simultaneously relate to ourselves as individual subjects and to others as part of collectives. As such, *Emotion in the Digital Age* will prove important reading for students and researchers in emotion studies, psychology, science and technology studies, sociology, and related fields.

Darren Ellis is Senior Lecturer in the Department of Social Sciences at the University of East London, UK, and co-author of *Social Psychology of Emotion*.

Ian Tucker is Professor in the School of Psychology at the University of East London, UK, and co-author of *Social Psychology of Emotion*.

Routledge Studies in Science, Technology and Society

For the full list of books in the series: https://www.routledge.com/Routledge-Studies-in-Science-Technology-and-Society/book-series/SE0054

Emotion in the Digital Age

Technologies, Data and Psychosocial Life

Darren Ellis and Ian Tucker

LONDON AND NEW YORK

First published 2021
by Routledge
2 Park Square, Milton Park, Abingdon, Oxon OX14 4RN

and by Routledge
605 Third Avenue, New York, NY 10017

First issued in paperback 2022

Routledge is an imprint of the Taylor & Francis Group, an informa business

© 2021 Darren Ellis and Ian Tucker

The right of Darren Ellis and Ian Tucker to be identified as authors of this work has been asserted by him/her/them in accordance with sections 77 and 78 of the Copyright, Designs and Patents Act 1988.

Publisher's Note
The publisher has gone to great lengths to ensure the quality of this reprint but points out that some imperfections in the original copies may be apparent.

British Library Cataloguing-in-Publication Data
A catalogue record for this book is available from the British Library

Library of Congress Cataloging-in-Publication Data
A catalog record has been requested for this book

ISBN 13: 978-0-367-54009-8 (pbk)
ISBN 13: 978-1-138-09103-0 (hbk)
ISBN 13: 978-1-315-10832-2 (ebk)

DOI: 10.4324/9781315108322

Typeset in Times New Roman
by Deanta Global Publishing Services, Chennai, India

In memory of David Tucker. Ian X

Contents

Acknowledgements

This book follows from our previous Social Psychology of Emotion (2015) book, which finished with a realisation of the growing influence of digital and data practices on our emotional and affective lives. We would like to thank Routledge for including this book in their Studies in Science, Technology and Society Series (particular thanks to Neil Jordan and Alice Salt).

We would like to acknowledge the funding provided to support research discussed in the book, including the "Social Media and Austerity" projects funded by EPSRC Communities and Culture Network and discussed in Chapter Five. The University of East London (UEL) also partly funded the empirical work on a project entitled "Experiences of Social Media" in Chapter Four. Additionally, the work in Chapter Six was supported by UEL School of Psychology funding.

The ideas developed in this book have emerged through many hugely valuable conversations and discussions with colleagues and friends. We would like to thank them all, as they have been invaluable to the completion of this book. In particular, we would like to thank Steve Brown, John Cromby, Lewis Goodings, Dave Harper, Ava Kanyeredzi, Anna Lavis, Laura McGrath, Paula Reavey, Tony Sampson, Buadaplup Sánchez-Escribano, Paul Stenner, and Angie Voela. We owe you all a drink (or two).

Last, but not least, we thank our families: Nicola, Katherine, Noah, Lily, Isaac, Otto, and Arthur.

1 Emotion in the digital age

Why emotion, why digital?

Digitised emotion almost seems contradictory. Can emotion be simulated through digits? The cold binary codes of zeros and ones may appear in tune to the logic of cognition in the mind, but can they emulate the emotional affairs of the heart? Claims that emotional activity can be captured, identified, recognised, and potentially simulated digitally have become increasingly prevalent (Fry, 2019; McStay, 2016; 2018). Additionally, not only are we imbuing digital technologies with emotion, but technologies are emotionally engaging us, as digitality has exponentially increased. Throughout this book, we plot some of the ways these relationships are forming. To these ends, the book draws together relevant philosophies, theories, and models of emotion to detail some of the ways that processes categorised as emotion are being mobilised by digital technologies. We start with processual, relational, and psychosocial approaches to think about the emergence of emotion and affective life through relations between bodies, collectives and technologies. Our approach is necessarily selective given the reach of digitality into all areas of life. We focus of four areas of significance to the study of emotion in a digital age: Emotion-related artificial intelligence, social media, digital mental health, and surveillance.

Discussion of the impacts of digital technologies often focuses on their technical capabilities rather than the underlying social and psychological processes. Moreover, it is often what this means for future life that is discussed; a portrayal of a future digital life acts as the meaning framework for considering digital technologies in the present. Digital technologies are often judged in terms of their potential, from providing more tailored shopping experience through behavioural economics to more automated work environments. However, analysing life in a digital age through the concept of emotion allows for more breadth and depth of digital activity to be explored, which allows for a sense of psychological life to feature. This is important because 1) The *human* is often used as a category to critique digitality – with the latter deemed to be some kind of threat to and/or enhancement of the former; 2) where digital activity is related to human activity, it often includes a definition of a pre-existing individual in mind. Focusing on emotion allows us to draw upon a range of theory, from the social sciences, philosophy, and broader scientific theory and practice, to interrogate the emergence of digital life. Avoiding a reductionist approach that locates emotional activity solely at the level of the physiological is important to draw out the limits and borders of digital life. Our approach is to address emotion as encompassing and transcending psychological, social, and physiological categories. Moreover, it is not something to be set against other categories of psychological life, which has often been the case historically – such as the distinction between emotion and rationality, or, more recently, emotion and cognition (England, 2019). Such categories are not bounded distinct entities, but rather, can be thought of as co-constituting elements of psychological life. Emotions are rarely felt in isolation from beliefs, memories, perceptions, attitudes, etc. Indeed, our whole psychological life is infused with emotion, which is inherently related to social and historical context, both individually and collectively.

The scope of this book is broad, and we will not succeed in covering all areas pertaining to emotion in a digital age. The saturation of our social worlds with digital technologies means that there are very few areas of everyday life that are not, or cannot, be mediated by technology. There are the emotional relationships we develop with personal technologies, such as mobile phones, computers, and fitness trackers. There are the emotional relations made possible by the internet, which include new forms of communication (e.g., online forums), as well as new practices that can elicit emotional responses (e.g., becoming frustrated with online tailored advertising). There is the breed of new technologies that claim to be able to identify, label, and potentially manipulate emotion. Technological advances have made it possible to process facial expressions and capture physiological responses, leading to claims that such activity brings emotion into the reach of the digital. Finally, although not exhaustively, there is the development of robots and virtual agents that are designed to interact emotionally. Each one of these areas is worthy of a book in itself. Our analysis is selective, focusing on areas we argue are key issues for life in a digital age, namely emotion-related artificial intelligence, social media, digital mental health, and surveillance. We will see that these areas intersect, and as such, are not discrete domains, but rather, operate as prominent arenas in which emotion is at stake in relation to digitisation and datafication.

A word on terminology

The terms emotion and affect are often presented together and used inter-changeably. Sometimes, this is acknowledged, with a reason provided (or not!). Part of the issue is how to articulate their use without providing a clear definition of each. In this book, we aim to use the terms as they are deployed by those we discuss. Where this is not possible, we will state so. In the sections in which we discuss the emotional and/or affective implications of a digital technology (e.g., when it is not explicitly designed to relate to emotion/affect, but we claim it does), we will provide a definition. We fully acknowledge existing theory that frames affect in terms of processes that impact upon individual and social life in ways that are presented as non-cognitive and/or non-conscious, for instance, in psychoanalysis, critical media studies, and philosophy. Many of these feature in the field of affect studies that has emerged strongly in the last 15–20 years (Ahmed, 2004; Ash, 2015; Clough, 2007; Gregg & Seigworth, 2009; Leys, 2017; Thrift, 2008). There is also prominent use of affect in relation to affective neuroscience, which emphasises neurological activity, for example, in relation to mood disorders (e.g., depression and anxiety) as well as a broader set of psychological activity (Davidson et al., 2002; Panksepp, 2010; Stein, 2003). The prominence of neurological activity in such accounts means that questions of cognition and/or consciousness do not commonly feature.

Whilst affect has featured in approaches that emphasise non-cognitive and non-conscious approaches (Wetherell, 2012), emotion has often been used in accounts that emphasise the importance of culture and language in the development of meaningful experiences that can be categorised in emotional terms (e.g., fear, love, and anger) (Harré, 1986). Emotional categories have been thought of as being culturally-specific references used when discussing and representing our feelings, for instance, the use of emojis as visual representations of feeling. The term *emotion* has more cultural currency than *affect,* as well as being core to mainstream psychological models. Such models have garnered increased prominence through their central role in the development of computerised attempts to capture and categorise physiological expressions as different kinds of emotion, for instance, the widespread use of universalist models of a basic set of emotions in artificial intelligence- (AI) based technologies (e.g., facial expression recognition).

This book considers emotion and affect as core concepts to understand life in a digital age. They form part of the overall psycho-social operation of experience, not just discrete psychological forms operating psycho-biologically "within" people. Throughout the book, we argue that there is more at stake, emotionally, than is often considered. For instance, emotion is not just operating at the level of facial expression but is a more fundamental part of how we orient to ourselves and our environments. Emotion and affect are important parts of the ways we experience the world, both in relation to ourselves as individuals and to others. As our lives increasingly operate in and through digital practices, and processes of datafication therein, the dimensions of emotion and affect through which we engage and feel our ways through the world are mediated by digital and data practices. Emotion and affect are implicated in terms of the relations we have with digital and data practices, as well as being a core design aim of the technology (e.g., affective computing). This requires an expanded analytic unit, which goes beyond focusing on the impact of the functional aim of emotion-related technologies.

We recognise the lack of a universally agreed definition for either emotion or affect. We also note important attempts to frame processes associated with emotion and affect through other concepts, such as *feeling,* e.g. Cromby (2015). However, we are reluctant to rely on an alternative concept to describe the psychological and social processes associated with existing concepts of emotion and affect. Creating an additional concept is likely to create as many problems as solutions and can end up subject to the same accusations of essentialising as theories of emotion and affect. As such, we follow the tradition of using both terms. In places, we will use *affective life* as a generic term (e.g., when not discussing specific emotional and/or affective activity) (Greco & Stenner, 2008; Despret, 2004). We will not follow other non-essentialist attempts in terms of only using affect (as a way of avoiding the reductionist baggage of mainstream psychological theory), as much of what we discuss concerns major psychological models. We also do not want to exclude the value of emphasising the role of cultural practices in the formation and maintenance of emotion categories (i.e., the impact of language and meaning in definitions of emotion). The scope is broad, but one which we hope draws sufficient and valuable attention to developing theoretical and empirical understandings of emotion and affective processes in a digital age.

Computation and emotion

The advent of computation catalysed much thinking about the potential for technologies to intersect with psychological processes. In the first fifty years of computation, this mostly focused on intelligence and then more discrete categories of cognition (Wilson, 2010). This is primarily due to the dominance of the information processing model of psychology that emerged in line with increased computation in the mid-20th century. Mainstream psychology claimed that minds work like computers, processing sensory information to form thoughts, perceptions, and memories (Varela, Thompson, & Rosch, 1991). Cognitive psychology has modelled emotion, but not to the same extent as the so-called "mental processes" of intelligence, perception, attention, and language processing. These were deemed more readily explainable in computational terms and fit into the historical prioritisation of rationalist thought over emotional feeling (Ellis & Tucker, 2015). This is not to suggest that emotion has never featured in computer science, as early attempts used a therapeutic context as the basis for exploring the potential for technologies to mimic human communication. For instance, Weizenbaum's Eliza programme used natural language processing to recreate a patient-doctor consultation (Weizenbaum, 1984). To Weizenbaum's surprise, the computer science field came to suggest that Eliza could create emotional responses of support for users. Whether this was by design or not, the programme has been influential in the growing field of digital mental health (which we will discuss in more detail in Chapter Five). The emergence of a designated field of "Affective Computing" has become one of the most prominent areas focused on emotion and technology (Calvo et al., 2015; Picard, 2000). Heavily influenced by psychological theory regarding universal emotional expression, multiple emotion recognition experiments have emerged since the mid-1980s and continue apace. Affective computing is concerned with emotion as expressed at an individual physiological level and the potential for digital technologies to identify and categorise such activity. Such work is deemed to have significant potential to inform industry practices, such as in commerce, as well as governments, in terms of national security (Bullington, 2005). Large scale generation of data from individuals has led to concerns regarding control and use of data. In recent years, data generation about emotional and affective life has increased significantly, in a variety of sectors, from advertising to health sectors (McStay, 2018). Emotion-related technologies have been studied mainly in the physical sciences (e.g., computer sciences), which have focused on the technical advances being made. A social scientific analysis is important for two reasons; 1) to evaluate how emotion theories are used in, and by, the physical sciences in relation to new technological attempts to define and manipulate emotion; and 2) to highlight some of the broader social and psychological implications of living in societies in which digital technologies are increasingly powerful social agents.

Life at the intersection of emotion, affect, and digitisation

Why call the present *a digital age*? Firstly, it is important to note that throughout the book we often use the term *a digital* age, despite the book's title being *Emotion in the Digital* Age. These are similar terms, but we are keen to avoid essentialising the current time as *the* defining digital epoch, as there may well be others in the future that take new directions and consequently present new challenges. As such, we often use *a digital age*, in addition to the title's *the digital age* (which was the publisher's preference). In terms of the aims of the book, we use the term *digital age* in the sense of most contemporary uses, namely to acknowledge the ubiquity of computing technologies in almost all aspects of human life. We are not, though, focusing on *digital forms* of emotion, which would be to enter long-standing philosophical debates about whether machines can be programmed to feel (although this question does arise in places in the book). Emotion has been thought of as constituting analogic processing, whereas digitality implies a more binary system of *positive* or *negative, on* or *off, one* or *two*. The analogue includes *and* rather than just *or, yellow-blue-red-green* rather than just *black* and *white*, and every other *colour* and *shade* possible. The underpinning binary logic of digitality relates to the operation of neurons, in that they are either on or off and they either fire a charge or do not. The nervous system has been argued as being more stochastic (probabilistic) and analogue than many computer simulations would have us believe. For example, Wilson (2010) documents how McCulloch and Pitts (1943) understood a neuron's threshold for activation as alterable. The threshold which dictates firing is more analogue than digital, as it "varies across a spectrum of possible values and will be altered by chemical variables (ionic concentrations) and electrical variables (after potentials) that are also continuous rather than discrete" (Wilson, 2010, p. 125). While emotional and affective processes can be framed as analogic, they are often thought of as existing on dimensions representing, for example, arousal (amount of) and valence (type of). It is this contradiction between the digital life of computers and the analogical life of emotion and affect which has captivated imaginations of science fiction writers for millennia.

We have previously articulated a narrative of the important factors pertaining to social psychology and emotion (Ellis & Tucker, 2015). This ended with a brief discussion of "digital emotion", by which we considered how studies of

emotion and affect may have to change in relation to the proliferation of digital technologies in societies (rather than framing a *digital version* of emotion).
The current book picks up where *Social Psychology of Emotion* left off. Our
approach is *broad* in the sense that it generally avoids speaking about specific
emotional categories in relation to digital life, for instance, concepts such as
love, fear, disinterest, concern, shame. These commonly understood categories
are important and valuable (e.g., the work on shame of Eve Sedgwick and Adam
Frank (2003), but ours is a broader concern with emotional and affective life in
a digital age. This is not to deny existing studies of specific emotion categories,
but this does not mean that such processes innately relate to such categories
and therefore, can only be understood according to the parameters of existing categories. For instance, an experience named as fear can co-exist with (or
transform into) one relating to excitement. We do not ascribe to a view that an
emotion (e.g., fear) exists in the form of a potentialised pattern of physiological
and psychological activity that is *triggered* by life events. Significant critiques
exist of the universality of emotional categories (some of which we will discuss
in Chapter Two).

The rapidly increasing technological interest in emotion is operating as a (re)
newed scientific claim as to emotional and affective life. This is not solely about
researching emotion, but about the ways that new technologies are claiming to
intervene with and inform emotion. A *technological expertise* is being claimed,
based on the idea that technologies are now able to unpick some of the secrets
of emotional understanding in ways not possible before and in ways out of the
reach of human perception (e.g., interpreting micro-facial expressions). The role
of industry and commerce is significant in these moves, and the imperative for
university-based research to produce "impact" beyond the academy often means
pushing at an open door when developing industry-academic partnerships for
technological research with emotion. Given that many of the technologies we
discuss are new, there is limited research to date as to their emotional and affective impact. Therefore, in certain chapters, our coverage will be on the claims of
new emotion-related technologies, what model of emotion they propagate (which
we will think of in terms of *version*), and their potential impact. In other areas, we
draw on original research to highlight emotion-related technologies in action and/
or to analyse people's *experiences* with digitality. The scope of the book includes
emotion-related digital technologies AND emotional and affective impact of mass
digitisation of everyday life. The latter includes digital technologies more broadly
(e.g., social media) and not only those designed specifically with emotion in mind
(e.g., so-called *emotional AI*). The limited focus on *specific* emotion categories
may come as a disappointment to readers interested in particular parts of digital
life and emotion, e.g. the politics of hate often argued to be facilitated by public
social media such as Twitter (Ott, 2017). Our approach will demonstrate how
key areas of digital life are impacting upon, and intersecting with, emotional and
affective life beyond the boundaries of individual categories. This is not to suggest
that attention to specific categories is unimportant, but that the remit of this book
requires a broader approach.

Overview of emotion in a digital age

Chapter Two introduces the philosophical orientations pertaining to emotion and affective life that shape our thinking throughout the book. Although the relationships between human bodies and technology have exponentially increased, researching the psychological impacts of mass technologization of society are not new. We trace some key events in the history of emotion and technology to demonstrate that concerns about technology have been both a research tool in relation to emotion as well as the focus of psychological research since the earliest days of the discipline. Theories of emotion have attempted to address both aspects, with a dominance of individualistic, largely psychophysiological, models featuring in psychological research, and approaches addressing emotion and affect as more social and distributed processes featuring predominantly in studies of the impact of technologies on affective life. Both have increased in line with the rise in use and presence of digital media in society (Ellis & Tucker, 2015). Chapter Two provides some historical context to emotion-technology research, prior to discussing claims as to the inherent relationality of emotion and technology. We will draw on Vinciane Despret's *version*, a concept used to frame a practice-based analysis of emotion, emphasising context as opposed to universality; theories that have been inspired by Gilles Deleuze and Felix Guattari on *affect;* and Gilbert Simondon's work on *individuation* and *affectivity*. Moreover, Chapter Two details our approach which incorporates processual, relational, and psychosocial theories to think about emotion and affective life through collectivities, bodies, and technologies. The value of concepts emphasising process and relationality is that they shift the analytic starting point away from established taken-for-granted forms (e.g., universal emotional categories) to a concern with *emergence of* individual forms as part of broader sets of relations that are always *in the making*.

Chapter Three explores the development of technologies using forms of artificial intelligence (AI) to try to track, identify, interpret, replicate, and potentially manipulate emotion activity (much of which has been developed in *affective computing*). AI has been associated with emotion across media, the military, the state, private industries, and academia. The affective computing market is predicted to reach $90 billion by 2024 and is now constituted by a range of areas. These include (but are not exhausted by) capturing emotion through facial expression, bodily expression, speech, text, physiological data such as skin conductance and heart rate, and senses such as touch. Chapter Three details the underlying models of emotion that are drawn upon within the affective computing field. It starts by looking at Manfred Clynes's theory of essentic forms, which suggests that emotion-based expressions are traceable through parts of the body, such as the finger, and are universal across cultures. Clynes's theory, alongside Charles Darwin and Paul Ekman, put forward notions of the universality of emotion (basic emotions). These theories have been useful to people who want to develop technologies that can, for example, measure and recognise human emotion, as they offer elegant models of emotion that have been engineered into technologies. We look at some of the ways that they have been modelled through, for example, facial expression recognition systems (such as within the iBorderCtrl technologies) and Affective Tutoring Systems (such as Affective AutoTutor), wherein students' emotions are recognised and manipulated. Our critical analyses include, for example, Lisa Feldman Barret's extensive constructionist-neuroscientific work. We argue that affective computing technologies are some way off from being able to develop something like an *emotion-chip* which Rana el Kaliouby (CEO of Affectiva) suggests will run in the background of numerous technologies, generating a constant emotional pulse. And yet, we do have systems like the iBorderCtrl scheme presently running, that uses facial micro-expression recognition to pre-screen travellers and detect deception. The algorithms programmed into the detection system can generate lasting and negative impact on people's lives, particularly when, for example, algorithms automate discrimination.

Chapter Four looks at some of the entanglements between bodies, emotion, and social media. Throughout this chapter we raise questions such as: What draws us to spend an increasing amount of our lives using social media? Do they enable new forms of emotional and affective expression? How do social media attempt to mobilise and manipulate emotion? What are the broader affective implications of living in environments saturated with social media? And how is emotion modelled and conceptualised in the social media context to facilitate research and capitalise it? We explore these questions through focusing on key areas pertaining to social media in relation to emotion and affective life: Motivation and theories of desire, personal information, emoticons and emojis, and sentiment analysis, considered alongside notions of digital and affective capitalism. Understanding emotion related to social media is a nascent but blooming field of study. Research seeking to understand emotional engagement with social media has largely been based in theories of motivation that tend to draw on cognitive and behavioural psychological theories. Motives are configured as internal needs that social media have the potential to fulfil, enabling self-actualisation and individuation, for example, through programming sociality. Here, the psychological subject is framed as having a number of internal constructs that are relatively fixed and stable. These models help computer scientists to develop social media platforms that can collect data that represent these internal constructs and to further compartmentalise and categorise in order to fit them into data-sets and algorithms, which can be manipulated and commodified. This chapter also examines a variety of sentiment analysis initiatives that have been developed in attempts to capture affective life online through, for example, collecting personal information, emoticons, and emojis. Again, it is argued that these are modelled on impoverished versions of emotion.

Chapter Five looks at the field of mental health and how it is becoming increasingly digitally mediated. A broad range of digital developments in mental health services has been proposed, from providing advice and guidance to people suffering with various mental health difficulties, through to creating digital versions of established treatments and therapeutic interventions (e.g., Cognitive Behavioural Therapy [CBT]). The App Industry has seen considerable potential in direct marketing digital aids to common mental health difficulties such as stress, depression, and anxiety. Indeed, Apple's App Store and Google's Play Store each has tens of thousands of mental health-related apps on offer. There is also an appetite for machine learning and big data analytics to gather previously unattainable large-scale data sets, which can be used to design digital tools using artificial intelligence to interact with, and offer support to, individuals experiencing mental ill-health. Mental health care in a digital age is consequently claimed to look very different to previous services, which were location based (e.g., institutions, community) and which utilised specific forms of treatment (e.g., medication, psychological therapies). Digital forms of support are not tied to specific locations, and do not always use specific interventions. They can be temporally and spatially ready to hand, and consequently, not so reliant on real-time access to mental health services. As such, they have considerable potential to intersect with individuals' ongoing emotional experiences, both in relation to their underlying distress, as well as positive feelings that forms of support are designed to deliver to help with the management of mental ill-health. In Chapter Five we look at two apps that have been designed to help people manage mental health issues. The first is a peer support forum, *Elefriends*, designed and run by the UK mental health charity. The second is a totally automated app that does not include any real-time human intervention, called Woebot.

Chapter Six focuses on emotional responses and potential impacts of *digital surveillance,* which refers to the capture, storage and use of data through everyday interactions with technologies. This includes practices not explicitly targeting emotion (e.g., the capture of social media data). Studies of surveillance have tended to focus on the technical and operational capacities of technologies such as CCTV, as well as those whose primary purpose is not explicitly surveillance, for instance, understanding the quantity and quality of data captured by *big tech* companies, along with their use of data. Critical theory has claimed that new digital technologies have facilitated the commodification of information (Thrift, 2008) and that we are increasingly living in *societies of information.* This work has coalesced into the field of surveillance studies, which has broadened its scope beyond the traditional visual forms of CCTV surveillance to the idea that digital technologies have facilitated new forms of surveillance through the capture, storage, and use of information pertaining to individuals' *private* lives. This ranges from government and organisational data capture (e.g., big tech companies) through to social media facilitating new ways for individuals to watch each other. In this chapter, we focus on affective responses and potential impacts of datafication. Previously, we have looked at experiences of surveillance through the spatial lens of the concept of affective atmospheres (Ellis et al., 2013) and surveillance-apatheia (Ellis, 2019). Chapter Six builds on this body of work by looking at what we term the derivatives of the datafication of the body. This chapter was left until last, as it encompasses many of the themes from the previous chapters. Surveillance practices are increasingly ubiquitous and are a central node that both affects, and in turn, is affected by, emotion. The final chapter offers some concluding thoughts and *next steps* discussion of important considerations for future social scientific understanding of emotion and affective life in a digital age.

References

Ahmed, S. (2004). Affective economies. *Social Text, 22*(2), 117–139.

Ash, J. (2015). Technology and affect: Towards a theory of inorganically organised objects. *Emotion, Space and Society, 14*, 84–90.

Bullington, J. (2005). 'Affective' computing and emotion recognition systems: The future of biometric surveillance? *Proceedings of the 2nd annual conference on information security curriculum development: InfoSecCD, '05*, 95.

Calvo, R. A., D'Mello, S., Gratch, J., & Kappas, A. (Eds.). (2015). *The Oxford handbook of affective computing*. Oxford; New York, NY: Oxford University Press.

Clough, P. (Ed.). (2007). *The affective turn: Theorising the social*. London: Duke University Press.

Cromby, J. (2015). *Feeling bodies: Embodying psychology*. Houndmills; Basingstoke; Hampshire; New York, NY: Palgrave Macmillan.

Davidson, R. J., Pizzagalli, D., Nitschke, J. B., & Putnam, K. (2002). Depression: Perspectives from affective neuroscience. *Annual Review of Psychology, 53*(1), 545–574.

Despret, V. (2004). *Our emotional makeup: Ethnopsychology and selfhood*. New York, NY: Other Press.

Ellis, D. (2019). Techno-securitisation of everyday life and cultures of surveillance-apatheia. *Science as Culture*. Online First.

Ellis, D., & Tucker, I. (2015). *Social psychology of emotion*. London: Sage.

Ellis, D., Tucker, I., & Harper, D. (2013). The affective atmospheres of surveillance. *Theory and Psychology, 23*(6), 716–731.

England, R. (2019). The cognitive/noncognitive debate in emotion theory: A corrective from Spinoza. *Emotion Review, 11*(2), 102–112.

Fry, H. (2019). *Hello world: How to be human in the age of the machine*. New York/London: Norton.

Greco, M., & Stenner, P. (Eds.). (2008). *Emotions: A social science reader*. London: Routledge.

Gregg, M., & Seigworth, G. (Eds.). (2009). *The affect reader*. New York, NY: Duke University Press.

Harre, R. (1986). *The social construction of emotion*. Oxford: Blackwell Publishing.

Leys, R. (2017). *The ascent of affect: Genealogy and critique*. Chicago, IL; London: The University of Chicago Press.

McCulloch, W., & Pitts, W. (1943). A logical calculus of the ideas immanent in nervous activity. *Bulletin of Mathematical Biophysics, 5*(4), 115–133.

McStay, A. (2016). Empathic media and advertising: Industry, policy, legal and citizen perspectives (the case for intimacy). *Big Data and Society, 3*(2).

McStay, Andrew (2018). *Emotional AI: The rise of empathic media*. London: Sage.

Ott, B. L. (2017). The age of Twitter: Donald J. Trump and the politics of debasement. *Critical Studies in Media Communication, 34*(1), 59–68.

Panksepp, J. (2010). Affective neuroscience of the emotional BrainMind: Evolutionary perspectives and implications for understanding depression. *Dialogues in Clinical Neuroscience, 12*(4), 533–545.

Picard, R. W. (2000). *Affective computing* (first paperback edition). Cambridge, MA; London: The MIT Press.

Sedgwick, E. K., & Frank, A. (2003). *Touching feeling: Affect, pedagogy, performativity*. Durham: Duke University Press.

Stein, D. J. (2003). *Cognitive-affective neuroscience of depression and anxiety disorders.* London; New York, NY; Florence, KY: Martin Dunitz; Distributed in the USA by Taylor & Francis.

Thrift, N. (2008). *Non-representational theory: Space, politics, affect.* London: Routledge.

Varela, F. J., Thompson, E., & Rosch, E. (1991). *The embodied mind: Cognitive science and human experience.* Cambridge, MA: MIT Press.

Weizenbaum, J. (1984). *Computer power and human reason: From judgment to calculation.* Harmondsworth, Middlesex, England; New York, NY: Penguin.

Wetherell, M. (2012). *Affect and emotion: A new social science understanding.* Los Angeles, CA; London: SAGE.

Wilson, E. A. (2010). *Affect and artificial intelligence.* Seattle, WA: University of Washington Press.

2 The history and emergence of emotion-technology relations

This chapter will discuss the philosophical orientations pertaining to emotional and affective life that shape our thinking throughout the book. This involves exploring key events in the history of emotion and technology to demonstrate that concerns about the psychological impacts of mass technologisation of society are not new. Technology has been both a research tool in relation to emotion as well as the focus of psychological research since the earliest days of the discipline (Malin, 2014). Theories of emotion have attempted to address both aspects, with a dominance of individualistic, largely psychophysiological models featuring in psychological research and approaches attempting to address emotion and affect as more social and distributed processes featuring in studies of the impact of technologies on affective life. Both have increased in line with the rise in use and presence of digital media in society (Ellis & Tucker, 2015). The aim of this chapter is to provide some historical context to research, prior to discussing claims as to the inherent relationality of emotion and technology.

Early psychological research on emotion and technology

A presenteeism often features in coverage of the impact of digital technologies on everyday life. Significant digital developments in recent times (e.g. smartphones, internet, social media) have been portrayed as a new and previously unheralded manifestation of a powerful role for technologies in contemporary life. Indeed, this is a large part of the motivation for writing this book. However, relations between emotion and technologies have a long history. The context of early technological efforts to capture and intervene in emotional life resonate with many of the current issues surrounding emotion in a digital age. In the late 19th and early 20th centuries, psychology was establishing its scientific credentials through developing new methods of experimentation. This meant a move away from methods that were deemed unscientific, such as introspection and psychoanalysis, towards approaches that focused on collecting more measurable physiological data (Ellis & Tucker, 2015). During the early 20th century, new studies emerged that aimed to capture emotional activity "in real time" (e.g. Dysinger and Ruckmick's cinema studies – discussed below). These form the nascent links between emotion and technology and underpin much work addressing emotion in a digital age (e.g. emotion-related artificial intelligence). The links between emotion and technology did not only feature in terms of technology being a new methodological tool, but also in terms of new psychological studies of the impact of new media on emotion.

During the early 20th century, new media technologies were emerging that were deemed to have significant emotional power, e.g. cinema. The sociological impacts of cinema as a new form of mass media were not understood, and there was much concern about the potential power of the new mass media of cinema to impact emotional life, particularly with regards to children, who were seen as emotionally vulnerable. The Payne-funded cinema studies of Dysinger and Ruckmick (1933) are a prominent example of a new technology emerging with perceived potential to shape emotional life. The concerns about cinema at the time resonate with contemporary concerns about digital media, e.g. widespread coverage of portrayals of social media having negative impacts on young people's mental health (Berryman, Ferguson, & Negy, 2018; Calancie et al., 2017).

Other developments in the early 20th century framed emotion as something that can be recognised and captured by technology and that doing so provided more authentic knowledge than the existing technique of introspection (Malin, 2014). Physiological activity was taken as a direct route to emotional activity, one not clouded by consciousness (as it was deemed to be with introspection). The premise of this work at the time was that technologies can "know" emotion better than humans, because they can identify the specific underpinning physiological activity in a way that escapes human conscious awareness. For instance, we do not know the extent of heart-rate change or skin-conductance activity that occurs when experiencing emotion, but a technology, such as a psycho-galvanometer, does. Understanding emotion was deemed to require a technological solution in terms of identifying and capturing underlying physiological activity.

Malin (2014) makes the point that these moves were part of a technologisation of science and emotion, in which the physicality of the body was privileged as the site at which the truth of emotion could be discovered. All that was needed was the technological means to do so (a position that remains to the present day). This could be taken a step further in terms of thinking of emotion as technological, because it was deemed to be physiologically based. This meant that to control technology was to control emotion, which, at the time, was still seen as unpredictable and unconstrained, as something not subject to psychological control by consciousness (Ellis and Tucker, 2015). The sense of control was based on the idea that technologies could objectively identify and interpret emotion, which other methods (i.e. introspection) were not deemed able to do. In psychology, new technologies, such as psycho-galvanometers and sonoscopes, provided the means to capture physiological activity associated with music and speech. This was welcomed, as it helped buttress the move away from introspection to a newly scientific experimental psychology, in which the "truth" of psychology could be discovered in newly formed laboratories. Despite introspection being prominent in the early experimental research, such as in the Leipzig laboratory of Willhelm Wundt, the concern with relying on self-reporting in introspection shifted the privileged location of psychological insight from consciousness to physiology, and it was technologies that facilitated this move. The argument was that introspection "failed" because it did not provide people with understanding of their physiology, whereby technology did.

The privileging of physiological data in terms of emotion continues to dominate much emotion-related technology activity, as we will see throughout this book, but the idea that 21st-century digital technologies are the first to intersect with emotion is misleading. Emotion has always been thought of in relation to technologies of the time, given that the latter are core agents in constructing our social and physical worlds. The nature of technologies changes over time, and therefore, so does the specificity of the arguments made. Indeed, the cultural context shapes understanding of technologies, which becomes a resource for how we frame our own experience in relation to technology: "[P]eople experience media technology within a particular context for understanding technology itself" (Malin, 2014, p. 238). As Ian Hacking (1999) pointed out, there is a feedback loop in terms of cultural knowledge and individual experience, in which part of the experience of technology comes from awareness of the cultural knowledge of technology's role in society, for instance, contemporary debates about excessive internet use and addiction leading to people asking themselves if they are becoming addicted (Monacis et al., 2017; Karaiskos et al., 2010). This is why Malin argues that we need to be concerned with the "systems of emotional dispositions" (2014, p. 248) that surround living in technologically-mediated worlds. To focus only on physiology is to miss the active role of cultural knowledge in the emergence of emotional experience. Physiology does not operate in a vacuum.

Psychophysiological approaches have been a prominent part of the history of the psychology of emotion. As psychology was taking shape as an experimental discipline, the observable nature of much psychophysiological data was a keen attraction. The preceding work in laboratories such as Wundt's had also attempted to develop experimental evidence of emotion, but its method of introspection and more complex theory of emotion did not so readily fit a scientific approach in the same way the psychophysiology of "emotional expression" research did. This led to a *selective* model and understanding of the psychology of emotion to develop throughout the 20th century – which had its roots in Darwin's (1965) work on emotional expression – and was developed through the facial expression work of Ekman during the middle half of the century (Ekman, Sorenson, & Friesen, 1969; Ekman & Friesen, 1971; Ekman et al., 1987). The pre-20th century work attempting to articulate the multiple psychological processes associated with emotion was gradually lost from mainstream research. This included work exploring what distinctions exist between different emotion-related terms and associated experiences, e.g. affect, passion, sentiment, will, and feeling. Subjecting any or all of these to experimental scrutiny was difficult (Ruckmick, 1936), and the desire for observable data for experimental studies meant models based on facial or bodily expressions came to the fore. To some extent, this has not changed to this day, e.g. use of AI-technologies such as face and body recognition technologies.

The early psychological studies of emotion were attempting to empirically describe something of emotional experience. It was widely held that awareness of what emotional experience felt like existed, due to everyone having such experiences, but developing a definition which can be operationalised was far more difficult (Ruckmick, 1936). The methods and technologies of the experimental studies used came to help shape the definitions and understandings that emerged. For instance, the desire for observable data led to studies and models based on various bodily expressions to predominate. The more nuanced studies of Wundt, in which he tried to operationalise studies providing insight into subjective emotional experience in all its *thickness*, gradually fell by the wayside, as expression-based studies surged ahead. This did not entirely eradicate the problem of a lack of a unified definition of emotion upon which to develop studies. Indeed, there was not even a unified terminology to draw upon, with multiple terms used.

Digital *versions* of emotion

The lack of an agreed upon universal definition of emotion persists to this day (Greco & Stenner, 2008). This has led some scholars to not think of emotions as defined aetiological entities, but to consider the individual, social and cultural practices through which knowledge (and subsequently experiences) of emotions emerge. Such a move is premised on the argument that we do not assume a discrete set of emotions existing outside of the practices through which they come to be expressed and understood (Ellis & Tucker, 2015). While everyone *knows* emotion in terms of their own feelings and experiences, knowledge and understanding of emotion are produced through practices that involve discourses, technologies, and bodies intersecting. The philosopher of science, Vinciane Despret (2004), points to this as a paradox. Bodies have intimate knowledge of emotion, and yet, academically, we exist with multiple ideas and forms of knowledge of what emotion is and how it operates. The question then becomes, how have existing theories and categories come to be; what are/were the theoretical and empirical conditions that *translated* research data into established models, and what are the implications of said models? Despret offers the concept of *version* to frame a practice-based analysis of emotion, which focuses on context dependency rather than universality. Despret acknowledges the diversity of understandings and models of emotion and explores how different versions have emerged, e.g. through the scientific endeavours of psychology. Despret uses the term *version* as a way of keeping *open* to analysis the multiplicity of theories and models of emotion; *version* "always relates back to multiplicity and keeps the existence of other versions in mind" (p. 23). Despret's approach does not prioritise one version over others. Indeed, it relies on the other versions, as they become knowledge-variants of emotion that any given version is known in relation to, e.g. basic emotion models can be critiqued with sociological accounts.

Despret was concerned with the psychologisation of emotion through experimental research during the second half of the 20th century. How did emotion come to be configured and translated in psychological laboratories in such a way to produce findings that led to specific psychological categories of emotion? Moreover, how do these fit into the broader suite of emotional theories in the social sciences and philosophy? Despret acknowledges the prominence of psychology as the scientific discipline of emotion, and as such, the primary power in terms of cultural and academic knowledge of emotion (which, for centuries beforehand, had been the remit of philosophy). For example, the social psychological experiments conducted by Richard Lazarus. By introducing multiple variables in his experiment, Lazarus introduces several *social* elements, in the form of culturally-defined values, that frame the social situations that shape the responses of participants. Despret discusses Lazarus's experiment involving participants viewing a film depicting an Australian Aboriginal circumcision ceremony. The experiment involved three groups, each viewing the film with a different commentary; one explaining the surgical procedure in detail ("traumatic" commentary); one emphasising how the ceremony is seen as a "joyful" experience; and the final one without commentary. Lazarus claims that the emotional intensity of the experiment was highest for those hearing the "traumatic" commentary. This led to Lazarus claiming that participants' (cognitive) evaluation of an event plays a significant role in emotional events. The point Despret makes is that evaluations in the experimental setting are shaped by participants' social and cultural experience (e.g. values and beliefs). Evaluations are not made in isolation but relate to a set of wider considerations and encultured experiences. As such, the evaluations made by participants in Lazarus's experiment are, in effect, social ones, and inform as much to the importance of culture to emotion as they do cognition. To understand them, one needs to understand the participants' psychological and social experience.

For Despret, emotion comes to signal something about the relationship an individual has with the world. The focus becomes on the nature of these relationships, e.g. whether emotion indicates "agreement or disagreement with the world" (2004, p. 178). In this view, the function of emotion is to inform and provide insight regarding an individuals' relationship with their social and cultural environments. This *socialising* of emotion was the translation of emotion enacted by the social psychology experiments of Lazarus. This is a *relational* theory in terms of a psychological version of emotion seen as intrinsically linked to the social environment. These are not theoretically framed as *separate* entities, but as existing on a continuum – as *connected*. Emotion is accordingly considered as the manifestation of processes that involve psychological AND social dimensions. Social psychology not only translated emotion into *social* events in the experimental setting, but as subsequently having a social life in the form of becoming categories by which people come to interpret their own experiences. Models emerging from experimental settings come to be ways for people to understand themselves. Despret extends this point by analysing William James's theory of emotion – a founding theory of psychology. In "suggesting another way of reading our emotions, James induces a new experience of them, that is to say, a new experience with emotion and, from that moment on, a new emotional experience with the world, another way of affecting oneself and of letting oneself be affected" (Despret, 2004, p. 203). What kind of "new experiences" of our emotions are made possible in a digital age?

Despret's concept of version renders emotion as cultural products. This provides a historical context to emotion categories, with certain emotions in the past no longer *existing*, e.g. melancholia was a common emotional disposition during the medieval period, but largely disappeared in 20th-century psychiatric terminology – to be replaced by *depression*. This is not a form of relativism, in terms of arguing that the experiences categorised as melancholia no longer exist, but rather, a different system of knowledge exists to which they are subject. Another example of this temporal contingency is the fact that the word *emotion* did not exist until the 19th century (Dixon, 2003), preceded by a terminology of the *passions*. Emotions become cultural products that contribute to the constitution of the historical period of the time and operate in relational processes between bodies and cultural practices of knowledge production (e.g. psychological experience). A consequence of this is that "emotions disappear when they no longer have a world in which to grow, while others are transformed when the world changes" (Despret, 2004, p. 187). The current book is one attempt to track the *transformation* of emotion as the world changes through mass digitisation. What does digitisation do to emotion? Which existing models of emotion are brought to the fore by digital research and practice? Are new emotion categories emerging due to digitisation of life? These will come to be the forms of emotional knowledge that feed into individual embodied knowledge and become the ways people come to interpret their own emotional experiences.

Version is a form of critique grounded in practice that does not result in judging different models against each other in terms of arguing which is *best*, but a way of keeping all as part of the reflective practice of understanding the range of emotional knowledge that exists. In an area as broad as emotion and affect, we think this is a valuable move, and it is one we aim to use as a directive throughout the book. This openness to analysis is useful for tracking emotion in a digital age, given the scope of the area, i.e. the spread of *the digital* into most areas of life. Throughout this book, we aim to remain "open" to the multiplicity of theories of emotion across the physical and social sciences, philosophy, science and technology studies, and cultural studies.

An additional contribution of thinking in terms of *versions* is the acknowledgement of the *enacting* of emotions in situation-specific ways. It does not suggest that different versions relate to the taking of multiple perspectives (e.g. psychological, sociological, biological) on a single emotional form. This would be a nod to multi-disciplinarity, but one underpinned by a reification of emotion. Instead, *versions* theoretically attend to emotion as enacted by the knowledge practices that claim to explain them. Despret captures this perfectly when stating "[v]ersion makes the world exist in a possible manner" (2004, p. 31). The development of theories based on bodily expressions of emotion is a key example of this, for instance, the (re)newed focus on psychophysiology shoring up psychological models under threat of seeming out of date (e.g. those which rely heavily on Ekman's Basic Emotion Model). A formal distinction between the practices we focus on and the knowledges we develop about them emerges, which has implications for notions of authenticity that are important in theories of emotion. For instance, attempts to develop forms of "artificial emotion" based on machine learning rely heavily on a claim to authenticity through machine readable physiological activity. Technologies are imbued with the capacity to bypass "inauthentic" consciousness *of* emotion by providing direct recognition of emotion expressed physiologically. Thinking in terms of a range of socio-material practices enacting multiple *versions* of emotion troubles this, as it does not rely on a notion of authenticity, which itself requires the possibility of being inauthentic to position itself against. This is an important move, as notions of authenticity are often important pillars of technological uses of emotion. They also threaten to simplify the knowledge produced, as they reduce the density of lived experience to a layer of psychophysiological expression. For instance, even if we were to accept the view that an emotion, such as anger, can be universally recognised, this does not mean that it is experienced in a universal way. Recognition can inform as to what emotion is present, but it does not explain how or why it emerges in each situation. An approach is needed that can speak to recognition, experience, and context dependency.

In the chapters that follow, we analyse different *versions* of emotion at work in the areas of artificial intelligence, social media, digital mental health, and surveillance. In relation to existing theory and literature, analysing emotion and affect in a digital age means covering the range of emotion models that underpin technological attempts to capture, read, and mimic emotion (e.g. AI), as well as the broader emotional implications of living in societies with greater digital presence. The chapters will adopt a similar structure. First, each chapter details the theory of emotion that is being recruited to underpin the technological development (e.g. emotion-related AI, social media). Then, we analyse what is enhanced, disrupted, and developed in terms of emotion by the technology, and finally, we describe the emotional implications of "living with" the technology. Emotion is at stake in multiple ways in relation to digital technologies, and it is important to articulate the multiplicities that emerge. We are not focused on defining a unified emotion, but rather on tracking and revealing the relational stakes at play in the emergence and operation of emotion in a digital age. In doing this, we are leaning towards approaches whose unit of analysis extends beyond the individual body (be it in relation to physiology, neurology, or cognition). One of the motivations for writing this book is the belief that emotion and affect are central to understanding life in a digital age, beyond their presence in specific body-technology relations. Part of developing understanding is about focusing on technologies not just in terms of their functional design, but also the broader impact of their use, e.g. how people feel when they realise that they are subject to covert face-recognition. This is about considering emotion and affect as agents of functionality in terms of the relations we have with our bodies and those of others that underpin psychological and social life. The aim of the current book is to gain insight into how such processes are being altered and (re)configured in and through the mediating practices of digital technologies.

Affective living with digital technologies

The approach of Despret encourages us to think of technologies not just as tools with which to discover emotional facts, but as agents that come to co-constitute social and psychological life. This shifts attention away from thinking about WHAT emotion is in a digital age to think about HOW different versions are enacted in relations between human bodies and technologies. This book aims to analyse emotion in relation to technologies, such as machine reading of bodily expressions and sentiment analysis, through to a broader analysis of the affective implications of living in environments subject to greater use of emotion-related technologies. The relational approach developed looks at what kinds of practices are enacted by new technologies. We are not only focused on understanding the models and theories of emotion that underpin new emotion-related technologies, but also the emotional impact of living in social worlds subject to their greater use. This involves extending the unit of emotional analysis to incorporate the social, relational, and cultural layers of emotional activity. Emotion is not only the result of physiological pressures, but also flows through relationships across life (e.g. personal, professional) and comes to shape the relations we have with the material objects with which we live (Miller, 2008). This aligns with social scientific thinking of emotion operating not just at a cognitive and/or psycho-physiological level, but also as a wider relational force that can shape bodies from *outside* (Brown et al., 2019; Tucker, 2006). This includes classic literature, such as Hochschild's (2012) sociology of emotions, to theories emerging from social psychology, human geography, and cultural studies. No single unified concept of "relational emotion" or affect exists. One attempt to capture the range of existing theory led Gregg & Seigworth (2009) to offer eight strands of affect theory, which they front up as being "by no means fully comprehensive" (p. 8). For Stenner (2017), there are three main strands: Work in queer studies influenced by Eve Sedgwick; psychoanalytically informed psychosocial theories; and work in cultural studies and critical theory drawing on the writings of Spinoza and Deleuze (e.g. with Massumi (1996) being a key exemplar). Additionally, affect has supplemented existing concepts, highlighting the indeterminacy of forces shaping spaces and environments, e.g. *affective atmospheres* (Ash, 2013; Bille, Bjerregaard, & Sorenson, 2015; Bissell, 2010; Ellis et al., 2013) and *affective assemblages* (Anderson & McFarlane, 2011; Duff, 2014; Marcus & Saka, 2006; Sampson, 2017). Here, the distinction between emotion and affect features, as it has throughout historical accounts, with non-individualistic accounts often developing theories of affect rather than emotion (Ahmed, 2004; Anderson, 2006; Gregg & Seigworth, 2009; Tucker, 2011; 2013).

It is the third strand that has catalysed theories of affect as grounded in embodied experience without reducing it to a set of internal processes. This has been particularly prominent in critical social psychology, human geography, and cultural studies (Ellis & Tucker, 2015). The attraction of Spinoza's thinking, both in its original form and as articulated through a Deleuzian lens, centres on his argument that bodies should not be understood in a vacuum, but only *as* the relations with other objects through which they come to be. Spinoza's affect is immediately non-reductionist and in essence, a *social* account of the operation of bodies. To understand the powers and capacities of an individual body, one needs to extend the unit of analysis to map the other bodies interacted with. For Spinoza, relations operate as the movement of power, rendering one body in a relation more powerful and one less. To understand a body, one needs to understand the extent of its capacity to act, namely what it can "do" and how this is determined through relations with other bodies. This immediately takes effect *outside* of the body, which differs from Bergson's (1988) concept of affectivity as the unique way we know our bodies from *within*, rather than from *without*, as per other bodies. Deleuze used Spinoza's concept of affect as a jumping off point for his own writings on affect as the motions of a body-in-process, operating through multiple connections with other human and non-human bodies, potentialised for new relations to emerge, and not driven by an internal set of functions whose properties remain consistent over time and space. Moreover, relations are not discretely located, but extend across the porous boundaries that are commonly taken to define individual bodies (e.g. the skin). Affect is used to name the movement of forces *through* the body and, by consequence, is not adequately understood by traditional notions of interiority and exteriority (i.e. affect is not thought to be contained within the body). A topological analysis develops, as the movement of affect is not dependent on a geometric sense of scale and space, but a more fluid, malleable spatial understanding of relationality. For instance, one can feel *closer* to a friend on the other side of the world, when interacting via social media, than to a stranger we sit next to on a bus. Distance and proximity are not primary in a topological sense of affect.

The relational thinking that underpins Deleuzian-influenced theories of affect means not just focusing on processes at work inside the body, be it the feelings of psychophysiological activity and/or their associated cognitions, but rather, to think of emotion as one part of a broader system of affect that is not dependent on the notion of an individual body to explain it. Instead, it brings in the wider array of objects and subjects that constitute our social worlds, including discourses, spaces, technologies, and their intersectionality. No single *object* is rendered primary or analysable in a vacuum. Accordingly, to understand an individual, one needs to analyse the system (or space) of relations through which it takes life. Relations emerge, not individual beings and objects. Analysis needs to attend to the ways that relations emerge and come to be, not their finished form. What is taken as *the psychological* expands beyond the individual body, as any part of a relation can take psychological form (whether it is internal or external to the body). This attaches potential affective weight to non-human objects and materiality, such as digital technologies. This is not to suggest that technologies have emotional attributes (although, in his later writing, Deleuze, with Guattari, suggested that works of art *have* affect [1994]), but that they are elements and dimensions of relations that originate and propagate emotion. Deleuzian notions of affect have featured in analysis of young people and education (Ringrose, 2011); mental health spaces (McGrath & Reavey, 2015; 2016, Duff, 2011; 2014);

vital memory (Brown & Reavey, 2015); and more. The notions of relational and inter-connected affect align well with the questions regarding emotional life in a digital age. The extent of digital technologies' elicitation, capture, and propaga-tion of data is blurring traditional notions of interiority, exteriority, individuality, and collectivity. For instance, the incessant absorption of data into systems of *big data*, in which a notion of *individual* data disappears.

Existing writing on affect as a relational force in the emergence of emotion and embodied experience has been broad in focus, and as such, has not always directly attended to specific relations between bodies and technology, although examples that have include Hillis, Paasonen, & Petit (2015) on *networked affect* and Coleman (2018) on *structures of feeling*. A specific relational affective con-ceptualisation of the co-operation of bodies and technologies did emerge in the mid-20th century writings of philosopher and psychologist Gilbert Simondon. The lack of English translations of Simondon's work has contributed to its under-representation in the philosophical resources drawn upon in affect studies, criti-cal theory, and the social sciences more generally (Deleuze's work is far more prominent). For Simondon, relationality does not involve highlighting the rela-tions *between* existing individual forms but rather, names the process through which objects and subjects come to exist and operate. Relationality is central to the concept of individuation, which Simondon develops as a move away from a philosophy premised on the idea of a world constituted by the relations between separated *forms* and *substances*. Instead, it is the emergence of individual *forms* as part of systems of relations that take priority. Simondon rails against the phi-losophy of hylomorphism that permeated mid-20th century cybernetics, framing information as the mechanism of communicating a *signal* between sender and receiver. For Simondon, the cybernetic version of information did not inform as to the role of information in the genesis of new relations through which individual objects and subjects come into being. Information is a more powerful agent for Simondon than for the cyberneticists. For Simondon, the key is not to think of information as *substance*, as somehow existing *outside of*, or on the *periphery* of life processes/events, but to think of it as structur*ing*, not a structure itself (Iliadis, 2013). This was a radical departure from the cybernetic thinking of the mid-20th century. Simondon's concept of information is part of his broader philosophy of individuation, in which he departs from the Aristotelian position of distinguishing between *form* and *matter* as distinct properties of substances (hylomorphism). For Simondon, form cannot be separated from matter *within* a substance. For instance, in relation to the human body, Simondon argues that sensation does not exist separately from matter. There is no existing category *outside* of matter where sensation resides, awaiting the form-givingness of matter. Substances as *forms* emerge through processes in which no distinction is present (Iliadis, 2013). Simondon was focused on the emergence of individual forms, but through a phi-losophy that does not rely on identifying a set of inherent properties that underpin the operation of a given form.

Attending to the processes of genesis and formation of human and technologi-cal life is as important now as it was during the early days of computation and cybernetics that influenced Simondon. He is arguably one of the most important thinkers of human-technological life and was a key influence on later thinkers such as Gilles Deleuze and Bernard Stiegler. His is a psycho-social approach (Simondon's approach is typically referred to as a hyphenated 'psycho-social' rather than the non-hyphenated version common in contemporary psychosocial theory), in which psychological and social/collective dimensions are intrinsically linked as co-emergent parts of a singular process of individuation. What he refers to as *psychic* and *collective* are not distinct forms that communicate *through* information, but rather they are *in-formed*; information is the mode of emergence they take. In arguing for an anti-substantialist position, Simondon faced the problem of how to articulate the nature of the psychological individual, the pillar of so much philosophical thought. How to think of psyche and collective without referring to an additional substance that somehow gives them form? To avoid recourse to substantiality, Simondon thinks of psychic-collective individuation as a *continuation* of pre-individuation. This allows him to conceptualise the psychological individual without *separating* it from other dimensions of emergence and sociality. If what he referred to as the *psychic individual* is truly individual, then it is rendered a separate substance to social/collective life. Simondon's answer to this problem was the concept of individuation, with the psychological individual an always-connected dimension of the process of individuation, without developing into a separate substantial being.

In effect, Simondon moves the analytic unit *back* from individual bodies to a preindividual realm of potentialised energy. Its creative potential conceptually requires it to *exceed* the individual (human and non-human forms). The process of individuation operates as a genesis of relationality, which means that an individual being (e.g. a human body) is seen as always-already part of a relational operation and emergence. This means that "psychic life" is not just the *interior* life of the individual (as a substantial form). It is the *interior* part of a set of relations. Psychic reality is not *closed* in a substantialist way but is *open* in a relational form. But what does being *open* mean; what is an individual open to? This is the next consequence of Simondon's anti-substantialism. If the individual body is not substantially different to the *collective*, then this means that it must *carry* something of the collective (preindividual) with it as an ever-present companion in the activity of living. Therefore, Simondon talks of psychic and collective individuation as a *singular* process. Individual bodies are psychic AND collective simultaneously; both are dimensions of a body's existence.

This raises questions for how we understand activity that is traditionally thought to operate *internally*, e.g. personal emotions. If forms are not *given* but operate as relational becomings, it means that what is perceived as individual life cannot be entirely sustained and "resolved" internally. This is because individual beings are not only individual, but also are partially collective. As such, individual bodies operate and exist through ongoing orientations to themselves as individual bodies (psychic individuation) as well as to the collective world (collective individuation). It is these relations that "structure the individual" (Keating, 2019, p. 7). Analysis is ontogenetically at the level of the emergence of relations that come to structure individual bodies. This provides a deep and significant relation between "interiority" and "exteriority", as they become two dimensions of dynamic processes of individuation through which individuals come into being. An individual living being is required to orient to both itself and to its external environment; it has a dual-aspect dynamic being. It is here that Simondon's concept of affectivity works to define the psychological reality of individuation.

Affectivity is the activity of living as a *psycho-social* being facing the ongoing problem of orienting to oneself (interiority) and to the collective (exteriority) simultaneously. Simondon shows us that our individual being is not reducible to ourselves as individuals, because our ongoing being is constituted by individual AND collective dimensions. Indeed, the genesis of our emergence is structured through relations. Affectivity is not about the relations we, as pre-constituted individual bodies, have with our surrounding environments. Individual and environment are not two substantial domains that exist independently and communicate as distinct beings. Affect designates the way social and individual life emerges AS relations (Combes, 2012). It is through affect that Simondon claims that individual being is "divided" (or polarised) through the double orientation to interiority and exteriority. Simondon's theory of affect relates to theories that situate affect as non-conscious, as he states that the division that affect signifies occurs prior to perception, and as such, constitutes a more general relation, akin to Whitehead's (1985) notion of feeling as the core aspect of relationality of all objects and entities. Simondon, though, does offer a specificity with his concept of affect as a core part of the genesis of living beings, which can be psychologised. Affect operates as a vital part of the emergence and operation of individual psychological beings. Crucially, this does not mean psychological life is bounded and distinct from exterior "social" life but rather, is an integrated dimension of processes of individuation.

Consider the following thought experiment regarding relationality:

> You enter a busy train carriage with all the seats taken apart from one. You sit in the vacant seat and start reading a book. Your experience is as an individual in a train carriage with multiple other bodies. There is nothing untoward about your experience. Several stops later your attention is drawn away from the book to the carriage, and you notice that all, bar one person, has disembarked. Your experience of the space of the carriage has changed. The one remaining person is sitting immediately next to you. What felt perfectly normal when you sat down, now feels strange. Being so close to another person in an otherwise empty carriage feels like an enforced intimacy that is disconcerting. You want to get up and move to another seat but are concerned that this will make your feeling of discomfort visible to the other passenger.

In this example, nothing has changed in your position, or that of the remaining passenger. What has changed is the relation with the other passengers. In a full carriage it feels perfectly okay to sit immediately next to another person. In a near empty carriage, it feels strange. The experience is entirely relational and changes despite your body remaining static and unmoved. It is the change in the relations with other passengers that alters your experience. The feeling of that situation is fundamentally relational. Moreover, it is that way for both passengers in this example. You are part of the collective for the remaining passenger, who now also potentially feels awkward at the transformed sense of proximity once the carriage emptied. Each body is simultaneously individual and collective.

Simondon's relational approach distinguishes him from subsequent philosophers of technology. For instance, Stiegler (1998) sees technics as "processes of exteriorisation" (p. 17). This prioritises the human individual through claiming that technologies draw out *interiorised* psychological processes, such as memory (e.g. technology reduce the need for memory, because things can be recorded by technologies rather than relying purely on cognition). For Stiegler, technologies *extend* human processes beyond the flesh and bones of the body to the informational realms of technologies. Simondon does not prioritise the human (psychological) in such a way, as for him, life is always-already human and technological. Emotion operates as the next ontogenetic step, it works "on" preceding affects in the formation of more structured and conscious orientations of the relations of an individual being to itself and its environment. It is a structuring process that situates the individual in a more consciously meaningful way with its environment. Here, the environment is not taken in a general sense but rather, as the immediate and local *milieu* with which the living being individuates. What we think of as a psychological subject "can then be conceived of as the unity of being as an individuated living being, and as a being that represents its actions through the world to itself as an element and as a dimension of the world" (Simondon, 2009, p. 8). Individual bodies come into being as part of relations with elements that constitute the milieu. This is not about the psychological and social as distinct realms, but the milieu as a more expanded unit of analysis that does not reduce the operation and becoming of individual beings to their bodies (human and non-human). The individual is therefore fundamentally about a relation *within* and a relation *without*. These are not sequential but are simultaneous and involve *action*. The individual subject is an agent of its own individuation in terms of intervening in the *problem* of its own existence. Simondon's theory of pre-individuation and affect shift thinking away from constituted living beings towards the stage of their genesis. This involves thinking *prior* to the formation of individual emotional beings.

Individuation and data

The setting of the analytic unit *prior* to the constitution of individuals speaks to the reality of life in a digital age. Bodies and data form new relations of individuality and collectivity. Data generated from and by bodily activity form the bulging databases *as/of* collectivity. There are multiple relationships at work between bodies and digital technologies, from creating new ways of connecting to our pasts, allowing us to follow very closely the day to day activities of family and friends, to becoming aware (or possibly not) about processes of commodification of our personal lives, friendships, and relationships. Core to these processes is data and how to conceptualise the impact of mass generation of data associated with the activity and motion of individual bodies. Attempts to conceptualise *data subjects* are emerging in response to mass datafication. For example, Goriunova (2019) suggests that data are not *representative* of bodies; their content and activity cannot be reduced in entirety to the bodily activity from which they were generated. This notion troubles concepts such as *data traces* and *data doubles* that rely on an established identified self to be traces and doubles *of* (data doubles are discussed in more detail in Chapter Six). If data are not representative, then what are they, and how should (and do) we relate to them? Data can be multiple, as can bodies, which means that two systems or multiplicity co-exist. Data can exist and operate in a range of different systems. Shopping loyalty schemes create data relating to our grocery purchases; travel companies create data about the journeys we take; insurance companies create data about where we live and the type of accommodation we live within; mortgage companies create data about income and marital status; schools create data about parents' place of work and phone numbers; mobile phone companies create data about where we carry and use mobile devices. These are fragments of data that relate to the activities and movement of bodies but are often considered as unifying in relation to an individual living body. In attempting to conceptualise the *digital subject*, Goriunova (2019) draws attention to the inherent complexity of the computational practices underpinning the data ecosystems that feed on the activities of individual bodies. Instead of thinking of a unified singular entity (akin to a data double) "the digital subject is in fact a set of dynamic processes that have the structures of computational actions, models, and socio-political cultures. It is a process in which no exact or stable state is significant or valuable; what matters is the algorithmic interpretation at the moments data can be used, sold, or otherwise acted upon" (p. 132). What matters, for Goriunova, is what has value. This could be commercial value for a retailer in the case of a loyalty shopping scheme, or health and safety value in the case of a school recording parents' place of work and contact details. Moreover, data must work algorithmically. They need to operate in a computational system that has clear objectives. This troubles the idea that the design and operation of data ecosystems relate to the activity and experiences of a unified singular subject. The lived body and data can be thought to operate as distinct, albeit related, systems of reality. Data are not straightforwardly representative of the body. For Goriunova, this creates a *distance* (rather than a relation) that constitutes the digital subject, which is neither a representation nor a discrete subject in the classical sense. This is not a distance created by mass digitisation. It could have been said to exist in pre-digital times that were also subject to attempts to represent the body through media (e.g. letters, telegrams, etc.). Datafication has, though, created a new intensity to the distance between bodies and data. This distance can be thought of as part of a process of individuation, in which data = collective and body = individual. To follow Goriunova, data make new forms of individuation possible (e.g. *digital subjects*).

Data can, consequently, be thought to operate as a realm of (preindividual) potentialised action in terms of enacting current and future individual forms of bodily activity and experience. Moreover, bodies carry part of future collectives, in terms of the continual generation of data that their activity facilitates when interacting with digital technologies. The non-representational *distance* Goriunova discusses can be (re)configured as part of Simondon's dual dimension *individual-collective* system of reality. While Goriunova's argument hinges on a notion of the digital subject, our analysis concentrates on the emotional dynamics of body-technology assemblages that operate non-reductively and non-representationally. For instance, what does the data generated by a face recognition camera tell us about the emotional experience of a body? Does the fact that a smile is expressed reliably indicate happiness? Could the person be masking another emotion for fear of upsetting their interlocutor? Our digital environments have created new forms of individuality and collectivity through the movement of data. Concerns about privacy and the ethics of data capture have emerged in response to the ways that bodies connect to myriad other objects through data. For instance, communicating with a friend through social media feels personal and individual, and yet, in doing so, data is contributing to the social media's (collective) database to be profiled and used for advertising. Individuality cannot operate without collectivity (through data). As such, we can think of data as part of the process of individuation through which individual bodies are continually presented with and which exist as a form of potential tension. Data come to act as part of the *collective* part of the dual-aspect psychic AND collective individuation through which bodies emerge and operate in life. It is this reality that we seek to explore throughout the book.

Simondon offers a valuable contribution at this stage because he spoke about affect as a core part of the process of individuation, incorporating a psychological point of view, as part of the relational and processual becoming of individual body-technology forms. This speaks to core concerns of this book, namely what kind of relational forms are emerging between bodies and digital technologies in our data-rich social worlds and how emotional and affective life are implicated in such processes. This develops the non-determinist and non-essentialist approach we stated as an aim in the introduction. Simondon's concept of affect does not relate to, nor inform, a categorical account of emotion. Nor does it enlighten cultural understandings of the meaning-making through language of emotion categories. What it does do is place affect at the centre of the emergence, operation, and motions of psychosocial life as a body in the world.

Digitally mediated processes of emotion and affect

The psychosocial approach developed throughout the book is premised on the idea of emotional and affective life being subject to specific digital interventions, as well as part of the relational emergence of bodies that are simultaneously individual and collective. The range and extent of interaction with digitisation varies and depends on our place in the world and the spaces and places we inhabit. For instance, the opening of the next chapter highlights the use of face-recognition AI in border control. This is something we have limited control over, should we decide to travel (or be required/forced to). Alternatively, for many people, the digital elements of the relations through which we exist and operate are the everyday technologies of social media and the internet. The potential for interacting with digital activity of some sort is significant. Key to understanding their impact is developing a non-reductionist and non-substantialist approach that does not focus solely on the *digital* as the primary force, nor rely on an essentialist view that digital and human are two pre-existing domains of activity communicating via information. Digital activity is being absorbed into existing practices and relationships (e.g. family message groups) as well as creating new ones (e.g. political arguments on Twitter).

The subsequent chapters are informed by the theoretical discussion in this chapter, to analyse the specific models and approaches to emotion in key areas of digital life. There are, of course, many areas that constitute digital life, and we have chosen a selection we think are important, namely artificial intelligence; social media; digital mental health; and surveillance. Each chapter demonstrates how emotional and affective life is implicated and operates in potentially multiple ways, including the models that underpin each area and their subsequent broader emotional impact on psychological and social life. Key to our approach is understanding that living in digitally mediated environments involves relations that are not static and fixed, but that emerge through processes that are multiplex and contingent. Emotion is not only operating at a psychophysiological level, but also through the objects, texts, and images that constitute our social worlds. Digital networks operate through the generation of data through images, text, and sounds (e.g. emojis, gifs). A mass materialisation of emotion and affect is underway, which, while not completely new, is creating new ways of connecting and interacting with ourselves and others. For instance, specialist apps designed to support people experiencing mental distress are creating new ways of understanding and relating to our bodies. Social media are producing archives in which the present is not forgotten but is available in perpetuity to be scrolled through and accessed. This *stored sociality* is previously only possible through technologies such as photographs and home video recordings. These archives are not just available for individual users, but to be commodified for the commercial interests of the social media providers.

Technologies are not solely tools for human use, but also cultural artefacts. In contemporary social worlds, digital technologies are very much part of the cultural consciousness, with frequent claims as to their impact on the world (e.g. social media and young people's mental health). This has an emotional impact on life as well. Digital activity enacts new processes of individuation, with affect orienting bodies to these new dimensions. Artificial intelligence and machine learning are being designed and deployed in several areas, from retail to national security, with many more promised to come. The rise of social media in the previous 10–15 years has been exponential, with billions of worldwide users undertaking their daily lives in concert with social media platforms. Mental health support is rapidly exploring the potential to develop new digital forms of support, which can be less expensive and more accessible than in-person services. Finally, the scope of data collection and storage that these digital media hold presents numerous opportunities for surveillance, not just in the traditional sense of CCTV, but the monitoring of personal data and information (so-called *data* or *digital* surveillance). These digital technologies are mediating the relations people have with themselves as individual bodies and with the environment around them. Emotion and affect are implicated in the emergence, operation, and anticipatory form motional relations take. Bodies move in concert with a variety of digital technologies designed to monitor and capture data about emotion. While these need analysing in and of themselves, we also argue that the very relations through which such body-technology patterns emerge can take affective form, which is something not always considered in design.

This chapter acknowledges that the history of emotion is not unified, and as such, contemporary emotion-related technologies do not stand on solid uncontested foundations as to what emotion and affect are and how they should be studied. Analysis needs to consider what models and theories of emotion and affect are at play and anticipated, in relation to digital technologies. Throughout the book, we are driven by two main concerns: 1) To discuss existing theory and practice in relation to key areas pertaining to emotion in a digital age. This is important to understand the theories of emotion that underpin technological developments such as AI; 2) To frame emotion as central to the relationships we have to ourselves and to the *datafied* world around us. This involves a *broader* concern about the operation of individual and social life and the emotional dynamics of living with data hungry technologies. Understanding emotion in a digital age requires this dual approach. This is the Simondonian influence in terms of pre-individuation. Bodies and technologies take form as part of processes, rather than emerging from *within* each entity as distinct *substances*. Data, technologies, and bodies are structuring dimensions of motional processes that come to constitute conscious and non-conscious emotional and affective experience. What we feel as emotions are actions that orient us to our own bodies and those of others (collectivity). The category of *relation* is central to our discussions throughout the book. Much of the content we cover focuses on emotion in an individualistic manner, as something residing and operating within the skin of the body. We seek to keep analysis open to consider bodies as individual AND social. Not all the technologies we discuss are in widespread use yet, so our analysis is in places anticipatory in terms of considering their implications for future emotional life. Analysing through a psycho-social lens involves incorporating a dimension of non-organic materiality (Simondon's sociality/collective); considering bodies as simultaneously organic and non-organic. This concept of relationality is not entirely captured when thinking of individual (organic) and social (partially non-organic) as separate entities. Instead, bodies can be thought of as carrying an element of non-organic life *with* them, in terms of bodies being the source of a continual generation of data by technologies (e.g. social media). It is the generation of data from bodily activity regarding emotional and affective life that is the focus of this book. Bodies operate in almost constant contact with technologies. Data is generated from these body-technology relations. This is not just the *giving* of data *by* bodies, nor the *taking* of data *by* technologies. It operates relationally. Our aim throughout this book is to explore the centrality of emotion and affect to relations between bodies and digital technologies. We must consider the potential emotional and affective impact of mass digitisation and datafication. This involves considering emotion, not in terms of the feelings of an already constituted individual being, but as forms of knowledge and experience enacted by social practices. Emotion and affect are ways through which we relate to ourselves and to others. Digitisation and datafication are creating new ways of relating to ourselves and others and hence, are impacting emotional and affective life. This is the underpinning principle of the book. Not every digital and/or data practice we discuss focuses explicitly on emotion, but, we argue, it has the current and future potential to be part of the emotional and affective fabric of our social worlds.

References

Ahmed, S. (2004). Affective economies. *Social Text, 22*(2), 117–139.

Anderson, B. (2006). Becoming and being hopeful: Towards a theory of affect. *Environment and Planning D: Society and Space, 24*(5), 733–752.

Anderson, B., & McFarlane, C. (2011). Assemblage and geography: Assemblage and geography. *Area, 43*(2), 124–127.

Ash, J. (2013). Rethinking affective atmospheres: Technology, perturbation and space times of the non-human. *Geoforum, 49*, 20–28.

Bergson, H. (1988). *Matter and memory.* New York, NY: Zone Books.

Berryman, C., Ferguson, C. J., & Negy, C. (2018). Social media use and mental health among young adults. *Psychiatric Quarterly, 89*(2), 307–314.

Bille, M., Bjerregaard, P., & Sørensen, T. F. (2015). Staging atmospheres: Materiality, culture, and the texture of the in-between. *Emotion, Space and Society, 15*, 31–38.

Bissell, D. (2010). Passenger mobilities: Affective atmospheres and the sociality of public transport. *Environment and Planning D: Society and Space.*

Brown, S. D., Kanyeredzi, A., McGrath, L., Reavey, P., & Tucker, I. (2019). Affect theory and the concept of atmosphere. *Distinktion: Journal of Social Theory, 20*(1), 5–24.

Brown, S. D., & Reavey, P. (2015). *Vital memory and affect: Living with a difficult past* (1st ed.). New York, NY: Routledge.

Calancie, O., Ewing, L., Narducci, L. D., Horgan, S., & Khalid-Khan, S. (2017). Exploring how social networking sites impact youth with anxiety: A qualitative study of Facebook stressors among adolescents with an anxiety disorder diagnosis. *Cyberpsychology: Journal of Psychosocial Research on Cyberspace, 11*(4).

Coleman, R. (2018). Theorizing the present: Digital media, pre-emergence and infrastructures of feeling. *Cultural Studies, 32*(4), 600–622.

Combes, M., & LaMarre, T. (2012). *Gilbert Simondon and the philosophy of the transindividual.* Retrieved from https://mitpress.mit.edu/books/gilbert-simondon-and -philosophy-transindividual.

Darwin, C. (1965). *The expression of the emotions in man and animals.* Chicago, IL: The Chicago University Press.

Deleuze, G., & Guattari, F. (1994). *What is philosophy?* New York, NY: Columbia University Press.

Despret, V. (2004). *Our emotional makeup: Ethnopsychology and selfhood.* New York, NY: Other Press.

Dixon, T. (2003). *From passions to emotions: The creation of a secular psychological category*. Cambridge: Cambridge University Press.

Duff, C. (2011). Networks, resources and agencies: On the character and production of enabling places. *Health and Place, 17*(1), 149–156.

Duff, C. (2014). *Assemblages of health: Deleuze's Empiricism and the ethology of life*. Dordrecht: Springer.

Dysinger, W. S., & Ruckmick, C. A. (1933). *The emotional responses of children to the motion picture situation*. New York, NY: MacMillan.

Ekman, P., Sorenson, E. R., & Friesen, W. V. (1969). Pan-cultural elements in facial displays of emotion. *Science, 164*(3875), 86–88.

Ekman, Paul, & Friesen, W. V. (1971). Constants across cultures in the face and emotion. *Journal of Personality and Social Psychology, 17*(2), 124–129.

Ekman, Paul, Friesen, W. V., O'Sullivan, M., Chan, A., Diacoyanni-Tarlatzis, I., Heider, K., ... Tzavaras, A. (1987). Universals and cultural differences in the judgments of facial expressions of emotion. *Journal of Personality and Social Psychology, 53*(4), 712–717.

Ellis, D., & Tucker, I. (2015). *Social psychology of emotion*. London: Sage.

Ellis, D., Tucker, I., & Harper, D. (2013). The affective atmospheres of surveillance. *Theory and Psychology, 23*(6), 716–731.

Goriunova, O. (2019). The digital subject: People as data as persons. *Theory, Culture and Society, 36*(6), 125–145.

Greco, M., & Stenner, P. (Eds.). (2008). *Emotions: A social science reader*. London: Routledge.

Gregg, M., & Seigworth, G. (Eds.). (2009). *The affect reader*. New York, NY: Duke University Press.

Hacking, I. (1999). *The social construction of what?* Cambridge, MA: Harvard University Press.

Hillis, K., Paasonen, S., & Petit, M. (Eds.). (2015). *Networked affect*. Cambridge, MA: The MIT Press.

Hochschild, A. R. (2012). *The managed heart: Commercialization of human feeling*. Berkeley, Los Angeles, CA: University of California Press.

Iliadis, A. (2013). A new individuation: Deleuze's Simondon connection. *MediaTropes ejournal, IV*(1), 83–100.

Karaiskos, D., Tzavellas, E., Balta, G., & Paparrigopoulos, T. (2010). Social network addiction: A new clinical disorder? *European Psychiatry, 25*, 855.

Keating, T. P. (2019). Pre-individual affects: Gilbert Simondon and the individuation of relation. *Cultural Geographies, 26*(2), 211–226.

Malin, B. J. (2014). *Feeling mediated: A history of media technology and emotion in America*. New York, NY: New York University Press.

Marcus, G. E., & Saka, E. (2006). Assemblage. *Theory, Culture and Society, 23*(2–3), 101–106.

Massumi, B. (1996). The autonomy of affect. In P. Patton (Ed.), *Deleuze: A critical reader*. Oxford: Blackwells Publishing.

McGrath, L., & Reavey, P. (2015). Seeking fluid possibility and solid ground: Space and movement in mental health service users' experiences of 'crisis'. *Social Science and Medicine, 128*, 115–125.

McGrath, L., & Reavey, P. (2016). "Zip me up, and cool me down": Molar narratives and molecular intensities in 'helicopter' mental health services. *Health and Place, 38*, 61–69.

Miller, D. (2008). *The comfort of things*. Cambridge, UK: Polity Press.

Monacis, L., de Palo, V., Griffiths, M. D., & Sinatra, M. (2017). Social networking addiction, attachment style, and validation of the Italian version of the Bergen Social Media Addiction Scale. *Journal of Behavioral Addictions*, *6*(2), 178–186.

Ringrose, J. (2011). Beyond Discourse? Using Deleuze and Guattari's schizoanalysis to explore affective assemblages, heterosexually striated space, and lines of flight online and at school. *Educational Philosophy and Theory*, *43*(6), 598–618.

Ruckmick, C. A. (1936). *The psychology of feeling and emotion*. New York, NY: McGraw-Hill.

Sampson, T. D. (2017). *The assemblage brain: Sense making in neuroculture*. Minneapolis, MN: University of Minnesota Press.

Simondon, G. (2009). The position of the problem of ontogenesis. *Parrhesia*, *7*, 4–16.

Stenner, P. (2017). *Liminality and experience: A transdisciplinary approach to the psychosocial*. London: Palgrave Macmillan.

Stiegler, B. (1998). *Technics and time: The fault of Epimetheus* (R. Beardsworth, Trans.). Stanford, CA: Stanford University Press.

Tucker, I. (2006). Towards the multiple body. *Theory and Psychology*, *16*(3), 433–440.

Tucker, I. (2011). Somatic concerns of mental health service users: A specific tale of affect. *Distinktion*, *12*(1), 23–35.

Tucker, I. (2013). Bodies and surveillance: Simondon, information and affect. *Distinktion: Scandinavian Journal of Social Theory*, *14*(1), 37–41.

Whitehead, A. N. (1985). *Process and reality: An essay in cosmology: Gifford Lectures delivered in the University of Edinburgh during the session 1927-28*. New York, NY: Free Press.

3 Artificial intelligence and emotion

Machine *reading* of emotion and affect

At the time of writing, a new European border patrol scheme has been announced, using artificial intelligence (AI) to identify potential illegal immigrants at the border of Hungary, Latvia, and Greece. The iBorderCtrl scheme plans to use "smart" lie-detection software, via an Avatar of a human border control officer, to analyse the facial micro-expressions of those attempting to cross the border. The scheme has been developed from a project that has received significant EU funding (ca. 4.5 million euro). The publication of this scheme has created much controversy (Heaven, 2018). iBorderCtrl is one of the latest examples of the increased use of AI designed to capture and label emotion through facial expressions. This "basic emotion" model, initially developed by Darwin (2002) in 1872 in *The Expression of the Emotions in Man and Animals* and later developed by Ekman (2004), suggests that authentic emotions "leak" through micro facial expressions, outside of an individual's control. The lie detection software is based upon what the producers call an aggregated risk-based approach. These forms of actuarial justice that utilise digitised data are becoming increasingly common within technosecurity systems (Hannah-Moffat, 2019). Digital technology is used to prevent crime by aggregating markers associated with crime risk factors. In this instance, emotion-based markers (so called micro-expressions), are part of an assemblage of data, including fingerprints, palm vein recognition, face matching, and document authenticity. The data are then run through the risk-based assessment tool (RBAT) and, additionally, used to build up a database to help identify new algorithms of risk.

The *lie detector* border control scheme relies on a model of emotion as identifiable through physiological expression (although the developers state a human border guard is required to make the final decision). This relates to the history of lie detection through a polygraph, meaning many-graphs or writings, as it is used to monitor multiple bioregulatory modifications, namely pulse rate, respiratory rate, skin conductivity, and blood pulse. John A. Larson invented the polygraph, or what he termed the cardio-pneumo psychogram, in 1921, for criminal investigatory purposes. He was the first American police officer to obtain an academic doctorate. Larson eventually realised that his invention was being used in methodologically incorrect ways with negative consequences for criminal justice. Toward the end of his life he reportedly stated, "Beyond my expectation, through uncontrollable factors, this scientific investigation became for practical purposes a Frankenstein's monster, which I have spent over 40 years in combating" (Alder, 2009, p. 249). The polygraph has subsequently been extensively used in lie detection activities; for example, in the USA, it has been used by the Federal Bureau of Investigation (FBI), the National Security Agency (NSA), the Central Intelligence Agency (CIA), and the Los Angeles Police Department (LAPD). Researchers, such as the National Research Council, continue to question its efficacy, e.g. questioning whether the data interpretation is subjective and idiosyncratic. Bruno Verschuere (with colleagues) suggests there is no scientific basis for methods used for lie-detection (Goeleven et al., 2008; Meijer et al., 2016; Verschuere et al., 2009) – work that led to him receiving the Ig Nobel Prize in psychology – a so-called *satiric* prize, awarded to research that is unusual and humorous, but assessed as offering significant insight for future research. Similarly, as we will see throughout this chapter, emotion-related AI, or which often features in the area of affective computing, has the potential to become a Frankenstein monster if incorrectly used or misunderstood. Leys (2017) notes that its popularity is largely down to its perceived objective approach to the study of affects, bypassing the complications of cognition, consciousness, and subjectivity. This is very appealing to those in government and industry keen to use AI to identify emotional activity and intention. Notwithstanding the significant political and ethical problems of border patrol, the underlying science is questionable. Additionally, it is well known in psychology that emotion is not easily separable from subjectivity, consciousness, and cognition; it is not, as is often portrayed, an extractable element. Emotional and affective life is not easily quantified for computational use. Emotional and affective phenomena have evolved over millions of years, and attempting to engineer them in machines is an extremely complex task, particularly when many different definitions exist. Using emotion based microexpressions as a basis to automatically detect deception on EU borders may seem like it is an efficient mechanism, however, many would argue that affect detection technology is insufficiently developed, e.g. in relation to iBorderCtrl, it has been claimed that "this implementation can lead to the implementation of a pseudoscientific border control" (Boffey, 2018).

This chapter explores the development of technologies using forms of AI in emotion-related data (much of which has been developed in "affective computing"). Our focus is on the efforts made to try to track, identify, interpret, replicate, and potentially manipulate emotional activity. AI has been associated with emotion across media, the military, the state, private industries, and academia. The discipline of affective computing has grown considerably in the last twenty years and is now constituted by a range of areas. These include (but are not exhausted by) capturing emotion through facial expression, bodily expression, speech, text, physiological data such as skin conductance and heart rate, and senses such as touch. Affective computing also involves areas focusing on affect generation, such as in virtual characters and emojis and physical robots (informed by techniques of labelling posture, gesture, and motion in dance) (Picard, 2000). Much of this work aims to create "emotional agents" (virtual and/or physical) capable of social interaction with humans. Affective computing is a field of significant size and growing influence, especially in industry. It remains a sub-field of engineering, though, which recruits existing models of emotion from psychology (primarily) and the social sciences. As such, it is important to analyse the theories of psychology that underpin the models that affective technologies develop and the associated labelling of emotion therein.

The dawning of emotion-focused artificial intelligence

Accounts of AI permeate human history. They date from at least Homer's Iliad, in which we are told about robots made by the Greek god Hephaestos, right up to contemporary science fiction. It was not until the 1940s that the goal of what Pamela McCorduck (2004) called "the thinking machine" was becoming realisable. Sedgwick and Frank (2003) define this time (from the late forties to the mid-sixties) "the cybernetic fold", wherein the development of computation was claimed to facilitate meaningful insight regarding the workings of the brain. Computational approaches to human processes were, for a long time, focused on intelligence as a rationalistic information-processing operation. This was influential in the development of cognitive psychology, which used computational models to conceptualise psychological processes, particularly intelligence, memory, attention and perception. The importance of models of cognition to the development of AI cannot be understated (Dreyfus, 1979). A reciprocal relationship emerged in which models of computation influenced psychological theories of cognition, which fed back into subsequent technological attempts to understand intelligence. What is clear is that cognition, and a particularly rationalist version of it, constituted the model of psychology that computer science drew upon in the design and development of what came to be known as artificial intelligence.

Dreyfus offered a seminal critique of AI in his *What Computers Can't Do* (1979) and *What Computers Still Can't Do* (1992), in which he argued that situational knowledge is core to intelligence. It is not just about knowledge operating in a universal way across contexts, but about being aware of situational factors. For Dreyfus, intelligence is context dependent, and computers cannot develop situational knowledge. Human knowledge develops through a range of skills and experiences. For Dreyfus:

> our sense of our situation is determined by our changing moods, by our current concerns and projects, by our long-range self-interpretation and probably also by our sensory-motor skills for coping with objects and people-skills we develop by practice without ever having to represent to ourselves our body as an object, our culture as a set of beliefs, and our propensities as situation → action rules. All these unique human capacities provide a "richness" or a "thickness" to our way of being-in-the-world and thus seem to play an essential role in situatedness, which in turn underlies all intelligent behaviour
>
> (1992, p. 53)

Dreyfus defines *intelligent behaviour* as founded on a set of life experience, skills, and activities that are required to understand the context dependency of situations and which cannot be *programmed*. To claim otherwise is to suggest that a *pure* intelligence exists, outside of contextual influences, which can be learnt by computers. The successes taken as evidence for AI were operating within very limited parameters. There were two ways that machines could be measured according to Turing (1950). The first was a form of abstract activity, such as playing a game of chess, and the second was to construct a machine "with the best sense organs money could buy" (Turing, 1950, p. 460) to allow it to learn like a child, for example, pointing out to it the names of things. Wilson (2010) suggests that early developments constructed either chess-like or child-like AI machines. The chess-oriented approach places cognition as of primary importance to intelligence, for example, information processing, problem solving, decision making, reasoning, pattern recognition and perception (Wilson, 2010), although of course, calculation was one of the central features of early models. This had been the dominant model, but more recently, the child-like approach has emerged and increased in prominence, for example, central to many AI models are machine learning programmes, where systems improve with "experience".

Despite the criticisms about the limited scope of artificial intelligence, which made it unable to account for forms of "situated knowledge", technological developments continued apace. Emotion did not feature strongly in much AI literature. This is most probably a reflection of emotion's repression and relegation from scientific thought. There has been a tendency to write emotion out of psychology in the 20th century, which is a legacy of some earlier philosophical and theological beliefs (Ellis & Tucker, 2015). For example, emotion was often associated with animalistic and primitive aspects of humanity, tied to mechanistic involuntarism, and considered as leading to immorality, vice, and sin, whereas reason was considered a divine property that ought to have emotion under its control, providing humans with volition and right moral judgment. Some have presented this as a "reason-emotion" tension, which is unique to humans, and is something that should not be programmed into technologies (Beavers, 2009). Against this general tendency, affective computing has focused on developing machines and algorithms that understand and replicate emotion, so that they can be perceived as *emotional* but remain wholly in the domain of rationality (Cowie, 2015). The idea being that machines develop the necessary understanding about emotion that facilitates emotional interactions with others, but that feeling emotion is not necessary. This idea underpins a lot of contemporary affective computing work, which operates on the premise that understanding of emotion can be developed through machine-readable activity.

Affecting computers

The last twenty-five years has seen a steady flow of research development in academia and industry on emotion-related machines, particularly in the field of affective computing that relates to, arises from, or deliberately influences emotions

(Picard, 1995). Researchers within the interdisciplinary field of affective computing are interested in a range of quite diverse phenomena that occur between humans, digital technology, and affect-related processes. For example, conceptualising how affective activity influences the interactivity between humans and technology, and the design, implementation, and mimicry of affective systems in digital technologies. A note on terminology is important here. Picard has stated that the reason she named the new research area *affective computing*, is because it sounded more scientific than *emotional computing*. Affective computing is being developed for a range of potential applications, for instance, formal and informal learning, games, robotics, virtual reality, autism research, healthcare, music, reflective writing, and security.

Rosalind Picard's work has been at the forefront of affective computing. At MIT, she developed her work with the Vision and Modelling Group, which worked on emulating technologies related to signal processing, pattern recognition, and mathematical modelling within the perceptual sciences. Picard's focus was on image processing. For example, she was involved in developing a model that was a precursor to the Google Images system. Her desire to help machines to "see" is where her journey with emotion began. Moreover, she was investigating mechanisms of perception in relation to decision making, which involved exploring "how people perceive what is in a picture" and "how they decide what the contents of an image are" (Picard, 2000, p. ix). The associated human mechanisms of perception and associated decision making had previously been modelled through reductionist notions of cognition, for example, as being purely rational and emanating from logical processes. She went on to position emotion and affect (terms that appear interchangeable for Picard) as vital aspects of perception and decision making.

Following a philosophical tradition going back for millennia, Picard was particularly focused on the link between perception and feeling. She suggested that when perceiving something, we are fundamentally biased by what we feel. When perceiving an object, our interest is seized by the feelings that accompany the perception. This was missing from computers that treat all incoming photons as equal. Thus, for Picard, humans emotionally select which perceptions to focus upon. These processes may or may not be conscious. Up until this point, computers and computer models did not account for this perceptual bias. Humans are struck by bright colours, distinct smells, quick movements, loud noises, etc., all of which affectively engage and bias attention. There is a form of natural selection of perceptions that occurs through a feeling-led bias.

To denote her understanding of this emotionally-led perception bias, Picard draws on an array of theories. For example, the work of Cytowic (1993) on synaesthesia, wherein patients' brains behave as if the senses are cross-wired and so can, for example, feel shapes on their palms as they taste food (Picard, 2000, p. 5). This tends to heighten perceptual experience, and therefore the expectation would be that the higher cortices where the senses come together would have increased activity. For example, the parietal lobe's tertiary association would be expected to increase in cerebral blood flow, as this is where the three senses of vision, touch, and hearing converge, but, in fact, it was subcortical areas of the limbic system where heightened activity occurred during an episode of synaesthesia, an area typically understood to be the seat of emotion, part of the limbic system, or what others have called the emotional brain (LeDoux, 1996). This led to the belief that the limbic system plays a significant role in perception. Picard argues that contrary to prior belief, perception occurs in both cortex and in sub-cortex regions, hence "Things are not being perceived without going through a system that attaches valence to the memory-positive or negative, like or dislike" (2000, p. 6). Picard includes other examples of how perception is affected by these lower cortical structures; such as depression biasing the judging of a facial expression (Bouhuys, Bloem, & Groothuis, 1995). LeDoux (1996) also notes two neural pathways for perception; one which goes straight to the limbic system and allows one to react to stimuli immediately (feeling-led), whilst the other goes through the cortex and is slower, but enables a much more accurate assessment of the situation (thought-led). Although this is a rudimentary and dualistic distinction, the point is, one incorporates less volition, but more emotion, than the other.

The belief that perception and associated cognition is imbued with emotion was becoming more acceptable (e.g. Damasio, 1994), although this was something that had, for at least two millennia, been understood as the case, but largely screened out of psychology (Ellis & Tucker, 2015). The question for affective computing was how to quantify this in computational terms. Picard states "We all know from experience that too much emotion can impair decision making, but the new scientific evidence is that *too little emotion can impair decision making*" (Ibid, p. x). Picard's work is underpinned by her belief that for computers to be truly intelligent and interact with humans, in other words, to develop AI, will require emotional intelligence, e.g. the capacity to recognise and express emotion (Picard, Vyzas, & Healey, 2001). Much of Picard and her colleagues' work was underpinned by two fundamental dimensions: Arousal and valance. Arousal (the amount of affective activity) tends to be measured through psychophysiological activity, such as heart-rate and skin-conductivity, whilst valence, the form/quality of emotion, tends to be identified, through facial expression.

Picard qualifies her almost synonymous use of the terms emotion and affect by stating they are adjectives describing either physical or cognitive components (Picard, 1997, p. 24). These definitions, however, did not sufficiently encapsulate the forms of processes that she wanted to distinguish, leading to her adoption of the term *sentic*, which relates to a particularly unusual understanding of emotional expression developed by Manfred Clynes (1977). Clynes had a multitude of interests, a polymath, and has many patents to his name. He is an accomplished pianist and has developed a sophisticated body of work culminating in integrating his interests in emotion, music, and neurophysiology. The invention that Clyne developed which initially attracted Picard to his work was the sentograph, a machine which he claimed was able to measure emotion (or what he termed "sentic states"). Clynes's understanding of emotion is relatively eccentric and spiritual. He felt that Western thought, throughout the so-called age of reason, had "driven a painful wedge into his being, dividing him from himself as well as his fellow beings and natural environment" (Clynes, 1977, p. xx). His work on sentics was Clynes's attempt to "reunite man's divided nature" (ibid). He drew on the belief that emotional expressions (sentic states) are genetically programmed and can reveal "the simple elegance of nature's plan within us" and "the communication of emotion is designed according to specific laws, we can discover a new sense of belonging to nature and recognize our common brotherhood" (ibid). Different sentic states have developed at different stages of evolution (p. 203). He puts forward the idea that similar sentic states have evolved in different species as nature displays preferred solutions (p. 202). He sees this as evidence of "design" in the universe. He states,

> Physicists admire the "elegant design" implicit in natural law-*that* in fact appears to be a source of its beauty, as well as of the awe and wonder which physicists often experience. Why then should we not permit ourselves to accept the possibility that design may be implicit in the more complex molecular organisation?

Given molecules are the same throughout the universe but have had different evolutionary paths to actualise "*through random influences of potential existence inherent in natural order*" (pp. 203–204), Clynes believes sentic states (or emotions) to be born out of similar natural laws. He suggests that humanity has reached a stage, wherein people can strive to actualise selective sentic state potentialities. He states, "Culture, seems to be in accord with the direction of evolution" (p. 204). Interestingly, Clynes, along with Kline, coined the term *cyborg* in a paper for the journal Astronautics in 1960 entitled "Cyborgs and Space", wherein they discuss the altering of human bodily functions to meet the requirements of space travel. "The cyborg deliberately incorporates exogenous components extending the self-regulatory control function of the organism in order to adapt it for new environments" (Clynes & Kline, 1960, p. 27). He goes on to develop his interest in the cyborg and space travel in relation to the artificial induction of sentic states to maintain emotional health in space, in which he introduces a form of meditation called the "sentic cycle", through which individuals experience basic emotion states in a specific order over a period of half an hour. The states are no emotion, anger, hate, grief, love, sex, joy, and reverence. These relate to, but do not match, the six basic emotions of the classical view. One of the points that Clynes makes is that being able to name a sentic state enables the individual to have more control over it, and that there exist potential sentic states yet to be actualised in this way. One such state that he advocates is being *apreene*; a sentic state which nurtures the quest for new ideas, expressed by tilting the head slightly to the right and slightly upward, "the body feels light, and there is a characteristic sensation of sideways expanding pressure in the forehead between the temples" (p. 205) etc. This state induces a "specific intellectual fervour, an openness, receptivity, enthusiasm, a readiness to receive" (p. 205). Clynes notes that once a sentic state's essentic form has been identified, the state can be eulogised, practiced, and cultivated, and giving it a name further enables that process.

To distinguish the form of the sentic state, Clynes developed the sentograph, a machine designed to capture and label emotion (sentic states) through bodily expression, as represented by intentional finger pressure. According to Clynes, it measures "the forms of the vertical and horizontal components of transient pressure on a finger rest as functions of time" (Clynes, 1977, p. 222). Clynes suggests that each sentic state is characterised by a "precise dynamic form" that he calls an "essentic form" (1977, p. xx). These forms, or sentic states, can be expressed, according to Clynes, through various modes, for example, through tone of voice or parts of the body. It has a spatiotemporal form, entailing a clear beginning and end.

To produce the essentic forms, the sentograph required the use of the middle finger. Clynes stated, "The dynamic pressure of a single finger rest has the possibility of being readily repeatable, and can be easily measured, and thus can become a standard means for measuring and comparing various expressive forms" (p. 27). This worked by exerting finger pressure on a sensor (sentograph) to express emotion. Clynes claims to have found distinct patterns from the finger exertions that represented anger, love, grief, sex, reverence, joy, and trust. An essential feature of the measure is the direction of the pressure of the finger. He gives precise instructions to participants to sit in a certain way so that, for example, the upper arm is held forward by a ten-degree angle and the forearm is slightly downward at a fifteen-degree angle. He claims that the expressive action emanates from the torso and it is not a lifting of the finger but "a transient pressure exerted through the arm" (p. 27). Hence, two transducers are used to measure the vertical pressure and the horizontal component. The participant is asked to express, for example, anger, with the finger pressure action thirty to fifty times. The repetition, Clynes argues, enables the fantasy of anger to grow in intensity. These are then averaged by The Computer of Average Transients (CAT). Clynes measured these alongside EEG (electroencephalogram) and a variety of arm muscles (electromyograms – EMG). He claims to have found the same patterns across a variety of cultures, including Mexico, Japan, and Bali; therefore, like Ekman and Darwin before him, he assumes to have found universal emotional expressions. The difference, though, being that Clynes's model is one of intentional action (i.e. middle finger press) rather than the involuntary expression underpinning facial expression work. Thus, the essentic forms are considered by him as natural words of emotion communication that arose before speech.

Mortillaro and Scherer (2009) in the *Oxford Companion to Emotion and the Affective Sciences* state that Clynes's sentograph methodology has been widely criticised, although they do not offer any references. In a chapter on *Emotional Expression in Music*, in the *Handbook of Affective Sciences*, Gabrielson and Juslin (2003) state that further studies have yielded mixed results. Gorman and Crain (1974) found that participants produced results that were just above chance. Trussoni, O'Malley, and Barton (1988) could not replicate Clynes's findings, neither could Nettelbeck, Henderson, and Willson (1989). Hama and Tsuda (1990) and De Vries (1991) do supply support for Clynes's theory. Additionally, the highly respected affective neuroscientist Jaak Panksepp writes about undergoing

Clynes sentic cycle meditation and then conducting an experiment using EEG and ERD (event related desynchronisation) measures. Panksepp states that the results were striking and that "such results show the power that feelings can have on higher brain activities" (1998, pp. 88–89).

Although support for Clynes's theory of essentic forms is limited, Picard's work heavily references his ideas in her seminal book and paper entitled *Affective Computing* (1995; 2000), in which she states in the acknowledgment that his "pioneering work into emotion argued persuasively for more attention on this topic, ultimately capturing my own" (Picard, 1995, p. 24). The fact that Clynes essentic forms are produced through computations of psychophysiological activity makes the concept attractive for affective computing, as it provides a way through which emotional expressions could be neatly captured and represented digitally. For example, Picard employs Clynes's concept of "sentic modulation" to represent the influence emotion has on bodily expression; namely voice inflection, facial expression, and posture, all of which could be digitised (Picard, 1997, p. 25). Sentic modulation is understood as a natural and mostly unconscious articulation of emotional states. These are usually considered involuntary and allow observers to guess a person's emotional state. Picard distinguishes these from moods, which she refers to as affective states that generally have a much longer duration. Moods are commonly the result, according to Picard, of repeated emotion activity. She states that sentic modulations come in all shapes and sizes, such as facial expressions, voice intonation, gestures, movements, postures and pupillary dilation; and those less apparent, but commonly measured for emotion activity: Heart rate, pulse, temperature, electrodermal response, perspiration, muscle action potentials, and blood pressure. Picard considers a range of factors through affective computing experiments; for example, there is a focus upon the intensity of the arousal, the form of the arousal, otherwise known as valence, the cause of the arousal, or induction, and the social display rule, or social expression, of the arousal.

Picard and her colleagues claimed to turn emotional expression into something computers could identify and process through pattern recognition programmes (digitised perception). Hence, machine learning was employed to read and aggregate emotional expressions of a variety of affective data. Many innovative data collection methods were developed, for example, the galvactivator, a glove-like device that tracked skin conductivity of a wearer. The development of the galvactivator was a joint project that Picard and her colleague Jocelyn Scherer produced which has subsequently been developed for many wearables. At the time of writing, Picard is the Chief Scientist at a company called Empatica, which has developed a wearable product called Embrace, which enables people to detect when they may be on the verge of having a seizure.

Prior to this, Picard worked with Rana el Kaliouby (who completed PhD research on a project entitled MindReader with the cognitive neuroscientist Simon Baron-Cohen). Baron-Cohen has pioneered autism research and together they built a video catalogue of emotional facial expressions to help people within the autistic spectrum with emotion recognition. LEDs on a pair of glasses would inform the user in real time, whether the person they were speaking to was engaged (green), neutral (amber), or bored (red). It was claimed to be 88% accurate. el Kaliouby went on to work with Picard at MIT, where they became leading figures in affective computing. It was during this time that Picard and el Kaliouby were encouraged by one of their then directors, Frank Moss, to commercialise their work outside of MIT. Picard was involved in two companies that reflect the development of her research: Emotional facial recognition research within the company Affectiva and galvanic arousal and associated physiological activity measured through watch-like wearables (Empatica). Affectiva was launched in 2009 and focused on el Kaliouby's MindReader which was reincarnated as Affdex. Millward-Brown (the world's second largest market research company) became a partner, investing $4.5 million. By 2014, they claimed to have had over 100,000 positive training samples of facial expression detection, with their algorithm for detecting facial expressions claiming to achieve over 90% accuracy. They sought more and more participants to generate larger data sets. For example, one project involved streaming SuperBowl ads online to viewers who agreed to be analysed via webcams while they watched. Affectiva's Affdex is now a key tool used in Madison Avenue's neuromarketing. Additionally, Affdex has been developed as a free app on Apple iPhones and now collects expression-related data from millions of faces around the world.

Affdex is designed to track four emotional classifiers: Happy, sad, disgusted, and angry. This relies on the FACS labelling system devised by Ekman and, as such, propagates a model of emotions as physiological phenomena. As one of the most successful affective computing technologies, it is playing a significant role in perpetuating a model of emotion as grounded in bodily expression, primarily the face. This is a selective model, and yet, is marketed as the pinnacle of technological expertise. The classic model of expressions based on six basic emotions has been subject to extensive critique (see Barrett et al., 2019 for a systematic review). As Barrett et al. (2019) point out, the classic model (or what they call the "common view") that has permeated society through its use in popular culture, is based on problematic underlying research. For instance, we have already discussed the foundation of this body of research that was formed through Clynes's *essentic forms* theory; additionally, it is widely acknowledged that there is a lack of evidence of the variability in facial expression of "basic emotions"; limited evidence stemming from studies in naturalistic settings; and moreover, the social context which shapes the emotional expression is disregarded. As such, affective computing technologies are based on foundations lacking scientific credentials when underpinned by the classical model of emotional expression. This is not to deny that emotional and affective life involves an expressive dimension. The question is, what categories of emotion are expressions related to? Developing a systematic way to identify and categorise these is of significant commercial interest for advertisers and retailers, and the simplicity of the classical view has resulted in its widespread use. One of the challenges these technologies face is that they depend on a fixed categorical emotion system, which is used to label facial expressions. This is only *capturing* emotion at the moment of facial expression. The movement and fluidity of emotional experience is much harder to capture through technologies such as AffDex. Researchers in the field have stated that facial expression recognition is far from a solved problem. It is frequently reported that while expression classifications work relatively well for posed expressions, identification and performance drops dramatically on recognising expressions during day-to-day activities, such as conversations (Gunes & Hung, 2016; Sariyanidi, Gunes, & Cavallaro, 2014; Zeng et al., 2008).

Once established, the technical efforts of affective computing primarily propagate a narrow reductionist account of emotional and affective life. The focus is on the mechanics of emotional activity, namely the question of how emotion operates within the body and how this can be used to design technologies to capture and interpret emotional data. Emotion is considered as operating primarily through physiological activity that is expressed by the body and which expert technological solutions are required to accurately identify. A broader sense of the emotional-affective implications of affective computing as technologies is not included in analysis. Neither are any of the multiple critiques of the universalist-tendencies of psychophysiological models addressed or acknowledged. Understanding an emotional event in a given moment (e.g. when purchasing a product) requires insight regarding context, e.g. why an individual is experiencing an emotion. Interpreting context can require relating an emotional event to broader life experience. For instance, a person may choose a product because of a memory of using it as a child, or it being the preferred choice of a loved one who has passed away. Emotion recognition technologies are capturing only one dimension of the emotional processes through which we make decisions. Despite these apparent limitations, the attraction of designing technologies to categorise and understand emotional activity is significant, and spans several decades, sectors, and areas. Affective tutoring has been a prominent area of affective computing development. Delivering education through computers is of significant interest to educators, governments, and industry, although, as we will see, questions remain as to their impact.

Affective tutoring systems

Affective Tutoring Systems (ATS) have attempted to develop AI-based tools to engage with the emotional state of students (Sarrafzadeh et al., 2008). Calvo and D'Mello (2012) state that ATS research is a "highly interdisciplinary endeavour that spans psychology, education, computer science, engineering, neuroscience, and artificial design" (p. 4). The main issue that drives ATS is to determine the forms of affect experienced by students, establish their causes, and then regulate the states accordingly. In attempts to determine the affects, technological methods have been developed to categorise psycho-physiological activity including facial expressions, body language, voice, physiological activity, and text. Many systems attempt to use multimodal forms of affective analysis to predict learning; for example, Vail et al. (2016) examine facial expression, electrodermal activity, posture, and gesture; Su et al. (2016) use both facial expression recognition and textual analysis. ATS differ from affective computing systems in terms of utilising different models of emotional-affective life than those based on a basic emotions model (Russell, 2003). Given the title of the field, there is more emphasis on a language of affect, not emotion, in affective tutoring.

D'Mello and Graessner (2012) tracked students' affective states in an online tutoring session (Affective AutoTutor) by holding conversations with students using natural language attempting to replicate pedagogical and motivational strategies of human tutors. The Affective AutoTutor was developed to detect the emotional states of students through expressions of boredom, confusion, engagement, frustration, delight, surprise, and neutral. It is often thought that positive affects enhance the learning process, such as flow and engagement, and that negative affects, such as boredom, confusion, frustration, and lack of self-confidence, stifle learning (Calvo & D'Mello, 2012; Malekzadeh et al., 2015; Erez & Isen, 2002). D'Mello and Graessner argue that cognitive processes related to learning, such as inference generation, causal reasoning, problem diagnosis, and coherent explanation generation are accompanied by affective states. Throughout the learning process, there ought to be movements from negative affect that is experienced when, for example, the learner makes mistakes, and from mild ones, such as irritation, up to severe states of rage, through to positive affective states experienced when, for instance, tasks are completed and challenges are conquered, such as, flow, delight, and eureka moments. They suggest that learning necessarily involves deep combinations of cognitive processes and affective states. Rather than draw on the generic six basic emotions, they refer to boredom and confusion, for example, as cognitive-affective mixtures rather than emotions *per se*. The underlying psychological model used to develop the system derived from cognitive disequilibrium theories that have a long history of research in psychology (for example, Piaget, 1952).

To empirically research the role of affective-cognitive processes in learning, D'Mello and Graessner recorded students for 30 minutes using the AutoTutor system, with their posture and face expressions, along with screen capture, recorded. These were linked together and played back to the student participants alongside the tutor's synthesised speech, printed text, students' responses, dialogue history, and images to create the context of the tutorial interaction. Students were asked to disclose which affective state was enacted at twenty second intervals, and they could also suggest what states may have been enacted between these intervals. The students were given a checklist of the seven cognitive-affective states to choose from. The results support the hypotheses regarding the learning underpinned by specific cognitive-affective states. For example, flow and confusion, and confusion to frustration.

A recent search by one of the current book's authors (Ellis) identified that Affective AutoTutor was no longer being developed. This was followed up with an email query to one of the developers, Graessner, who replied:

The National Science Foundation grant ended on Affective AutoTutor so that particular system had no follow-up research. It also had many sensors for affect detection that made it difficult to run a large number of participants. So we ended up with other versions of AutoTutor with fewer sensors and a focus on responding to particular emotions, such as confusion or boredom/disengagement.

(Graessner [email], 2019)

Of note, here, is that affective computing in relation to affective tutoring systems is relatively unsophisticated. Although D'Mello and Graessner claim to have been able to conduct what they refer to as a fine-grained analysis of cognitive-affective states, the detection method was human (self-report). This is not supportive of the position (discussed in Chapter Two) that technologies provide more authentic access to emotion as psychophysiological phenomena. Self-reporting is commonly thought to be an unreliable method of emotion detection and, indeed, runs totally against affective computing's goal of computer-generated affect detection. D'Mello and Graessner's research did not facilitate clear and uncontested detection of the cognitive-affective states argued to underpin learning. Perhaps this was a factor in the lack of follow on funding for the system.

Despite the ending of the Affective Auto Tutoring system, a review by Petrovica, Anohina-Naumeca, and Ekenel (2017) identified a range of emerging research in the area including analysing posture, eye tracking, gaze pattern, facial expressions, acoustic features (e.g. speech intensity energy, volume, duration, and pauses), skin conductivity, heart rate, muscle activity, and many more, analysing affect through self-assessment (e.g. the self-assessment manakin SAM). Petrovica et al. (2017) conclude that the *basic emotions* (anger, disgust, happiness, fear, sadness, and surprise) are not often experienced in the learning process, and so suggest that the identification of basic emotions is largely insignificant for the adaption of the tutoring process. Hence, most of the work that has been produced by affective computing in relation to detecting basic emotions was of no use. Boredom, confusion, engagement, frustration, delight, and surprise, for example, are what they see as a combination of cognitive and affective states and so are not as detectable through facial expressions.

The field of affective computing presents multiple challenges, including technical, theoretical, and ethical challenges. Technologies based on a basic/classic model have clearly had some success, particularly in marketing and advertising, e.g. Affectiva, while in other areas, such as affective tutoring, the basic emotions model has proved less successful. What researchers in the field of affective tutoring distinguish as cognitive-affective states are not as explicitly expressible (detectible) as the basic emotions. Theoretical attempts to integrate emotion with other psychological processes, such as perception, have emerged, but the technologies developed have relied very much on the idea that emotions are expressed through physiological activity, which can be captured, quantified and categorised computationally. The next section presents an interesting example of emerging theory designed to further the affective computing cause but in a more controversial area, namely whether computers can be developed that not only detect and replicate emotion but are also able to *feel*.

Towards an inclusive computational model of emotion

An interesting area of theory in affective computing is the work of Guadalupe Sanchez-Escribano (2018, p. 62), an engineer attempting to develop an inclusive computational model of emotion. He painstakingly reviews the ways that models of emotion have been used in the development of artificial systems and suggests a washing machine analogy. He argues it is important to think about the structure, purpose, and operation of a man-made system in relation to the biological system it is trying to replicate. For example, affective computing engineers should first decide upon what emotion does in a biological agent, then search for relevant analogies in artificial systems. He thinks it absurd to think of the artificial system's requirements as being the same as the biological system. The washing machine was developed to reproduce the human work of washing clothes, but not in such a way that replicates the way humans wash clothes. It was far more practical to analyse the effects of washing clothes, i.e. removing dirt, stains, and smells. Contemporary washing machines, therefore, do not replicate human movement, but are more effective washers than humans. Steven Shaviro (2016, p. 50) makes a similar point in *Discognition*, stating that since the 1950s, computer engineers and computer scientists have sought the holy grail of AI only to be disappointed, with limited success. They were hampered by the misconception that computers could think like human beings and that humans think in a way analogous to how computers operate. If computers ever do come to think, it is likely to be in a very different way to human modes of thought. Shaviro states affective computing:

> is much more concerned with enabling computers to "read" human emotional responses, than it is with eliciting anything like the affective states of computers themselves. The latter, should they ever come to exist, are likely to be quite different from anything that we are accustomed to.
>
> (p. 51)

So, if a machine could be designed to feel, it is likely to feel in very different ways to how humans feel. Sanchez-Escribano conceptualises the potential feeling of emotion in artificial systems through Damasio's distinction between emotion and feeling. In *The Feeling of What Happens*, Damasio states that we know we have an emotion when the sense of a feeling is created in our minds (Damasio, 2000, p. 54). The feeling emanates from a variety of neural patterns (maps) that represent changes in the brain and body, constituting, for Damasio, the emotion. Replicating this in a machine is, for Sanchez-Escribano, not so much a philosophical problem as an engineering problem. He understands the problem as one of symbolic representation, in other words, how can the feeling of the emotion be represented in an artificial system? Sanchez-Escribano delineates mechanics that he considers as relating to conscious and non-conscious processing. In accordance with Turing's (1937, p. 259) notion that machines are only conscious about what they can *read*, he states that machines are only aware of the data that they *receive*. Again, using Damasio's notion of maps and images as analogous to machine processing, Sanchez-Escribano develops the notion of c-maps and c-images (computer maps and computer images). Damasio uses the term maps and images when discussing feelings; maps are neural patterns which underlie the mental images. Damasio states that images that we see in our mind are not facsimiles of the particular (real) object, but a set of correspondences between physical objects and the dynamics of the human organism. In this way, Damasio understands feelings as symbolic representations of, in this instance, emotions:

> There is no picture of the object being transferred from the object to the retina and from the retina to the brain. There is, rather, a set of correspondences between physical characteristics of the object and modes of reaction of the organism according to which an internally generated image is constructed.
>
> (Damasio, 2000, p. 54)

Sanchez-Escribano's computational version of Damasio's distinction between maps and images frames some c-images as being accessible to the system, constituted as knowledge, whilst others are not. This, for Sanchez-Escribano, is "the computational conceptualization" of being conscious, or being capable of using this data as "knowledge" and also, in the case of it not being accessible, it is "not being conscious of" or in other words "not being capable of use" (2018, p. 155). The question is how this relates to sentience and animal experience. For example, the input of information and the output of behaviour (input-output relationship) for any event is predictable with machines. This is not so with animals, even some of the least neurologically complex of animals, the fruit fly, does not behave in programmed, deterministic ways. They spontaneously generate behaviour which is influenced by numerous contextual (environmental) and complex internal (biological) phenomena. They are not passively responding to stimuli, but actively altering behaviour in relation to the environment. However, perhaps if multiple sensors were engineered onto a machine that was able to respond to all forms of environmental factors, the behavioural responses – could, theoretically, be as complex as a fruit fly? It is a philosophical question as to whether this represents some form of active agentic behaviour constituting sentience.

Sanchez-Escribano develops a computational theory grounded in existing neuropsychological research regarding emotion. The following section draws on contemporary neuropsychological emotion research, which offers a different view of how emotion operates in the brain. The *constructionist* theory of Lisa Feldman Barratt offers a theory of emotions as goal-directed actions involving complex patterns of neuronal activity. For Barratt, emotions are not the manifestation of specific neuropsychological patterns of activity triggered by environmental stimuli, i.e. they are not pre-existing forms, but are action-oriented processes enacted *neuronally-anew* on each iteration.

Constructionist models of emotion

As we have seen, the reliance on theories that have emerged from emotion recognition experiments remains strong in affective computing. This is largely due to the promises made about a realm of authentic emotion that is machine readable (as this is the aim of affective computing). Within neuroscience, this position has been critiqued extensively, with advocates of a more constructionist approach to emotion emerging. Lisa Feldman Barratt grounds emotional activity in the brain, but in a way that incorporates social and cultural influence. The latter is at odds with the universalist principles of Basic Emotion Theory (and its variants), as it introduces a co-production of emotion processes through physiological and socio-cultural processes. Barratt's constructionist approach holds that emotional processes are not passive reactions to external stimuli, but are active constructions pertaining to the social context and the emotional cues and activity of other actors. Emotions are not viewed as a set of universal entities located physiologically that are triggered by external stimuli. Instead, they are framed as socially-situated actions that operate in relation to other bodies in the production of social life. Barratt defines this as "[A]n emotion is your brain's creation of what your bodily sensations mean, in relation to your context" (2018, p. 30). She proposed that even though we experience others and ourselves as producing discrete emotions, and that we have used a terminology of discrete emotion for millennia, evidence does not bear out their actual existence in brain structures. This is often referred to as the *emotion paradox*.

Constructionist approaches require a neural plasticity to allow for a model that argues emotion expressions are context-dependent, because the brain must be able to deal with new experiential information. No one form could retain the emotional potential to underpin activity across a potentially unlimited set of contexts. Instead, Barratt offers a terminology of *instances* and *categories* of emotion rather than singular universal forms. The constructed nature of emotion makes recognition and identification difficult, because the physiological expression taken as the manifestation of emotion is only part of the process. It does not inform as to the context through which it emerged. This is one reason why Barratt feels the classical basic emotion model's claims to universality are invalid. Moreover, the brain is seen to create emotions in relation to the goals of a particular social situation. Emotions are not deemed to reside *within* the brain-body, awaiting triggering, but as active goal-based processes. Barratt's neuroscientific account of emotion argues that emotions are *instances* of activity, which emerge through different patterns of neurons on each occasion. Hence, they are not *stored* in a single neural form (an argument shared by Sanchez-Escribano). Barratt is critical of the recognition experiments that underpin Basic Emotion Theory, arguing they demonstrate the significant influence of priming in terms of pre-categorising facial expressions. Barratt's own studies, without pre-categorisation, produce far lower accuracy response rates. The fervour that emerges in relation to new technological developments tends to mask existing critiques as to the validity of underlying experimental evidence, particularly given the public and commercial interest in machine learning and recognition. Constructionist accounts are yet to feature in affective computing due to the complexities of mapping and quantifying multiple relations between psychophysiological activity and social context. And yet, they offer important insight as to the challenges facing affective computing, given the complexity of theories as to neuropsychological reality of emotion.

AI-mediated futures

There is little doubting the continued growth and presence of affective computing, and we have not discussed all the areas in which affective computing technologies are currently being developed and applied (e.g. digital mental health, which will be discussed in Chapter Five). It is an area of significant commercial interest, which makes it highly likely to continue to develop, premised on the view that affective computational tools will increase in sophistication and therefore, significant potential exists as to their current and future utility. As it stands, current technological attempts to capture, interpret, and potentially manipulate emotion are in a nascent stage. Limited success has been achieved with affective computation technologies built upon classical models of *basic* and *universal* emotion. Attempts to *read* emotion according to core *basic* categories remain lacking, although it is argued that they are improving (McStay, 2018). In addition to the problems they have with providing insight regarding emotional and affective *experience*, at a technical level, they are only as good as the data upon which they are programmed (Fry, 2019). For instance, if a new technology is programmed with discriminatory data, it will produce discriminatory outputs. One can think of the example of the recruitment algorithm developed by Amazon that was designed to improve recruitment processes by identifying patterns of sought-after skills and expertise in candidate CVs. The problem was that it was based on CVs of existing staff, who were predominantly white and male. This was not factored into the design of the algorithm, and when it was used, it was found to discriminate based on gender, with even the mention of the word *woman* on the CV leading to it not being shortlisted. Thankfully, Amazon recognised this and ceased its use. The social implications of the development and use of emotion technologies are often not considered, due to the primary focus being on their technical capabilities.

Another persistent issue is the question of authenticity. The range of emotional expression data collected by Affectiva, for instance, is impressive, some 60 million *data points*. This situates it firmly in the area of big data (and the currency it has). Technologies are deemed to provide more accurate and rich insight regarding emotion than individuals can, as consciousness is viewed as an obstruction to accurate reading, not a help. The argument follows that people are not aware of the range of micro-expressions that faces display, and even if they were, self-reporting as to their meaning is claimed to be less accurate than machine reading (McStay, 2018). The question of authenticity hinges on a slightly different set of issues than universality and essentialism. To introduce a notion of authenticity is to (re)articulate a distinction between an objective physiologically-based realm of emotion and a psychologically-based, representative realm. This kind of dualism has been subject to extensive critique, and yet continues to perpetuate in relation to emotion technologies. This is what Whitehead referred to as the *bifurcation of nature* (1985), which aims to separate the world into a set of essential objective elements and the mind's representation and understandings of said elements. This is a distinction of primary and secondary qualities, with the essential objective realm taken as primary, knowledge of which is the driver of scientific endeavour.

Whitehead calls 'secondary qualities' *psychic additions* (1964), which ostensibly seem to be very much part of emotional activity. And yet, emotion technologies increasingly operate on a model that claims to be able to capture authentic emotions by bypassing the *psychic additions* of reflection and self-reporting. The body is claimed to be the level at which emotional truth is to be found, with machines presented as the means to do this accurately. This is a form of de-psychologisation of emotion, in which the role of conscious experience is precluded. Emotion is seen as primarily physiological, with conscious experience a layer of noise that can mask *authentic emotion*. This relies on a classical reductionist and dualistic model, in which the body (physiological expression), is seen not only as distinct from the conscious experiencing mind, but is primary when it comes to emotion.

Affective computing is a contemporary version of the process of the *scientisation of emotion* in the early 20th century (Malin, 2014 – discussed in Chapter One) – this time in the form of a *commodification of emotion*. A large proportion of affective computing research is undertaken with commercial interests in mind. This has run contrary to how Picard hoped it would develop; she desired what Zuboff notes as, "good-hearted" or at least "benign" use of the technology (2019, p. 285). Picard envisaged the technology to be used *for* the individual and that the data it produced should be owned by the individual, rather than it just being *about* the individual. She warned of the potential for affective computing to eventually be used by governments to manipulate and control the emotions of its subjects. Her endeavour and hope were that it would be used for life enhancing applications such as:

> helping autistic children develop emotional skills, provide software designers with feedback on users' frustration levels, assigning points to video game players to reward courage or stress reduction, producing learning modules that stimulate curiosity and minimize anxiety, and analyzing emotional dynamics in the classroom.
>
> (Zuboff, 2019, p. 285)

Instead, affective computing has succumbed to the pressures of large-scale commodification, which is of significant value to industry. Affective computing produces the idea of the individual as consumer, rather than a broader sense of the psychological subject. Twenty years after Picard's publication, according to a report in 2017, the affective computing market had grown from a $9.53 billion-dollar industry to a predicted $53.98 billion by 2021; this annual 35 percent growth is mainly due to the marketing and advertising sectors. In 2020, the marketandmarkets.com forecasts the global affective computing market size is projected to grow from USD 22.2 billion in 2019 to a staggering USD 90.0 billion by 2024. Interestingly, the report states that "Voice-activated biometrics used for security purposes help in providing access to authenticated users for performing a transaction, therefore, surging the use of affective computing solutions across the globe" (marketandmarket.com). Picard was eventually pushed out of the company Affectiva, as her ethical stance ran against commercial interests. Her original partner and now CEO of Affectiva, Kaliouby, boasts that the company now has the largest database in the world of emotion data (4.8 million face videos from 75 countries and counting). She has widely suggested in interviews that it is perfectly reasonable that an emotion chip will become the base unit of the emotion economy, running in the background of an array of technologies generating an emotional pulse. She claims emotion scanning will be taken for granted like a cookie, running in your computer tracking your emotion like it would online browsing. However, it is hard to see exactly how this will play out. How much actual use are these unidimensional models of emotion activity? For example, the affective tutoring system discussed above was not able to implement any basic model of emotion to facilitate *affective tutoring*. It soon found that affectivity and emotion in this context are far more complex and would require a whole host of technologies and sensors to incorporate affective computing into its system. Our reading suggests that an *emotion chip* having the kind of universal application that it is presently being hyped by Affectiva seems to be some way off (if at all possible).

Expression, context, and relational multiplicity

So far, we have covered key examples of AI-based affective computing technologies and presented key challenges to the theories of emotion from neurological perspectives that underpin computational attempts to reliably and validly capture and categorise emotion in neuropsychological terms. Despite the variance in approach to categorising emotional activity across affective computing, the widespread emphasis on reducing emotion to physiological activity renders a primacy on expressivity and essentialism. What is left out of such accounts is a sense of the broader dimensions of the system of relations through which emotional and affective life emerge and operate. Simondon's concepts of individuation, information, and affect in Chapter Two suggests that entities and relations are not separate, distinct parts of the world. What we see as perceivable instances of emotion are just visible parts of relations. The smile we express when looking at a product that elicits positive childhood memories is not an isolated event. This involves a temporal dimension, in terms of making emotions in the present indelibly linked to past life experience. The theoretical discussion in Chapter Two argues for a relational approach that situates emotional and affective activity in the context within which they emerge. Physiologically-based emotion recognition technologies rely on the notion that emotions have a definitive quality, which is expressed as a unique configuration of facial muscles, and that this quality resides *in the body*; it's inherent.

The quantification that affective computing requires can be distinguished from a qualitative sense of the *experience* of emotion and affect. Simondon's concept of affect names an emotionally rich activity of experiencing one's body as fundamentally relational and provisional, operating as a *relation of relations* Tucker (2018) – simultaneously a relation with one's own body (psychic) and a relation with others (collective). This can be thought of as an extension of Henri

Bergson's concept of affect (which he names *affection*) as qualitative *internal* states that constitute a uniqueness about the relation we have with our own bodies, as distinguished from the relations we have with other bodies, through perception. For Bergson, affection names the relation we have with our own bodies, which relies on feeling the sensations of the body. We come to know our bodies through *feeling* with them. This is different to the ways that we know other bodies, with the relation we have with our own body forming our *centre of representation*, "so that the other images range themselves round it in the very order in which they might be subject to its action; on the other hand, I know it from within, by sensations which I term affective" (Bergson, 1988, p. 61). Simondon's theory of affect retains the relationship with the collective (so-called *collective individuation*) as central – rather than distinguishing it as perception in the way Bergson does.

Simondon's extended concept of affect manifesting as individuality and collectivity offers a way of theoretically incorporating the specifics of social and psychological life. Whereas Bergson directs us to think that two different faculties are at work – perception (of other bodies) and affection (of our own body), meaning we are challenged to understand other bodies from a position of only having affective knowledge of our own body – Simondon makes both relations central to emotional and affective experience. In relation to affective computing, efforts such as Affdex do not acknowledge, nor incorporate, a sense of experience as simultaneously psychological and social. Instead, the analytic spotlight is shone only at physiological activity interpreted as emotion expression. There is no sense of how emotional and affective activity is central to how bodies operate as psychological AND social objects and subjects, for example, when people try to hide their feelings due to social context. Non-expressed emotional activity is much more difficult to track. Another limitation is lack of focus on the emotional impact of affective computing itself and its role as a social agent. For instance, one might ask how people feel about having their faces scanned by facial recognition technologies as they go about their daily lives, or indeed, potentially having emotion chips that read psychophysiological data in their computers. How does this feed into the emotional expressions that technologies categorise and make inferences about? Affective computing markets itself as the emotional expert that can discover authentic emotional activity beyond the capabilities of individuals and yet, does not address its role as a part of a digitisation of emotion, as an agent of emotional and affective *change* not *discovery*. Affective computing technologies are not passive tools that identify and categorise, but come to be actors in our social worlds, and as such, become part of what creates the emotional landscape against which social and psychological life exists. It is here that a more expansive approach that analyses the emergence of emotion in and through social and material situations is potentially valuable. Such an approach could help to demonstrate how the experience of emotion is always-already situational and relational. The example of neuromarketing based on face-tracking technologies can be seen in a relational way too. Surely, the way we respond to an advert depends on the context within which it is viewed, e.g. whether individually or with others? We may respond more positively to an advert for a product that is a favourite of a loved one, especially if we view it with them present.

To date, AI-utilising emotion-related technologies have failed to capture the role of emotion and affect as core ways in which we relate to ourselves (as subjects) and to the world. The focus on physiological expression offers only a narrow analytic spotlight, which is shorn of much of the rich multi-dimensionality of emotional and affective life. Despite claims to the contrary, so-called emotional-AI is limited and is a long way from interpreting the broad range of conscious and non-conscious processes that can constitute emotional and affective activity. As social scientists, we need to attempt to ensure we are part of research dialogues concerning new emotion-related AI developments, which are coming thick and fast. This may involve us operating outside our normal environments, e.g. working more closely with computer scientists in the design of new technologies. Moreover, there is significant need to offer social scientific insight of the emotional and affective impact of new technologies once they are in operation. The next chapter continues the discussion of areas in which emotional and affective life intersect with digital technologies, with a focus on social media.

References

Alder, K. (2009). *The lie detectors: The history of an American obsession*. Lincoln: University of Nebraska Press.

Barrett, L. F. (2018). *How emotions are made: The secret life of the brain*. London: PAN Books.

Barrett, L. F., Adolphs, R., Marsella, S., Martinez, A. M., & Pollak, S. D. (2019). Emotional expressions reconsidered: Challenges to inferring emotion from human facial movements. *Psychological Science in the Public Interest, 20*(1), 1–68.

Beavers, A. F. (2009). Between angels and animals: The question of robot ethics, or is Kantian moral agency desirable? *Proceedings of the Association for Practical and Professional Ethics, 18th Annual Meeting*, Cincinnati, OH (p. 13).

Bergson, H. (1988). *Matter and memory*. New York, NY: Zone Books.

Boffey, D. (2018). EU border 'lie detector' system criticised as pseudoscience. *The Guardian*, p. 2.

Bouhuys, A. L., Bloem, G. M., & Groothuis, T. G. (1995). Induction of depressed and elated mood by music influences the perception of facial emotional expressions in healthy subjects. *Journal of Affective Disorders, 33*(4), 215–226.

Calvo, R. A., & D'Mello, S. K. (2012). *New perspectives on affect and learning technologies* (Vol. 3). New York/London: Springer Science & Business Media.

Clynes, M. (1977). *Sentics: The touch of emotions*. London: Souvenir Press.

Clynes Manfred, E., & Kline Nathan, S. (1960, September). Cyborgs and space. *Astronautics*.

Cowie, R. (2015). Ethical issues in affective computing. In R. A. Calvo, S. D'Mello, J. Gratch & A. Kappas (Eds.), *The Oxford Handbook of Affective Computing* (p. 334–348). Oxford: Oxford University Press.

Cytowic, R. (1993). *The man who tasted shapes: A bizarre medical mystery offers revolutionary insights into emotions. Reasoning, and consciousness*. London: Abacus.

Damasio, A. (1994). *Descartes error: Emotion, rationality and the human brain* (p. 352). New York, NY: Putnam.

Damasio, A. R. (2000). *The feeling of what happens: Body and emotion in the making of consciousness*. London: Mariner Books.

Darwin, C. (2002). *The expression of the emotions in man and animals*. Oxford: Oxford University Press.

De Vries, B. (1991). Assessment of the affective response to music with Clynes's sentograph. *Psychology of Music, 19*(1), 46–64.

D'Mello, C., & Graessner, A. (2012). Dynamics of affective states during complex learning. *Learning and Instruction, 22*(2), 145–157.

Dreyfus, H. L. (1979). *What computers can't do: The limits of artificial intelligence* (rev. ed.). New York, NY: Harper & Row.

Dreyfus, H. L. (1992). *What computers still can't do: A critique of artificial reason*. Cambridge, MA: MIT Press.

Ekman, P. (2004). *Emotions revealed: Understanding faces and feelings*. London: Phoenix.

Ellis, D., & Tucker, I. (2015). *Social psychology of emotion*. London: Sage.

Erez, A., & Isen, A. M. (2002). The Influence of positive affect on the components of expectancy motivation. *Journal of Applied Psychology, 87*(6), 1055–1067.

Fry, H. (2019). *Hello world: How to be human in the age of the machine*. London: Penguin.

Gabrielsson, A., & Juslin, P. N. (2003). Emotional expression in music. In R. J. Davidson, K. R. Scherer & H. H. Goldsmith (Eds.), *Series in affective science. Handbook of affective sciences* (p. 503–534). Oxford: Oxford University Press.

Goeleven, E., De Raedt, R., Leyman, L., & Verschuere, B. (2008). The Karolinska Directed Emotional Faces: A validation study. *Cognition and Emotion, 22*(6), 1094–1118.

Gorman, B. S., & Crain, W. C. (1974). Decoding of "sentograms". *Perceptual and Motor Skills, 39*(2), 784–786.

Gunes, H., & Hung, H. (2016). Is automatic facial expression recognition of emotions coming to a dead end? The rise of the new kids on the block. *Image and Vision Computing, 55*, 6–8.

Hama, H., & Tsuda, K. (1990). Finger-pressure waveforms measured on Clynes' sentograph distinguish among emotions. *Perceptual and Motor Skills, 70*(2), 371–376.

Hannah-Moffat, K. (2019). Algorithmic risk governance: Big data analytics, race and information activism in criminal justice debates. *Theoretical Criminology, 23*(4), 453–470.

Heaven, D. (2018). AI to interrogate travellers. *New Scientist, 240*(3202), 5.

LeDoux, J. (1996). *The emotional brain*. New York, NY: Simon & Schuster Paperbacks.

Leys, R. (2017). *The ascent of affect: Genealogy and critique*. Chicago, IL; London: The University of Chicago Press.

Malekzadeh, M., Mustafa, M. B., & Lahsasna, A. (2015). A review of emotion regulation in intelligent tutoring systems. *Educational Technology and Society, 18*(4), 435–445.

Malin, B. J. (2014). *Feeling mediated: A history of media technology and emotion in America*. New York: New York University Press.

McCorduck, P. (2004). *Machines who think: A personal inquiry into the history and prospects of artificial intelligence* (25th anniversary update). Natick, MA: A.K. Peters.

McStay, A. (2018). *Emotional AI: The rise of empathic media*. London: Sage.

Meijer, E. H., Verschuere, B., Gamer, M., Merckelbach, H., & Ben-Shakhar, G. (2016). Deception detection with behavioral, autonomic, and neural measures: Conceptual and methodological considerations that warrant modesty: Deception research: Methodological considerations. *Psychophysiology*, *53*(5), 593–604.

Mortillaro, M., & Scherer, K. R. (2009). Bodily expression of emotion. In D. Sander & K. Scherer (Eds.), *Oxford companion to emotion and the affective sciences*. Oxford: OUP.

Nettelbeck, T., Henderson, C., & Willson, R. (1989). Communicating emotion through sound: An evaluation of Clynes' theory of sentics. *Australian Journal of Psychology*, *41*(1), 25–36.

Panksepp, J. (1998). *Series in affective science. Affective neuroscience: The foundations of human and animal emotions*. Oxford: Oxford University Press.

Petrovica, S., Anohina-Naumeca, A., & Ekenel, H. K. (2017). Emotion recognition in affective tutoring systems: Collection of ground-truth data. *Procedia Computer Science*, *104*, 437–444.

Piaget, J. (1952). The origins of intelligence in children (M. Cook, Trans.). W. W. Norton & Co.

Picard, R. W. (1995). *Affective computing* (M. I. T. Media laboratory perceptual Computing Section Technical Report No. 321) (pp. 1–26). https://affect.media.mit.edu/pdfs/95.picard.pdf.

Picard, R. W. (1997). *Affective computing*. Cambridge, MA: MIT Press.

Picard, R. W. (2000). *Affective computing. (First Paperback Edition)*. Cambridge, MA; London: The MIT Press.

Picard, R. W., Vyzas, E., & Healey, J. (2001). Toward machine emotional intelligence: Analysis of affective physiological state. *IEEE Transactions on Pattern Analysis and Machine Intelligence*, *23*(10), 1175–1191.

Russell, J. A. (2003). Core affect and the psychological construction of emotion. *Psychological Review*, *110*(1), 145–172.

Sánchez-Escribano, M. G. (2018). *Engineering computational emotion-A reference model for emotion in artificial systems*. Berlin: Springer.

Sariyanidi, E., Gunes, H., & Cavallaro, A. (2014). Automatic analysis of facial affect: A survey of registration, representation, and recognition. *IEEE Transactions on Pattern Analysis and Machine Intelligence*, *37*(6), 1113–1133.

Sarrafzadeh, A., Alexander, S., Dadgostar, F., Fan, C., & Bigdeli, A. (2008). "How do you know that I don't understand?" A look at the future of intelligent tutoring systems. *Computers in Human Behavior*, *24*(4), 1342–1363.

Sedgwick, E. K., & Frank, A. (2003). *Touching feeling: Affect, pedagogy, performativity*. Durham: Duke University Press.

Shaviro, S. (2016). *Discognition*. London: Repeater.

Su, S.-H., Lin, H.-C. K., Wang, C.-H., & Huang, Z.-C. (2016). Multi-modal affective computing technology design the interaction between computers and human of intelligent tutoring systems. *International Journal of Online Pedagogy and Course Design (IJOPCD)*, *6*(1), 13–28.

Trussoni, S. J., O'Malley, A., & Barton, A. (1988). Human emotion communication by touch: A modified replication of an experiment by Manfred Clynes. *Perceptual and Motor Skills*, *66*(2), 419–424.

Tucker, I. M. (2018). Deleuze, Simondon and the problem of psychological life. *Annual Review of Critical Psychology Special Issue*, 14, 127–144.

Turing, A. M. (1937). On computable numbers, with an application to the Entscheidungsproblem. *Proceedings of the London Mathematical Society*, *2*(1), 230–265.

Turing, A. M. (1950). Computing machinery and intelligence. *Mind*, *59*(236), 433–460.

Vail, A. K., Grafsgaard, J. F., Boyer, K. E., Wiebe, E. N., & Lester, J. C. (2016). Predicting learning from student affective response to tutor. Questions. *Proceedings of the 13th International Conference on Intelligent Tutoring System.* Zagreb, Croatia (pp. 154–164).

Verschuere, B., Rosenfeld, J. P., Winograd, M. R., Labkovsky, E., & Wiersema, R. (2009). The role of deception in P300 memory detection. *Legal and Criminological Psychology, 14*(2), 253–262.

Whitehead, A. N. (1964). *The concept of nature.* Cambridge: Cambridge University Press

Whitehead, A. N. (1985). *Process and reality: An essay in cosmology: Gifford Lectures delivered in the University of Edinburgh during the session 1927-28.* New York, NY: Free Press.

Wilson, E. A. (2010). *Affect and artificial intelligence.* Seattle: University of Washington Press.

Zeng, Z., Pantic, M., Roisman, G. I., & Huang, T. S. (2008). A survey of affect recognition methods: Audio, visual, and spontaneous expressions. *IEEE Transactions on Pattern Analysis and Machine Intelligence, 31*(1), 39–58.

Zuboff, S. (2019). *The age of surveillance capitalism: The fight for a human future at the new frontier of power.* London: Profile Books.

Retrieved from https://www.affectiva.com/how/how-it-works/.

Retrieved from https://www.iborderctrl.eu/Technical-Framework.

Retrieved from https://alumni.berkeley.edu/california-magazine/spring-2010-searchlight-gray-areas/truth-machine.

Retrieved from https://www.marketsandmarkets.com/Market-Reports/affective-comput ing-market-130730395.html.

4   Social media and emotion

What draws us to spend an increasing amount of our lives using social media? Do they enable new forms of emotional and affective expression? How do social media attempt to mobilise and manipulate emotion? What are the broader affective implications of living in environments saturated with social media? And how is emotion modelled and conceptualised in the social media context to facilitate research and capitalise it? In this chapter, we explore these questions through focusing on key areas pertaining to social media in relation to emotional and affective life: Motivation and theories of desire, personal information, emoticons and emojis, and sentiment analysis, considered alongside notions of digital and affective capitalism. Understanding emotion related to social media is a nascent, but blooming field of study. Existing research has revolved around a series of concerns, such as the desire to form and maintain relationships, for pleasure, to escape, for information, and to expand the self. Moreover, social media is often portrayed as fulfilling any number of human needs and drives. The captivating powers of social media have made them of interest to a wide variety of businesses, governments, and other institutions, all of whom are eager to pioneer ways of generating data related to peoples' conscious and unconscious emotional lives.

In this chapter, we first explore motivation (and what is later referred to as desire) in relation to social media and what kind of conceptualisation of motivation addresses the diversity and multiplicity of social media activity. Being able to categorise and quantify motivation has been of considerable interest for developers to augment social media platforms with the aim of enhancing and increasing usage. Social media are portrayed as new ways to reach emotional fulfilment, e.g. by continually swiping screens, using emojis, etc. These activities are framed as having affective potential that social media algorithms can plunder for their surplus value. The fact that these motivations and emotion-led desires are largely made possible by the corporate imperatives of contemporary tech-obsessed capitalism does not appear to quash people's desire to use social media. Delineating categorisations of one sort or another renders social media content into bite-sized data fit for market economics. This chapter focuses on key areas in which emotion is recruited in social media design and analysis, namely our motivations and desires for engaging with social media, along with exploring some of the main ways that emotionality is digitised and catalogued, namely through personal information, emojis, and sentiment analysis.

The term *social media* captures a wide range of platforms and associated activity, and we primarily use it to denote platforms as Facebook, Twitter, Instagram, Snapchat, and, to a lesser extent, YouTube and TikTok (among others). Social media activity can be motivated by a range of (sometimes contradictory) factors. For example, Twitter and other microblogging platforms are often used for instant updates on 'what is going on in the world', whereas Facebook commonly involves connecting with friends and family (although of course much over-lap exists across platforms). A joke meme circulating towards the end of 2019 characterised platforms according to four photographs of a person in each of the following social media contexts: Facebook, Instagram, Linkedin, and Tinder. In each photographic image they presented themselves differently in relation to the platform's perceived function. For example, on Tinder, they looked sexy, whereas on Linkedin, they looked professional, on Instagram, they looked young, and on Facebook, more family friendly. This chapter is not a fine-grained analysis of the specificities of different platforms but analyses social media platforms' more general relations to emotionality.

Desiring social media

The long-standing distinction between emotion and cognition figures in relation to existing models of motivation, despite it being subject to significant critique (see Ellis & Tucker, 2015). For example, Brewer and Hewstone's (2004) *Emotion and Motivation* states that social psychology has remained a predominantly cognitive discipline. However, they argue that incorporating a tripartite approach, which involves emotion, motivation, and cognition, helps to make the field much better balanced. Motivation was argued to be missing in early attempts in cybernetics to computationally replicate human behaviour. Silvan Tomkins made this point, and prioritised affect over motivation in his mid-20th century theory of affect. For Tomkins, the history of philosophy is littered with theories that subordinated affect to the drives (Leys, 2017). As such, theories of motivation were likely to be biased towards the drives. Tomkins proposed a significant shift in understanding, arguing that the *affect system* underpins motivation, not the system of drives; "it is the affects rather than the drives which are the primary human motives" (Tomkins & Messick, 1963, p. 16). This was an important moment in the history of theories of affect and emotion, and it significantly influenced the (re)emergence of affect studies in the social sciences and cultural studies in late 20th century. It also placed conceptual debates about the role of the drives and affect in motivation at the centre of cybernetics, which has been an important influence on contemporary studies of technology and emotion (e.g. emotional AI). Indeed, the relationships between affects, drives, motivation, and cognition continue to feature in and shape contemporary theories regarding motivation, emotion, and social media use.

Our approach takes heed of Tomkins's point in terms of registering an important role for motivation in relation to emotional processes. To understand the latter, one needs to analyse the former. We recognise that theories of motivation in psychology, since the mid-20th century, have primarily come from social cognition, but argue for an expanded approach to motivation that incorporates thinking from areas such as philosophy, humanistic psychology, and psychoanalysis. It is this broader discussion of motivation that helps to inform as to the emotional implications of social media activity. Conceptualisations of motivation in psychology are often tied to rational choice theories, and therefore, have been grounded in cognitive theory rather than emotion. This has certainly been the case for much social media research of motivation.

Motivation research in the social media context is an extensive research field. Clearly, gaining insight into what motivates people to use and sustain engagement with social media is of significant interest to social scientists (as well as for those who profit from their use). As the field is so wide, this section on motivation does not constitute the complete picture, however, it attempts to discuss and analyse what we have found as the most visible and dominant research in this field. Motivation is predominantly understood in the field through self-evaluation questionnaires and hence, each motivation is thought of as a variable that is malleable, for example, through the material world of tangible rewards, such as money, and more psycho-virtual rewards (e.g. increased "likes" and/or "followers"). A lot of the research that these theories are tied to tend to construct social media as fulfilling various gratifications (Chen, 2011; Dunne Áine et al., 2010; Huang et al., 2014; Mo & Leung, 2015; Park et al., 2009; Quan-Haase & Young, 2010; Raacke & Bonds-Raacke, 2008; Shao, 2009; Smock et al., 2011; Stafford et al., 2004; Whiting & Williams, 2013), creating a sense of psychological ownership (Karahanna et al., 2015) and increasing social capital (Best & Krueger, 2006; Burke et al., 2011; Ellison et al., 2007; Hofer & Aubert, 2013; Mo & Leung, 2015; Valenzuela et al., 2009; Williams, 2006). What is not forthcoming in the literature is how these motives are pre-scribed, socially produced, and can be thought of as not fixed, but more often unconscious, relational, processual, situational, social, political, and affect laden.

Existing research on social media and motivation tends to portray it as incorporating a fixed number of categories encapsulated under superordinate categories; for example: Social networking, information, self, escapism, and enjoyment (Chen, 2011; Dunne Áine et al., 2010; Ellison et al., 2007; Huang et al., 2014; Karahanna et al., 2015; Mo & Leung, 2015; Park et al., 2009; Quan-Haase & Young, 2010; Raacke & Bonds-Raacke, 2008; Shao, 2009; Smock et al., 2011; Whiting & Williams, 2013). The models of motivation used in social media studies, such as Uses and Gratifications Theory, Psychological Ownership Theory, and Social Capital Theory, are based within Rational Choice theorisations, which denote categories of motivation as fixed, stable, and operating as individual psychological constructs. This is reflected in the methodologies which rely upon questionnaires and surveys that seek to index individuals' self-reported motivations through pre-defined mental categories. This version of the psychological subject emerged as part of the cognitive revolution of the mid-20th century. Historically, theories have framed motivation-related processes as complex, and the subject of tensions between *reason* and *emotion*. For instance, Plato envisaged motivation as existing in a battle between reason and emotion. Motivation has commonly been related to conscious and cognitive processes, rather than the somatic-emotionally driven aspects, or what Tomkins denotes as affect systems, that have been culturally adopted over time.

Drawing on a range of disciplines (psychology, sociology, anthropology, and cultural studies), Jansz discusses what he understands as the "social embeddedness of human motivation" (1996, p. 472). He acknowledges that there are biological urges that motivate individuals, but stresses the importance of sociality and culture. The communicative interaction, as, for instance, a consequence of being a member of a particular social group, leads to the internalisation of culturally normalised affectivities (or motivations). These social motives, as he terms them, are not, however, taken on wholesale; they may be resisted by the individual because they conflict with other social motives. He argues that social motives may undergo modification throughout the internalisation process. Jansz uses the term "borrowing" to denote the way that social motives are reconstructed intrapersonally through communicative interaction, rather than simply copied through internalisation, and hence, they are then experienced as if they have derived from within the individual. Motivations, therefore, can become idiosyncratic, rather than overly socially and culturally determined and often nonconscious aspects of everyday life. Additionally, Jansz argues that the motivations may be nonconsciously in conflict with each other. This latter part is rather similar to how Leibniz and Nietzsche theorised motivation activity (see Smith, 2011).

Deleuze and Guattari (1987; 1987; 1994) offer a different way of thinking about motivation (Styhre, 2001). Following Leibniz and Nietzsche, Deleuze and Guattari think of desire as a complex configuration of drives and impulses. These have been constructed to allow for investment in a particular social formation (i.e. the capitalist formation). Desire is thus invested in the social formation. However, the social formation (capitalism) brings about a *lack*, which fits the common practice of thinking of desire in terms of lack. Desire though is not defined as a feeling of lack or absence; rather, desire *produces*, it is a creative force. It is the social infrastructure that creates the lack, not desire; "Why do people fight for their servitude as stubbornly as though it were their salvation", asked Spinoza (Spinoza quoted in Smith, 2011, p. 4). This question formulates clearly what Deleuze and Guattari understood as the fundamental problem of political philosophy, in other words "why do we have such a stake in investing in a social system that constantly represses us, thwarts our interests, and introduces lack into our lives?" (Smith, 2011, p. 74). This is because one's desires, the drives and affects, are not our own, but have been instituted into each of us through the capitalist infrastructure.

Deleuze's use of *interest* in place of desire is a move to insert rational choice theory in its proper context, argues Smith (2011). This school of thought tends to understand human nature economically, as always acting to secure and maximise one's own interest. A person may have a rational interest in using Facebook, for example, to widen their social circle, with the view of gaining social capital, to ultimately increase the chances of obtaining a specific job. This interest is only possible because it exists in a particular social formation. So, desire is invested in the social formation, which creates particular interests (e.g. having a particular job), which in turn creates the sense of lack, the person lacks a particular job, hence filling the lack by having the particular job is conceived of as increasing social and economic status. Smith suggests that another distinction between interest and desire is the rational and irrational, respectively. The pursuit of one's interests may be rational; for instance, using Facebook to widen one's social capital by being able to befriend assemblages of people who work in the field of interest. However, the underlying social formation, capitalism, for Deleuze and Guattari, was irrational. Smith uses a quote from an interview with Deleuze to illustrate his thinking:

> Reason is always a region carved out of the irrational-it is not sheltered from the irrational at all, but traversed by it and only defined by a particular kind of relationship among irrational factors. Underneath all reason lies delirium and drift. Everything about capitalism is rational, except capital. . . A stock market is a perfectly rational mechanism, you can understand it, learn how it works; capitalists know how to use it; and yet what a delirium, it's mad. . . It's just like theology: everything about it is quite rational-if you accept sin, the immaculate conception, and the incarnation, which are themselves irrational elements."
>
> (Deleuze, quoted in Smith, 2011, p. 75)

Deleuze and Guattari understood capitalism as fundamentally "schizophrenic", or what object-relations theorists would refer to as split (e.g. Klein's paranoid schizoid position (1946), rather than contemporary understandings of *schizophrenia* as a problematic psychiatric diagnostic category, Boyle, 2002). It is part of a social formation that constructs or restricts the flows of, for example: money, commodities, people, traffic, the words of a language, and, of course, the individual's drives. Thus, just as schizophrenia is at the heart of (capitalist) society, it is also at the heart of the self, "our society produces schizzos the same way it produces Prell shampoo or Ford cars, the only difference being that the schizzos are not saleable" (Deleuze & Guattari, 1987, p. 245). Social media is at the heart of the new digital capitalism with which we now live. Emotion and affect in the digital age are apprehended by social media as a way of shoring up the capital. Motivations are emotionally manipulated and constructed through digital capitalist algorithms, but are argued to create a sense of wanting more, an emptiness, or worse still, as Nash (2016) suggests in his analysis of emoji use on social media, *anxiety* is the only payment that the social media user is rewarded with.

The motivations and desires of the social media corporations to obtain more capital through social media data leads to users becoming both producer and consumer, or what Beer and Burrows (2010) refer to as prosumer, as our desires become entangled with theirs. This sort of collaboration, Pridmore (2012) suggests, leads the individual to subtly consent to divulging personal information.

We end up nonconsciously desiring to work for the corporation and hand over that which is often most personal to us; it is not simply information, but *personal* information, which, in turn, as will be discussed below, becomes *impersonal*.

Digitised emotional capitalism and communitarianism

The translation of sometimes-ineffable emotional and affective processes into digitised symbolic form through, for example, emoticons and emojis, is having huge cultural impact and facilitates mass data generation in relation to people's use of social media. Nash (2016) argues that emojis are a tool designed for the commercial benefit of advertisers. Pariser (2011) suggests they are presented as empowering tools for the individual user, but have a dark underbelly that is part of the filter bubble, creating an informational determinism where "you can get stuck in a static, ever narrowing version of yourself – an endless you-loop" (Pariser, 2011, p. 16). Following Deleuze and other notable affect theorists, Nash thinks about emojis through Simondon's ontogenesis, wherein the *process* of individuation is privileged over the *product* of the individual body (i.e. process over the product) – as discussed in Chapter Two.

Nash argues that social media exploit beliefs of individuality and agency prominent prior to the digital age. Like, for example, Beer and Burrows, (2010), Pridmore (2012), Fuchs (2017), and Zuboff (2019) have argued, users are understood as both producing and consuming the social network product, but not participating in its profits, nor do they participate in the potential opportunities of social media networking. Nash puts forward a notion of the potential of social media to enable what Simondon refers to as transindividuation – life as simultaneously individual and collective (discussed in Chapter Two). Instead of basing his ontology on a reality involving the interacting of already existing individual forms (which, for Simondon, would be an ontology), he argues for an onto-genetic positioning of individuals as emergent through a broader system of transindividuation (which always-already involves relations that are individual and collective). For Simondon, individuation is not a singular and unified process, but the individual is a multiplicity of individuations (or individualising individuations) (Simondon, 2005). Nash applies this notion to digital data, which he suggests exist as generic continuums and are not indexically related to their source. Digital data are individuating digital entities, which, to exist, require modulation through a set of protocols that are encoded in what Nash describes as:

> the set of digital data being modulated; the operationalized and reciprocal sets of digital data "doing" the modulating (ie, software, operating system, digital networks); and the associated milieu which all of these sets of digital data individuate (ie, *the digital* in the world).
>
> (Nash, 2016, p. 7)

Hence the digital data, in its generic form, is akin to Simondon's preindividual. Digital data constitute ecosystems that are in a sense *preindividual*, as they are aggregated systems of mass data generated from individual bodies, but in which the connection with the individual is lost through aggregation. Digital data within the interactive social network are, according to Nash, profoundly indeterminate. Importantly for Nash, this enables digital capitalism to thrive. Moreover, digital capitalism contributes to digital environments that can create anxiety for the *slave worker*. Rather than recognise the *collective* part of their being, the individual subject is encouraged by social media to do the opposite, to turn inward, which only reinforces a static sense of individuality. This inward-looking subject then becomes anxious, as the inherent tension that constitutes its existence cannot be *solved* internally, only in relation to the collective, and as such, the *turn inward* only perpetuates the tension. The commodity that prevails, anxiety, is a very poor substitute for transindividuality. Nash hails it as a disingenuous logic of digital capitalism. The touted empowerment of the individual (or selfie culture), is a seductively masked quantification of the self for the advertising of products.

> The bigger and more generic the demographic group the better: "it's gone viral" meaning millions of individuals are watching the same thing, retweeting, reblogging, and reposting the same thing. "Yes, we are all individuals!" (Monty Python, 1979)
>
> (Nash, 2016, p. 14)

Simondon argues that workers, in the Fordist industrial paradigm, are kept alienated from the production process by distinguishing between regulating the machine and operating it: The former is seen as a cultural act, qualitatively different to the latter, which is a technical act. Nash applies this distinction to the social media users, who are seduced through an emotive language of engagement, believing they are regulating the machine rather than simply operating it. These beliefs were partly borne out of the digital utopianism and the emergence of ideal online communities that were advocated by communitarianist ideologies in the 1990s. Communitarians tend to understand the community as that which gives one a sense of belonging, cohesion, and a common purpose. Raymond Williams (1961) points out that the term community is bound up with ideology; it often signifies, in discourse, an ideal and pure, uncorrupted social formation. The emotive language of community and hence, social media, points to groups of people with common ideals and aspirations, wherein the individual is responsible for the community. An early example of this was Rheingold's (1994) description of the WELL, an early online group.

> Excerpt from Rheingold (1994, p. xviii)
> "Daddy is saying 'Holy moly!' to his computer again!"
> Those words have become a family code for the way my virtual community has infiltrated our real world. My seven-year-old daughter knows that her father congregates with a family of invisible friends who seem to gather in his computer. Sometimes he talks to them, even if nobody else can see them. And

she knows that these friends sometimes show up in the flesh, materializing from the next block or the other side of the planet.

Since the summer of 1985, for an average of two hours a day, seven days a week, I've been plugging my personal computer into my telephone and making contact with the WELL (Whole Earth 'Lectronic Link) – a computer conferencing system that enables people around the world to carry on public conversations and exchange private electronic mail (e-mail). The idea of a community accessible only via my computer screen sounded cold to me at first, but I learned quickly that people can feel passionately about e-mail and computer conferences. I've become one of them. I care about these people I met through my computer, and I care deeply about the future of the medium that enables us to assemble.

I'm not alone in this emotional attachment to an apparently bloodless technological ritual. Millions of people on every continent also participate in the computer-mediated social groups known as virtual communities, and this population is growing fast. Finding the WELL was like discovering a cozy little world that had been flourishing without me, hidden within the walls of my house; an entire cast of characters welcomed me to the troupe with great merriment as soon as I found the secret door.

There is almost a messianic hope tied to the future of virtual communities by Rheingold, where transindividuation can occur within communities that are warm, fuzzy, and friendly, but this is contrary to the highly ambivalent spaces that many experience today, or the digital network anxiety of Nash. The emotive discourse of communitarianism leads to beliefs that individuals can turn to social media in good and bad times, and that they help people live a balanced, healthy life. Morozov (2013) argued that this utopian vision of the internet was bound to fail. He looks at how a variety of corporate and government desires have nudged and steered behaviour through such mediums as social media by way of this emotional manipulation.

Plundering personalities

A prime example relating to emotional manipulation was the Facebook emotion experiment conducted on 689,000 Facebook users by Cornell University and the University of San Francisco, where newsfeeds were manipulated in attempts to control the emotions that users were exposed to (Kramer et al., 2014). This study had significant ethical problems (e.g. lack of consent) but has been used as evidence for the power of social media to manipulate thoughts, feelings, and emotion. No doubt, this had some impact upon Cambridge Analytica's more recent use of social media manipulation, whereby 50 million Facebook users' personal information was captured without consent of either Facebook or the users. This data was targeted with the intention of manipulating voter behaviour. Most notably, the Analytica manipulation was linked to Donald Trump's US Presidential election campaign and the Brexit campaign in the UK. Analytica developed software to predict and emotionally influence ballot box choices, otherwise known as psychographic microtargeting. The whistle blower Christopher Wiley stated:

> We exploited Facebook to harvest millions of people's profiles. And built models to exploit what we knew about them and target their inner demons. That was the basis the entire company was built on.
>
> (Graham-Harrison & Cadwalladr, 2018)

Through developing a personality detection algorithm, they were able to detect a voters' orientation and craft messages aimed at nudging them towards a Trump or Brexit vote. Up until 2012, Facebook users were invited to take a psychometric test called myPersonality, an app developed by David Stillwell in 2007 at The Psychometrics Centre at Cambridge Judge Business School. Six million people took the test, and their data were shared with registered academic collaborators. According to Kanter and Kanter (2018), this led to 45 scientific publications. In 2008, Michael Konsinki joined Stillwell, and they claimed they were able to predict users' personalities. The theory of personality that it drew on was the five-factor model, which is supposed to measure a person's amount of: Openness to experience, conscientiousness, extraversion, agreeableness, and neuroticism (OCEAN). After the test, users could opt in to share their Facebook data with the researchers. Personality outcomes were then correlated with their Facebook likes. For example, people who liked Lady Gaga were most likely to be extraverts, and those who liked philosophy were most likely to be introverts. The suggestion is that the more data-points that can be harvested, the more reliable and powerful the predictions become. It was famously stated that with 150 Facebook likes, the system could predict a user's personality better than an individuals' friends could, and with 300 likes, it could outperform a spouse! (Youyou et al., 2015). Cambridge Analytica (as subsidiary of Strategic Communication Limited Group [SGL]) was partly owned by an American hedge fund billionaire, Robert Mercer. A data scientist, Christopher Wylie, went to work for Alexander Nix at SGL and introduced Wylie to Steve Bannon, who was the head of Donald Trump's 2016 US Presidential election campaign. Between them, they decided to combine microtargeting (a well-used political tool to target voters) with harvesting voters' personality information. Mercer invested $15 million into Cambridge Analytica to develop the idea, and Konsinki was approached by Wylie for the myPersonality data. For some reason, they were not able to obtain this data, and so a solution was developed by Aleksandr Kogan, who developed an app entitled thisisyourdigitallife, which incorporated the personality quiz. They paid users to take the test and to have their data collected, but not only was the data of the participants taken, the data of their Facebook friends were also harvested. Facebook's terms allowed this data from their friends to be taken unless they had changed their privacy settings. Within the Trump campaign, Analytica focused upon what it saw as potential voters who were hesitating, considered as having a personality type that is high on the neuroticism scale, and hence, deemed vulnerable to Trump's messages. Those in swing states were particularly targeted. This occurred through a Facebook feature known as "Dark Post", personalised ads only visible to the targeted individual.

Many psychologists and social theorists have, for the last 50 years, critiqued personality trait theories (e.g. Mischel, 1968; Kelly, 1970). Among the critiques are the following:

- Self-tests are relatively subjective and hence are low in validity; they require individuals to have insight into themselves and to be honest about themselves.
- There are many personality psychologies with a variety of competing traits that differ from each other.
- Many of the so-called personality factors, traits, and dimensions are context-dependent and widely fluctuate.
- Critical psychologists, arguing from social constructionism, are likely to argue against the validity of the very concept of personality, suggesting that it is an empty category, a reification.

We agree with these critiques, and view personality tests such as OCEAN as constructing overly simplistic notions of what they denote as *personality*. Unsurprisingly, significant questions have been raised regarding the effectiveness of Analytica's operations. For example, voter profiles are very weakly correlated with political values, and so voters are often mistargeted (Chen & Potenza, 2018). Other variables are more likely to correlate with potential Trump support, such as the Birther conspiracy theory. Prior to the Trump campaign, Analytica worked on the Ted Cruz campaign, during the Republican Primary in 2016. The psychographic model was reported in the New York Times by former Cruz aide Rick Tyler as unreliable; over half the people from Oklahoma that Analytica identified as supporters, in fact, favoured other candidates. The extra information that Analytica was offering does not give any more useful information than can be obtained from a public voter database, and it loses validity over time as voters change their minds. Although it may work to persuade consumers to, for example, buy a different brand of shampoo, something as core as a political belief is likely to be much more difficult to alter, it is argued. Critiques have therefore suggested that Cambridge Analytica has exaggerated its role in the election outcome, e.g. Kendall Taggart (2017) wrote that more than a dozen employees of Analytica, Trump campaign staffers, and executives at consulting firms stated that psychographics were not actually used in Trump's campaign:

> But interviews with 13 former employees, campaign staffers, and executives at other Republican consulting firms who have seen Cambridge Analytica's work suggest that its psychological approach was not actually used by the Trump campaign and, furthermore, the company has never provided evidence that it even works. Rather than a sinister breakthrough in political technology, the Cambridge Analytica story appears to be part of the traditional

contest among consultants on a winning political campaign to get their share of credit — and win future clients.

(Taggart, 2017)

Nix boasts that Cambridge Analytica had about 5,000 data points on every American citizen, but Taggert argues that this is common; campaigns and political consultants from both the left and the right buy data on voter demographics, from age and gender to magazine and website subscriptions. It is worth noting, however, that the development of what The Psychometrics Centre at Cambridge Judge Business School call a psychodemographic profile is very much under way. For example, on their web-page, they have a tool called Apply Magic Sauce, which is "a battery of scientifically robust predictive algorithms that analyse your online behaviour to predict your psychodemographic profile" (psychometrics.cam .ac.uk). These events garnered major media coverage, particularly in the light of national political elections (e.g. three UK General Elections between 2015 and 2019). As such, the use of data generated from people's digital activity by political parties and data brokers is becoming increasingly part of the cultural consciousness regarding digital life. This has the potential to shape individuals' experiences and feelings regarding data and information and what can be taken to be *personal* in a digital age.

From personal to impersonal information

The question of what constitutes personal and private information is central to life in a digital age, e.g. should data be considered as information *about* the self that is digitised and commodified through a range of digital markets? This section explores this issue through a study conducted by one of the authors (Ellis, 2018), which suggests that data has come to be understood by social media users as *impersonal* rather than *personal*. This hinges on a question of ownership, with users feeling that they no longer own data generated from their activity, as its generation was part of what Zuboff (2019) calls a *behaviour surplus* of the *big other* of surveillance capitalism. This very much contrasts the notion of the individuality of data in theories of motivation and personality discussed above. The laying down of personal information is the result of the inculcation of social media, requiring us to believe in a trade-off of the unspoken social-(media)-contract that we (often non-consciously) sign up to. We are bound to click to agree to partake, despite the numerous and fluctuating terms and conditions. But how do people understand the trade-off of personal information? Ellis's (2018) study on social media practices found that participants understood personal information as relatively impersonal, but emoticons and emojis as relatively personal expressions of the self.

The study involved sixteen semi-structured interviews on the topic of participants' "everyday social media use". A range of people were interviewed; the only inclusion criterion was that participants were adults and used social media daily. The analysis concerned people's social media usage, what sorts of information they share, and issues relating to security, trust, and emotional and affective activity. The interview protocol was structured around the following four specific themes: 1) *Background information*: The forms of social media platforms that were used, frequency of use, and reasons for preference; 2) *Personal information*: What forms (if any) of personal information are shared on-line and to whom; 3) *Trust*: How are issues related to trust negotiated with the platform and individuals within the network, what are the concerns (if any), and how might personal information be shared; 4) *Affective activity*: How might emotions and feelings be communicated and experienced online, how might this differ to offline activity, in what ways (if any) are emoticons used.

When asked about personal information, participants described it in similar ways to how marketers distinguish it. Phelps, Nowak, and Ferrell (2000) denote five categories of personal information used by marketers: Demographic characteristics, lifestyle characteristics (including media habits), shopping/purchasing habits, financial data, and personal identifiers (such as names and addresses). Personal information was discussed by the interviewees in much the same way. For example, typically participants stated that personal information was: *Where they ask you where you are from and your name* and *things that are already there, like relationships and date of birth*, with "they" presumably referring to social media service providers. Personal information was portrayed as something required by the platforms for their commercial interests. The social-media-contract is therefore fulfilled, through the generation and sharing of information commonly deemed to be *personal*. Part of the conceptual issue at work in relation to so-called personal data and social media is the apparent *fixing* of aspects of the individual self through data. Like the fixing of motivation and personality categories discussed above, the individual body becomes categorised according to fixed data points, in which a sense of the dynamism of bodies as mobile, feeling objects is at risk of being lost. This relates to the process philosophy of Albert North Whitehead (1978), namely his concepts of prehension, concrescence and actual entities. "The datum is abstracted and prehended by both the social media service providers and the user through processes of concrescence wherein fluid aspects of the self become frozen blocks of actual entities incorporating personal information" (Ellis, 2018, p. 21).

Data generated from individual bodies (so-called *personal* information) become what Whitehead would denote as actual entities (frozen, but fleeting moments of experience). They lose their dynamism and become a datafication of frozen or static representation of the self that is, in turn, categorised, quantified, and rendered for digital capitalism. What was considered personal becomes *im*personal, as it no longer refers to the movements and activity of an individual body, but becomes part of a large database. As such, individuals no longer have ownership of it, as we are, as Marx would have it, literally alienated from ourselves and perhaps, as Nash (2016) suggests, anxiety persists.

So, what is occurring here? How does this exchange operate, and are all the actors involved aware? It is difficult to remain unaware of the demand of social media for data and information, but does this translate into specific understanding of personal information in relation to social media? Are we forming new relationships with the self? Are parts of our very being becoming commodified and fragmented? It can be viewed as a process of virtual detachment from the self. What was once personal and private is becoming increasingly impersonal and subject to processes of networked publicness, e.g. becoming visible to others. What Whitehead considered to be actual entities of the self are increasingly prehended through acts of online concretion, through the social-media-contract.

One social media user in Ellis's study stated that he did not share personal information; yet when asked in what ways he communicated emotion online, he responded by saying that his Whatsapp status reflects his life. He framed his social media activity as a distinction between personal information and status, the latter involves his feelings "because status is how you feel at the current moment". His status update is considered less fixed than what is portrayed as personal information. The status entry affords more dynamic representations of feelings, or at least of how he wants to be perceived as feeling, rather than choosing from a predefined set of limited criteria. It is an actual occasion of the current, but already passed, moment. The process of actualisation solidifies the moment, feeling, emotion, and affect for all to see. But it appears ironically more *personal* than so called *personal information*. Perhaps these are non-consciously prehended as non-commodifiable information, and so, in some way, remain personal, shared only with a desired crowd.

Whitehead used the term prehension to name what he saw as an inherently non-reductionist and relational account of life. Prehension defines the ways in which human and non-human entities *appropriate* elements from other objects. Put simply, prehension is about a process of being shaped by the existence of other objects. Crucially though, it does not start from a position of conceptualising objects as distinct entities, but rather as always-already in connection and relations with others. They do not exist outside, or separately, from these relations. Prehension is a way to conceptualise this perpetual inter-connectedness, without reducing it to the level of individual conscious emotion. Prehensions are not psychological processes. They do not refer to a process originating from an individual subject or object, but rather to objects registering the presence of another's existence. This relates to what Aristotle called accidental changes, wherein the quality of an object is in some-way changed, for example, the temperature of a stone from the heat of the sun, or the reverberation of a guitar string being loosened or tightened. The stone emerges as part of a relation constituted through the prehension of the heat of the sun and likewise, the string prehends reverberations of the strum, but in different ways to how humans may feel the sun's heat and the strumming of a guitar chord. In a digital context, prehension denotes the appropriation of, and relations between, bodies and digital technologies. It encourages us to consider these relations beyond their impact as registered by an individual body, but as part of the broader "system of mutual relevance" (Whitehead, 2011, p. 184) that constitutes our social worlds. Systems are increasingly digitally mediated, albeit in ways that do not register, in entirety, at an individual cognitive or emotional level.

Emojification

Social media have emerged as digital systems that become *relevant* for bodies in multiple ways. One part of this is the visual realm of emojis and emoticons, which are designed as short-hand immediate ways to express the emotional content of a message. This hinges on the relationships between the visual effect of emojis and the underlying emotional dynamics of social media communication, as seen in the following extract:

> Erm the most personal stuff that gets up on-line are my emotions and thoughts and feelings at the time so it could be something like oh I'm so frustrated that I have missed the bus but then I wouldn't go deep into how I feel on Twitter or something like that.
>
> (Ellis, 2018, p. 22)

Perhaps significantly, the term "stuff" is used in place of *information*, which implies a less formal and a more transitory quality. This personal stuff includes feelings, emotions, thoughts, and, in this instance, "frustration". The frustration of missing a bus can manifest as a multi-layered emotional event, the specifics of which can be difficult to express through social media. It is more appropriate, in terms of the standard conventions of social media communication, to express the frustration through an emoji, e.g. 😟. This renders the multi-layered emotional dynamic created by missing the bus into a pre-categorised "snapshot" image, in keeping with the immediacy of social media communication. The emotion icon, emoticon, or, more precisely in this case, emoji, derived from the 1980s, wherein Scott E. Fahlman (a computer science professor at Carnegie Mellon University) developed a strategy for ensuring that any jokes that were posted on their digital bulletin board were not taken literally, as many sarcastic comments were. He states that this was important because:

> when using text-based online communication, we lack the body language or tone-of-voice cues that convey this information when we talk in person or on the phone. Various "joke markers" were suggested, and in the midst of that discussion it occurred to me that the character sequence :-) would be an elegant solution
>
> Fahlman, n.d.)

Emoticons, therefore, were first used on social media to curtail ambiguity. Today, emoticons are referred to as combinations of symbols that can be found on a qwerty keyboard, whereas emojis are pictures. When typing an emoticon, such as the following smiley face :), Microsoft Word and Outlook email will automatically turn it into an emoji. The AffdexMe app (discussed in Chapter Three) also actualises facial expressions captured on the camera phone as emojis (although it is not clear from the app what actual use this has). Vyvyan Evans (2017) argues that the "[E]moji is providing an inevitable step in plugging a gap in a new channel of communication: The digital ultimately "makes us more effective communicators in our twenty-first-century world of communication" (238–239).

Emojis reduce affective activity to a single picture, radically simplifying the complexity and depth of an actual occasion of emotion, hence the statement above "I wouldn't go into how I feel". From an actual occasion, certain prehensions are selected (Whitehead states these are positive prehensions), and others are deselected (negative prehensions). The latter are part of Whitehead's unifying philosophy, in which *all* other elements in a universe are potentially part of a given actual occasion. Of course, only a selection of the totality will come to be dimensions of a specific actual occasion, a process which Whitehead categorises in terms of positive and negative prehensions. Selection is not a conscious decision of an individual body, but is part of a broader manifestation of a system of relations into an actual occasion of an experiencing body. In terms of social media, this refers to a *selection* of a specific part of the *digital universe* (i.e. data ecosystems) that constitute social media environments. It is not just the use of an emoji itself, but the unifying of a set of data and bodily activity into an actual entity that manifests as use of the emoji. As such, in the extract above, the use of an emoji is the final part of the selective process.

The communication actualisations afforded to social media users are confined by the infrastructure of the platform. Emoticons and emojis qualify and fix the affective capacity of activity. The dynamic complexity of *missing a bus* is stripped, and in its place, we have a picture of what is described on emojipedia .org as "[A] yellow face with closed eyes, furrowed eyebrows, broad frown, and two puffs of steam blowing out of its nose, as if in a huff or fuming." This emoji was originally named *face with the look of triumph*, which is rather odd, as triumph, in our understanding, is nothing like frustration. Why would one be steaming from the nose in triumph? Neuroscientists have claimed that a form of emotional contagion can occur on sight of an emoji. Churches et al. (2014) state that the same sections of the brain are activated through the sight of an online smiley face as when seeing a human in the flesh smiling. This has not come about through some innate capacity, but through the cumulative experiences of the digitised smiley face. For example, the following emoticon : -) would not have affected the smiley regions of the brain prior to 1982, as it did not signify the smile then, but now that we see this as a smiley, it would also affect associated brain regions. This suggests that emojis can have a neural (somatic) affect. Not only do we consciously perceive something, but it also implies nonconscious affectivity. Research has also indicated that the areas of the brain that are activated by a smiley face are those associated with, for example, smiling, but not the part of the brain associated with facial recognition. In other words, seeing a person smiling in the flesh and seeing a smiley emoticon both activate the right inferior frontal gyrus, an area of the brain believed to be associated with emotional processing, but only the former increases activity in the right fusiform gyrus, the part of the brain associated with key face-processing region (Yuasa et al., 2006). In addition, Yuasa and colleagues also found that emoticons increase activity in the Broca's area of the brain, a region involved in text comprehension. Hence, emoticon comprehension straddle verbal and non-verbal comprehension. However, what researchers have found interesting, following Yuasa et al.'s (2006) findings, is that although the areas of the brain associated with face-processing were not previously activated by emoticons, it seems that over time, that has changed, and new neural-cultural responses to emoticons are emerging (Churches et al., 2014). Our brains have adapted and learnt to recognise and be affected by the smiley face emoji. This would suggest, therefore, that some non-conscious emotional contagion activity is occurring. This is a slightly disturbing bio-cultural phenomenon; it does beg the question, in what other ways are we being affected by social media?

Ellis's (2018) study specifically asked people about their use of emoticons and emojis, with three main uses discussed. Firstly, to reduce ambiguity by reinforcing the meaning that was given in the text. This finding is common within a variety of literature on emoticons. For example, the British newspaper, *The Telegraph*, published an article entitled Internet rules and laws, in which one of the laws concerned the importance of indicating when being sarcastic: "Without a winking smiley or other blatant display of humour, it is impossible to create a parody of fundamentalism that someone won't mistake for the real thing" (Chivers, 2009). This links to the earlier point about the reasons that emoticons were developed in Carnegie Mellon University. Secondly, people spoke about the emoticon or emoji being used to reduce complexity. For example, one person stated:

I would find it easier to express myself online reason being I get helped. I've got emoticons I have phrases I have got all sorts of things to give me help in hand to explain the way I feel just in case I can't use words.

Pre-prepared stock phrases and emoticons are wheeled out to help "explain" what is being felt. An emoji works as a visual representation that may be difficult to codify within the former language system. Reduced selection (negative selection) of a basic emotional expression facilitates communication, although it does not fully represent the event under focus (e.g. missing a bus), it enables some form of desired effect. Lastly, and perhaps most interestingly, one person suggested that the emoticon creates a form of desired deception. This affective activity is well described through the dramaturgical theory developed in the sociology of emotion (Ellis & Tucker, 2015) and is akin to an online version of what Goffman (1967) describes as face-work and later, Hochschild (1983) called emotion-work. The following extract shows how one person within the study uses emoticons, not to express how he is feeling, but to mask or obscure the feeling.

I: In what ways do you communicate your emotions and feelings online?
Rob: Erm statuses-smiley faces and photos.
I: So, emoticons are helpful?
Rob: Yes.
I: Are you more open to expression emotion and feelings online than you are offline?

Rob: Yes.

I: Can you describe why this is?

Rob: Because if you're face-to-face with someone and your offline you are showing your emotions more whereas when you are online it does not have to be taken so seriously.

Of interest here is how a notion of authenticity is introduced to differentiate between online and offline activity. Social media are presented as a more flexible space in which to exercise control over emotional dynamics of communication. Face-to-face interaction is presented as emotion in a more authentic form, whereas social media facilitates greater expressive scope because the body is not present, "showing your emotions" to others. Perhaps this maintains what Goffman understands as rituals of politeness, but goes further to hide what is being felt.

Commodification of emojification

The above examples of using emoticons and emojis illustrate how the actual entities derived through these symbols emerge through multiple desires. These were desires to explain, objectify, and to deceive, but also to fix and qualify affect wherein prehensions are stripped of their dynamic complexity. This is often used, particularly by corporations, to increase clicks, likes, friends, users, and related economies. Stark and Crawford (2015) see the emoji as a conduit for affective labour. They suggest that the emoji characters embody and represent "the tension between affect as human potential, and as a productive force that capital continually seeks to harness through the management of everyday biopolitics" (Stark & Crawford, 2015, p. 2).

As we know from the work of Hochschild (1983), emotional labour and, more recently, affective labour, concerns the ways that affective activity in the workplace and the market more generally has become central to functions of economic systems. Just as personal information has been commodified, the emoji face, declared Murray Spain "is a symbol of capitalism" (BBC Radio and Wise Buddha Creative, 2013 – cited in Stark and Crawford, 2015). Stark and Crawford argue that platforms such as Facebook use emojis and emotional signifiers in their user experience design for further "commoditization and monetization of social affect" (2015, p. 8). They set out a relatively bleak history of the rise of the emoji, one that is blemished with lawsuits and churned through capitalism to suck it dry:

> The patterns of use for emoji over time between friends and partners can become abstract and cryptic, or can degenerate to become pro forma: just plain basic. In the best case, there is a unique personal subtext to that exchange of a rainbow or the love-heart smile, many layers of unspoken meaning that would be difficult for intelligence analysts or machine-learning algorithm to parse. Nonetheless, this complexity has not stopped institutions from making the attempt, and commercializing emoji sociality in other ways.
>
> (Stark & Crawford, 2015, p. 6)

A/B testing is essentially an experiment, where two or more variants of a page are shown to users at random and statistical analysis is used to determine which variation performs better for a given conversion goal, such as likes, comments, and shares. Overall, it is widely claimed by marketers that emojis induce users to engage more frequently (Van Grove, 2013). As we will discuss below, Facebook, Twitter, and other social media platforms can include emojis for sentiment analytics. A view of Emojitracker.com portrays the relatively shocking amount and array of real-time emoji use on Twitter. It is quite amazing to visualise all this data, which is of much apparent value to digital capitalism. For example, Hubspot are keen to point out that their research shows that certain emojis enhance clicks. The following emojis are the top ten that increase engagement: 1😀 2🧥 3🎔 4🧕 5🕊 6♥ 7😔 8♥ 9😕 10♥ (https://blog.hubspot.com/marketing/best-emojis). Hubspot state that the list is likely to be biased, as these were the top ten around the time of Valentine's Day. Emoji engagement is defined as how they increase likes, comments, and shares. Hubspot suggest that it is of interest that none of the first five emojis are yellow faces, and that it may be advantageous to use less popular emojis in marketing campaigns. Their analysis is rather surface level, as they cannot, for example, state why the cherry emoji is so popular. An A/B testing kit is available on the Hubspot blogsite to download. These are used to prove emojis improve traffic and to show which ones particularly do so. For example, in a Facebook post, emojis are claimed to increase likes by 57%.

The most used emoji on Twitter is the "Face with Tears of Joy" 😂 for the third year running, but according to Google trends, the Face with the Tears of Joy was over-taken in 2016 by the red heart emoji ♥, which is the most used emoji (overall). 75% of the emojis used on Twitter are positive, but negative emojis increase in the evening (peaking at 9 p.m.) (brandwatch.com). The most clicked upon emoji, according to Hubspot, is the finger pointing emoji: White Right Pointing Backhand Index ☞ (Emojipedia.org), the simple reason being it is often used to literally point the user to *click here*. The website states that the most popular emoji used to click-through is the octopus emoji 🐙, followed by horse face 🐴, and then jeans 👖. They state, "why the octopus is in first place, we'll never know", although they do conclude that it maybe its "randomness that catches the viewers eye". This is something that will annoy corporations who desire only certainty. Prediction through behavioural surplus analytics of the fixed symbols, then, is not straightforward. Symbols are not always a given, but have shifting meanings. Although it is difficult to make much sense of, we can see through the Google Trends analytic tools that different emojis have more affective value in some countries above others, which speaks to the cultural specificity of these trends. For example, it seems that in the last five years, the octopus emoji 🐙 had the most interest in Algeria, followed by Saudi Arabia, whereas the red heart emoji ♥ had the most interest in Brazil, followed by Italy.

At the time of World Emoji Day on the 17th of July 2018, Facebook released some analysis of how emojis are used on the platform. There were very few surprises, although they included the least used emojis. These included Man in Suit Levitating: Dark Skin Tone 🕴. When attempting to look at the analytics of this emoticon on Google Trends, it stated that there was not enough data to reveal any statistics. Similarly, Man Playing Water Polo: Light Skin Tone 🤽 was also one of the least used. However, the Man in Suit Levitating: Light Skin Tone did have statistics to reveal, and it showed that it was popular in just the USA and India. Man in Suit Levitating: Medium-Light Skin Tone had enough data to reveal its use predominantly in the USA. Man in Suit Levitating: Medium Skin Tone also had enough data to reveal its use in the USA. However, Man in Suit Levitating: Medium Dark Skin and Man in Suit Levitating: Dark Skin did not have enough data for any analysis. These statistics are concerning in terms of pointing to a potential affective bias in emoji use that is racialised. Joe Veix, in Newsweek (2016), wrote a piece entitled *The Secret Ska History of That Weird Levitating Businessman Emoji*. Veix explains how the Man in Suit Levitating was taken from the early 1990s Microsoft symbol font called Webdings, which is still in existence on Microsoft Word, and for which, the letter m appeared as the following 🕴. This figure may be familiar to those who remember the British two-tone record label which featured, for example, a British multiracial SKA group called The Specials.

Vincent Connaire, who developed the font, thought that the image of the two-tone man fit with the black and white font, and as he had an album from The Specials featuring a song called "Jump", he thought it would be a good idea to have a jumping (pogoing) two-tone man. Seventeen years later, in 2014, the Unicode Consortium decided to include the pogoing rude-boy, but instead of the rude-boy, he became the levitating businessman (much more in tune with the new-tone). Ironically, however, the original two-tone character, created by Specials' keyboard player and song writer Jerry Dammers, was based upon a black reggae musician called Peter Tosh, a core member of the Wailers alongside Bob Marley and Bunny Wailer. Hence, emojis are often culturally adopted and produce and reinforce relative meanings. Like all language and discursive constructions, they can facilitate social bubbles wherein their meanings can be subtly politicised and create division. Thus, their use and value may reveal important sociological information and psychosocial affectivities, and so they require social scientists to detail and analyse their emergence in day-to-day life.

The table below is adapted from Wolny's (2016) classification of emoticons, emojis, and ideograms, compiled to develop a sentiment and emotion analysis of tweets. Wolney developed this in Poland, and so it is presumed that some of these depictions are culturally relative. Most striking is that, like most sentiment analysis, it is broken down into three overarching sentiments: Positive, negative, and neutral. This radically reduces the potential meanings, but it is presumed that for marketing purposes, if the hashtag was about a political party or product, this may be useful. Additionally, there is a distinct lack of so-called positive images, which would also bias sentiment towards the negative and neutral. Thirdly, as we have seen, emoticons, emojis, and ideograms can often be used in subversive or subjective ways. One example is the eggplant 🍆, considered as lucky in Japan to dream of on the first night of the new year, but quite often used elsewhere as representing a phallus. It was also banned for some time in 2015 on Instagram.

Table 4.1 The below table is adapted from Wolny (2016)

Sentiment Polarity	Emotion Classes	Emoticons and Emoji ideograms related
Positive	Happiness Laugh Grin	😊 😁 :-) :) :D :o) :] :3 :c) :>=] 8)
Negative	Sadness	😟 😫 😞 😔 🙀 >:[:-(:(:-c :c :-< :< :-[:[:{
	Anger	😠 😡 😣 💢 :-|| :@ >:(
	Cry	😭 😢 😥 😓 😪 😔 :'-(:'(
	Horror Disgust Great Dismay	😨 😷 😖 😫 💩 🍙 D:< D: D8 D; D= DX v.v D-'
	Skeptical Annoyed Undecided Uneasy Hesitant	😒 😕 😑 😞 >:> :/ :-/ :-.:-: =/ =: L=L :S >.<
	Cool Bored/yawning	😎 😐 |;-) 😵 🐻 👖 ♂ 😶
Neutral	Straight face No expression Indecision	:| :-|
	Surprise Shock	😮 😯 >:O :-O :O :-o :o 8O O_O o-o O_o o_O o_o O-O 😲 😳 😱 😨 😵 🙀 😯

In the above table, it is not clear why the cool face and the fist pump 😎 👖 were considered as negative. Was this a Polish or local cultural representation of something negative, or was it more subjective? Similarly, it was unclear why the rice ball 🍙 was included within the Horror, Disgust, Great Dismay category?

Novak et al. (2015) hired 83 human annotators to develop a sentiment map of the 751 most frequently used emojis. Again, the emojis were marked either negative, positive, or neutral. They found that most emojis are positive (particularly those most used) and they claim that there are no significant differences in emoji ranking between the 13 European languages that were included. Findings are aggregated, so, for example, a significant amount of the time the eggplant emoji is used, it would be very difficult to understand its valence without knowing more about the context through which it is used. Even if we had information that allowed us to know that it was being used to represent a penis, we would still need further information to judge it as having a positive, negative, or neutral valance. Sentiment analysis does not focus upon idiosyncratic uses of language, or in this case, emojis. As language and meaning is constantly shifting, for example, in the words of Run D.M.C., "Not bad meaning bad but bad meaning good!", sentiment analysis, although popular, seems to be very limited. However, Novak et al. (2015), developed a sentiment ranking for emojis positioned within a spectrum of positive or negative sentiment. Similarly, Wiseman and Gould (2018) look at how emojis can be used in highly personalised and secretive ways. They are repurposed, as they suggest, for something other than their intended use. Friends, family members, and close partners can repurpose them in ways that convey intimate and personal sentiments and that enable a localised language. This may be more widely used, such as the eggplant 🍆 for penis or the peach 🍑 for buttocks. However, emojis can also be quite idiosyncratic, such as a pizza slice 🍕 signifying love between a particular couple: "We love each other as much as we love pizza"; this came from a shared understanding that would not make much sense to people outside of this relationships (Wiseman & Gould, 2018). So, overall, social media platforms incorporate emojis to further facilitate human affective expression, and emojis are being rendered by digital capitalism as behavioural surplus markers. Yet, these are not as easy to psychologically interpret as was possibly initially hoped. Positioning a symbol (emoji) as representing a positive, negative, or neutral sentiment, affect, expression, opinion, or emotion is extremely limiting, but have sentiment analysis techniques of digital text incorporated more sophisticated models of affectivity?

Representing emotionality through sentiment analysis

The positive effects of putting emotions and feelings into words or labelling affect has been the bread and butter of psychotherapists for the last century. A large body of research discusses the merits (and indeed some of dangers) of disclosing or labelling affect (see, for example, Ellis & Cromby, 2009, 2011). Some have argued that affect is simply amplified by the labelling process, but lots of research, particularly in the emotional disclosure paradigm, argues for its regulative effect, particularly in relation to labelling so-called negative affect (Torre & Lieberman, 2018). Apparently, labelling emotion through social media use also has a regulative effect. Fan et al. (2018) used a rather novel approach to look at this through social media activity, or, more precisely, through disclosing how people felt on Twitter. They argue that previous affect labelling research had taken place within laboratory settings, and social media affords the potential to research naturally occurring affect labelling. As we saw in Chapter Three, emotions and feelings are difficult to measure in naturalistic settings, therefore, sentiment analysis has been touted as a way of measuring and gauging emotions represented digitally. Fan et al. tracked what they term "the evolution of specific emotions" of 74,487 Twitter users through a sentiment analysis. They analysed the emotional content of their tweets before and after they had explicitly reported experiencing an emotion. For example, the tweet might state "I feel angry" or "I feel sad", etc. After the labelling occurred, they found a rapid reduction in affect for those who reported feeling negative affect and a less rapid reduction in affect for those reporting positive affect. They cite two sources to substantiate the statement that sentiment analysis may reflect individuals' emotions. Upon further investigation, though, we found these claims to not be as robust as they would present. The first source was Beasley and Mason (2015), and they state that they found only a very weak correlation between sentiment analysis and how people "truly feel". The second study, Ziemer and Korkmaz (2017), did not find that sentiment analysis reflected individuals' emotions, but found that human raters were far better at predicting depression measures from text than computer word analysis, although, it should be noted, the latter was almost as proficient as human raters in predicting "pain catastrophizing and illness intrusiveness" (p. 122). Fan et al. (2018) assume that labelling an emotion on social media is equal to expressing emotion. The term *expression* requires some deciphering here, as it implies that something of the emotion that was being felt inside the individual is released through social media. Again, this suggests a kind of drive theory of emotion (affect), something that the designer of the sentiment analysis programme in the above case, the linguistic and word count programme (LIWC), Pennebaker, draws upon as a model for emotional disclosure (see Ellis and Cromby [2009] for critiques). Although it may be the case that forms of emotional disclosure have beneficial effects (wherein labelling is expression), the evidence for this is limited, and indeed, can have deleterious effects in some cases (Ellis & Cromby, 2011).

What it may be better at predicting is opinions, rather than some inner emotional truth. In fact, the term sentiment analysis and opinion mining are often used interchangeably. Liu states that sentiment analysis aims to analyse "opinions, sentiments, appraisals, attitudes and emotions" (2015, p. 1) in online written texts. What is the difference between opinion and sentiment? As stated above, everyday use of the term sentiment includes bodily feelings, whilst opinions are more about thought. Dictionary definitions tend to define sentiment as an attitude, appraisal, and judgment that has been prompted by a feeling, whereas an opinion is strictly formed in the mind. Sentiment analysis, within the social media context, originated not from psychology or sociology, but from computer science. Although the latter has had input into earlier forms of network analysis (from the 1940s), computer scientists borrowed concepts and models from psychology to base their psycho-linguistic models of sentiment analysis upon. In a book entitled *Sentiment analysis: Mining opinions, sentiments and emotions*, Liu (2015) includes a useful table of the different basic emotions from 14 basic emotion theories. As we have, elsewhere (Ellis & Tucker, 2015), Liu (2015) highlights the problematics of having such an abundance of competing theories without any agreed set of primary emotions. However, Liu notes that sentiment analysts need not "be concerned with the disagreement of theorists. For a particular application, we can choose the types of emotions that are useful to the application." (Liu, 2015, pp. 33–35). The usual way that emotions are analysed through sentiment analysis is classifying them as either having a positive or negative, (and sometimes) neutral valence.

The emotion annotation and representation language (EARL) system, developed by the Human-Attempting to enable a more nuanced sentiment analysis, Machine Interaction Network on Emotion (2006) (HUMAINE), classified emotions into ten forms of valences, each entailing up to six emotions (48 emotion types in all). These included: Negative and forceful, negative and passive, quiet positive, negative and not control, positive and lively, caring, negative thoughts, positive thoughts, reactive, and agitation. This is a relatively more complex version of sentiment analysis than is usually produced, but it is also of note to point out that the subtitles do not always appear very useful. For example, included under the *reactive* heading are: Interest, politeness, and surprise. It is difficult to see how these states are any more reactive than, for example, disgust or pleasure?

Indeed, as discussed when looking at emojis, meanings within language are context-dependent, and attempting to abstract terms from their context and label them as having either a negative, positive, or neutral valence can be very limiting and reductive. Within psychology and sociology, sophisticated forms of qualitative analysis have been developed to interpret the meanings that people bring to and enact through speech. Although sentiment analysis is attempting to become increasingly diligent to context through Natural Language Processing, it is still some way off from human processing and understanding of, for example, emotional tone and meaning within text. Sentiment analysts argue, however, that just so long as issues can be identified, then solution techniques can be developed and instituted into existing frameworks. The challenge facing sentiment analysis is how to move beyond framing emotion as relatively fixed and universal, to capture the more fluid, subjective, and transient ways that emotions emerge and operate. Fan et al.'s (2018) study was able to reflect some of this, in that participants' emotion-based text was tracked over time (before and after a particular representation of how the participant was feeling). Yet, we would argue that to denote these as *expressions* assumes particular conceptions and links between emotion, digitised textual representation, and expression.

Concluding thoughts

Everyday encounters with social media are imbued with emotional and affective activity, as they seek to hypnotically pull us in and sustain engagement. Motivation studies have framed social media as having the capacity to fulfil any number of human needs, leading to self-actualisation and individuation. It would be wrong to suggest that social media does not enable some important benefits to our lives, for example, developing and maintaining new personal relationships, keeping in contact with family members (near and far), enhancing professional networks, enabling forms of escape and entertainment. And yet, it is not a benevolent entity offering a well of human goods. It also requires something in return. Social media platforms are essentially driven by profit and are relatively unregulated; they are often hailed as the new frontier of the wild west. For example, Zuboff (2019), among others, discuss the behaviourist experiments that are conducted on us through social media that we are often not aware of. This new behaviourism is conducted outside of ethically-controlled university research contexts. Consent is often unknowingly given to these corporations through the terms-of-service (also known as click-wrap). We get wrapped up in a contract by clicking on the box in agreement with terms that we most likely have not read. In addition to these very long, laborious contractual documents, once clicked, they can be unilaterally changed at any time without user consent or knowledge. It is possible that the experimenters know only too well that motivations are not simply fulfilled through social media, but are fashioned by it. The architecture of social media has been created not simply to fulfil needs, but to create them. Rather than becoming means to an end, they often become an end in themselves, as they seek to draw us in through, for example, algorithms, or what Bucher (2018) refers to as *programmed sociality*. To facilitate these processes, research has tended to compartmentalise motivation phenomena by nominating categorical forms. Similar to how emotion has been categorised into particularised forms in the affective computing context, as discussed in the previous chapter, motivations are thought about in much the same way. Discerning discrete motivational forms facilitates their programmability into algorithms, supposedly feeding tailor-made tastes and drives. These are not always noticeable and, at times, surface and affect us in a variety of ways; as Bucher argues, they can become "strangely tangible in their capacity to create certain affective impulses, statements, protests, sensations and feelings of anger, confusion or joy" (2018, p. 94). Often, the algorithms get it wrong; for example, we no longer receive feeds from certain friends for no discernible reason. This may be a result of motivation phenomena being misconstrued, too narrowly understood, and moreover, misconceptualised. However, on aggregate, if statistics suggest that hits have increased, then little else, it seems, matters.

We have argued here that processes of motivation are more complex than are presently accounted for in much of social media research. They have drawn on theories that tend to base human functioning within behaviourist and rational choice models. Researchers need to be aware of some of the implicit and often obfuscated notions underlying the theoretical framework of motivation research in this context, such as, people use social media because it fulfils a natural need, some form of psychological ownership need, or self-actualisation tendency. Motivations are understood in this light as fixed psychological constructs. We included views from Jansz, Leibniz, Nietzsche, and Deleuze and Guattari, to illustrate more complex notions of motivation, which are attuned to the non-conscious, social context, political underpinnings, and emotional tone of motivation. In place of motivation, Deleuze and Guattari put forward a theory of desire to reflect this, which, of course, is much more difficult to model, but if we are to more accurately digitally configure motivation, in our opinion, the present limited views will require significant expansion.

Emotional labour, as Hochschild (1983) and, more recently, Ahmed (2004), have discussed, concerns the management of feelings and expressions required in the labour market to increase custom and hence profit. As we have discussed, along with Beer and Burrows (2010), Pridmore (2012), Fuchs (2017), Nash

(2016), and Zuboff (2019), social media users are not only consumers, but producers of the social media product, affective labourers. In this chapter, we looked at how personal information, emoticons, and emojis are used to this end. Our emotional lives online are especially plundered through forms of sentiment analysis. As some of the participants in a study we conducted suggest, they learn how to wheel out representations of emotion, affect, and feelings when required. Likes 👍, love ❤️, ha ha 😄, wow 😮, sad, and anger 😠 certainly have not only specified meanings, but a quantifiable value on Facebook, as we have seen, for example, through the work of Cambridge Analytica. Sentiment analysts are trying to develop methods to further enhance the capture of what is configured as our digitised emotionality. Again, laying down a framework, as Facebook has, which reduces emotional expressions to five emojis, is one way of simplifying, and thus quantifying the affective landscape of social media. Perhaps this is just enough to profiteer from our emotional labour? Again, the thought is, why complexify it, if it produces a desired effect? In other words, replicating the complexity of affective activity is not required for capital; just so long as the data can be aggregated, to the extent that it informs as to whether it is more likely to produce a positive, negative, or neutral (sentiment) value, it is of use. Social scientists have a role to play here. It is vital that the role of emotion is persistently investigated and theorised in the academy, not for capitalist ends but for human ends, perhaps increasing the likelihood of transindividuation and communitarianism. In the following chapter, in the digital mental health context, this is also important, as applications are developed through which to design, develop, and implement formal and informal forms of support for people with a range of mental health issues.

References

Ahmed, S. (2004). *The cultural politics of emotion*. Edinburgh: Edinburgh University Press.

Áine, Dunne, Margaret-Anne, Lawlor, & Jennifer, Rowley (2010). Young people's use of online social networking sites – A uses and gratifications perspective. *Journal of Research in Interactive Marketing, 4*(1), 46–58.

Beasley, A., & Mason, W. (2015). Emotional States vs. emotional Words in Social Media. In *Proceedings of the ACM web science conference*. Oxford, UK: Association for Computing Machinery, p. Article 31.

Beer, D., & Burrows, R. (2010). Consumption, prosumption and participatory web cultures: An introduction. *Journal of Consumer Culture, 10*(1), 3–12.

Best, S. J., & Krueger, B. S. (2006). Online interactions and social capital: Distinguishing between new and existing ties. *Social Science Computer Review, 24*(4), 395–410.

Boyle, M. (2002). *Schizophrenia: A scientific delusion?* (2nd ed.). London: Routledge.

Brewer, M. B., & Hewstone, M. E. (2004). *Emotion and motivation*. Oxford: Blackwell Publishing.

Bucher, T. (2018). *If...then: Algorithmic power and politics*. Oxford: Oxford University Press.

Burke, M., Kraut, R., & Marlow, C. (2011). *Social capital on Facebook: Differentiating uses and users*. Presented at the Proceedings of the SIGCHI Conference on Human Factors in Computing Systems, Vancouver, BC, pp. 571–580.

Chen, A., & Potenza, A. (2018). Cambridge analytica's Facebook data abuse shouldn't get credit for Trump: 'I think Cambridge Analytica is a better marketing company than a targeting company'. Retrieved July 12, 2019.

Chen, G. M. (2011). Tweet this: A uses and gratifications perspective on how active Twitter use gratifies a need to connect with others. *Computers in Human Behavior*, *27*(2), 755–762.

Chivers, T. (2009). Internet rules and laws: The top 10, from Godwin to Poe. *The Telegraph*, p. 23.

Churches, O., Nicholls, M., Thiessen, M., Kohler, M., & Keage, H. (2014). Emoticons in mind: An event-related potential study. *Social Neuroscience*, *9*(2), 196–202.

Deleuze, G., & Guattari, F. (1987). *A thousand plateaus: Capitalism and schizophrenia*. Minneapolis: University of Minnesota Press.

Deleuze, G., & Guattari, F. (1994). *What is philosophy?* London/New York: Verso.

Ellis, D. (2018). *Social media, emoticons and process, in: Affect and social media: Emotion, mediation, anxiety and contagion* (pp. 18–26). New York: Rowman and Littlefield.

Ellis, D., & Cromby, J. (2009). Inhibition and reappraisal within emotional disclosure: The embodying of narration. *Counselling Psychology Quarterly*, *22*(3), 319–331.

Ellis, D., & Cromby, J. (2011). Emotional inhibition: A discourse analysis of disclosure. *Psychology and Health*, *27*(5), 515–532.

Ellis, D., & Tucker, I. (2015). *Social psychology of emotion*. London: Sage Publications.

Ellison, N. B., Steinfield, C., & Lampe, C. (2007). The benefits of Facebook "friends:" Social capital and college students' use of online social network sites. *Journal of Computer-Mediated Communication*, *12*(4), 1143–1168.

Evans, V. (2017). *The emoji code: How smiley faces, love hearts and thumbs up are changing the way we communicate*. London: Michael O'Mara Books.

Fahlman, S. E. (n.d.) Smiley Lore :-) [Blog Post]. Retrieved from http://www.cs.cmu.edu/~sef/sefSmiley.htm.

Fan, R., Varamesh, A., Varol, O., Barron, A., van de Leemput, I., Scheffer, M., & Bollen, J. (2018). Does putting your emotions into words make you feel better? Measuring the minute-scale dynamics of emotions from online data. *ArXiv E-Prints*. Retrieved from arXiv:1807.09725.

Fuchs, C. (2017). *Social media: A critical introduction*. London: Sage.

Goffman, E. (1967). *Interaction rituals*. New York: Garden City.

Graham-Harrison, E., & Cadwalladr, C. (2018). Revealed: 50 Million Facebook profiles harvested for Cambridge Analytica in major data breach. *The Guardian*, p. 16.

Hochschild, A. R. (1983). *The managed heart*. Berkeley, CA: University of California Press.

Hofer, M., & Aubert, V. (2013). Perceived bridging and bonding social capital on Twitter: Differentiating between followers and followees. *Computers in Human Behavior*, *29*(6), 2134–2142.

Huang, L.-Y., Hsieh, Y.-J., & Wu, Y.-C. J. (2014). Gratifications and social network service usage: The mediating role of online experience. *Information Management*, *51*(6), 774–782.

Jansz, J. (1996). Constructed motives. *Theory and Psychology*, *6*(3), 471–484.

Kanter, J., & Kanter, J. (2018). Facebook is investigating another app created by Cambridge University academics after it hoovered up the data of millions of users. Retrieved from https://www.businessinsider.in/facebook-is-investigating-another-app-created-by-cambridge-university-academics-after-it-hoovered-up-the-data-of-millions-of-users/articleshow/64173953.cms.

Karahanna, E., Xu, S. X., & Zhang, N. (Andy), (2015). Psychological ownership motivation and use of social media. *Journal of Marketing Theory and Practice, 23,* 185–207.

Kelly, G. A. (1970). A brief introduction to personal construct theory. *Perspectives in Personal Construct Theory, 1,* 29.

Klein, M. (1946). Notes on some schizoid mechanisms. *International Journal of Psychoanalysis, 27,* 99–110.

Kramer, A. D. I., Guillory, J. E., & Hancock, J. T. (2014). Experimental evidence of massive-scale emotional contagion through social networks. *Proceedings of the National Academy of Sciences, 111*(24), 8788–8790.

Leys, R. (2017). *The ascent of affect: Genealogy and critique.* Chicago/London: University of Chicago Press.

Liu, B. (2015). *Sentiment analysis: Mining opinions, sentiments, and emotions.* Cambridge: Cambridge University Press.

Mischel, W. (1968). *Personality and assessment.* Chichester: John Wiley & Sons Inc.

Mo, R., & Leung, L. (2015). Exploring the roles of narcissism, uses of, and gratifications from microblogs on affinity-seeking and social capital. *Asian Journal of Social Psychology, 18*(2), 152–162.

Morozov, E. (2013). The real privacy problem. *Technology Review, 116,* 32–43.

Nash, A. (2016). *Affect, people, and digital social networks, in: Emotions, Technology, and Social Media* (pp. 3–23). London: Elsevier.

Novak, P. K., Smailović, J., Sluban, B., & Mozetič, I. (2015). Sentiment of emojis. *PLoS One, 10*(12), e0144296.

Pariser, E. (2011). *The filter bubble: What the Internet is hiding from you.* New York: Penguin.

Park, N., Kee, K. F., & Valenzuela, S. (2009). Being immersed in social networking environment: Facebook groups, uses and gratifications, and social outcomes. *Cyber Psychology and Behavior, 12*(6), 729–733.

Phelps, J., Nowak, G., & Ferrell, E. (2000). Privacy concerns and consumer willingness to provide personal information. *Journal of Public Policy and Marketing, 19*(1), 27–41.

Pridmore, J. (2012). Consumer surveillance: Context, perspectives and concerns in the personal information economy. In Handbook of Surveillance *Studies.* New York/Abingdon Oxon: Routledge.

Quan-Haase, A., & Young, A. L. (2010). Uses and gratifications of social media: A comparison of Facebook and instant messaging. *Bulletin of Science, Technology and Society, 30*(5), 350–361.

Raacke, J., & Bonds-Raacke, J. (2008). MySpace and Facebook: Applying the uses and gratifications theory to exploring friend-networking sites. *Cyber Psychology and Behavior, 11*(2), 169–174.

Rheingold, H. (1994). *The virtual community: Surfing the internet.* London: Minerva.

Shao, G. (2009). Understanding the appeal of user-generated media: A uses and gratification perspective. *Internet Research, 19*(1), 7–25.

Simondon, G. (2005). *L'individuation à la lumière des notions de forme et d'information.* Paris: Éditions Jérôme Millon.

Smith, D. W. (2011). Deleuze and the question of desire: Towards an immanent theory of ethics. In N. Jun & D.W. Smith (Eds.) *Deleuze and Ethics* (123–141). Edinburgh: Edinburgh University Press.

Smock, A. D., Ellison, N. B., Lampe, C., & Wohn, D. Y. (2011). Facebook as a toolkit: A uses and gratification approach to unbundling feature use. *Computers in Human Behavior, 27*(6), 2322–2329.

Stafford, T. F., Stafford, M. R., & Schkade, L. L. (2004). Determining uses and gratifications for the Internet. *Decision Sciences, 35*(2), 259–288.

Stark, L., & Crawford, K. (2015). The conservatism of emoji: Work, affect, and communication. *Social Media+ Society, 1*, 2056305115604853.

Styhre, A. (2001). We have never been Deleuzians: Desire, immanence, motivation, and the absence of Deleuze in organization theory. In: *Presented at the 2nd Critical Management Studies Conference* (pp. 11–13). Manchester, England.

Taggart, K. (2017). The truth about the Trump data team that people are freaking out about. *BuzzFeed News*.

Tomkins, S. S., & Messick, S. (1963). *Computer simulation of personality, frontier of psychological theory*. New York: John Wiley and Sons Inc.

Torre, J. B., & Lieberman, M. D. (2018). Putting feelings into words: Affect labeling as implicit emotion regulation. *Emotion Review, 10*(2), 116–124.

Valenzuela, S., Park, N., & Kee, K. F. (2009). Is there social capital in a social network site?: Facebook use and college students' life satisfaction, trust, and participation. *Journal of Computer-Mediated Communication, 14*(4), 875–901.

Van Grove, J. (2013, July 2). As Facebook gets serious about stickers, creator says so long. *CNET*. Retrieved from http://www.cnet.com/news/as-facebook-gets-serious-about-stickers-creator-says-so-long/.

Whitehead, A. N. (1978). *Process and reality: Corrected edition*. New York: Macmillan.

Whitehead, A. N. (2011). *Science and the modern world*. Cambridge: Cambridge University Press.

Whiting, A., & Williams, D. (2013). Why people use social media: A uses and gratifications approach. *Qualitative Market Research, 16*(4), 362–369.

Williams, D. (2006). On and off the'Net: Scales for social capital in an online era. *Journal of Computer-Mediated Communication, 11*(2), 593–628.

Williams, R. (1961). *Sociology of culture*. Chicago: Chicago University Press.

Wiseman, S., & Gould, S. J. (2018). Repurposing emoji for personalised communication: Why Means "I love you." In *Presented at the Proceedings of the CHI Conference on Human Factors in Computing Systems* (pp. 1–10).

Wolny, W. (2016). Emotion analysis of twitter data that use emoticons and emoji ideograms. In *25th International Conference on Information Systems Development: ISD2016 Katowice*, Katowice, Poland, University of Economics in Katowice.

Youyou, W., Kosinski, M., & Stillwell, D. (2015). Computer-based personality judgments are more accurate than those made by humans. *Proceedings of the National Academy of Sciences of the United States of America, 112*(4), 1036–1040.

Yuasa, M., Saito, K., & Mukawa, N. (2006). Emoticons convey emotions without cognition of faces: An fMRI study. In *Presented at the CHI'06 extended abstracts on Human factors in computing systems* (pp. 1565–1570).

Ziemer, K. S., & Korkmaz, G. (2017). Using text to predict psychological and physical health: A comparison of human raters and computerized text analysis. *Computers in Human Behavior, 76*, 122–127.

Zuboff, S. (2019). *The age of surveillance capitalism: The fight for a human future at the new frontier of power*. London: Profile Books.

Retrieved from https://www.psychometrics.cam.ac.uk/productsservices/apply-magic-sauce.

5   Digital mental health

Emotional health in a digital age

The field of mental health is becoming increasingly digitally mediated. A broad range of digital developments in mental health services has been proposed, from providing advice and guidance to people suffering with various mental health difficulties, through to creating digital versions of established treatments and therapeutic interventions (e.g. Cognitive Behavioural Therapy [CBT]). The App Industry has seen considerable potential in direct marketing digital aids to common mental health difficulties, such as stress, depression, and anxiety. Indeed, Apple's App Store and Google's Play Store each have tens of thousands of mental health-related apps on offer. There is also an appetite for machine learning and big data analytics to gather previously unattainable large-scale data sets, which can be used to design digital tools using artificial intelligence (AI) (e.g. chatbots). Mental health care in a digital age is consequently beginning to look very different to previous location-based services (e.g. institutions, community). Digital forms of support are not tied to specific locations but can be temporally and spatially ready to hand and, consequently, not so reliant on real time access to mental health services. As such, they have considerable potential to intersect with individuals' ongoing emotional experiences, both in relation to their underlying distress and through facilitating key aspects of support such as creating and maintaining peer relationships.

The development of digital forms of support in mental health can be linked to the promise of technologies to increase productivity while lowering cost (Wang et al., 2018). Mental health has experienced significant shifts in the location and form of support provided, from the institutional settings of 20th century psychiatry to the community-based systems present today. The use of digital technologies emerging in recent years ranges from online accessing of information by patients to the digitisation of established clinical interventions such as CBT. This chapter analyses some of what is at stake when technologies intersect, formally and informally, with experiences of emotional distress. Hence, the focus on emotion in this chapter is primarily in terms of experiences and feelings of emotional distress that constitute and connect to living with various forms of mental ill-health.

Digital materialities

We know that understanding the emotional challenges facing individuals living with mental ill-health is aided by analysing the relationships they have with the environments in and through which they live (Brown & Reavey, 2015; McGrath & Reavey, 2015; Parr, 2008; Philo, 2005; Tucker, 2011). Given the reduction of dedicated mental health spaces, such as in-patient services, community day centres, and support groups, people are facing a limiting of face-to-face opportunities for support. At the same time, digital options are growing. As such, digital devices and platforms are developing increased agency with the relations people have with the environments in which they live (Lupton, 2018). The reduction in dedicated mental health spaces makes it more difficult to build and maintain relationships with other people, which can be so valuable in terms of peer support (Tucker & Goodings, 2017, 2018). The growing proportion of "digital spaces" means that people face having to learn how to seek support in new, mediated ways. While "the digital" has huge power to connect, this does not, by definition, mean that existing support practices can easily translate into digital form (Tucker & Lavis, 2019).

Distress can take many forms, with psychiatric diagnostic categories often used as a definitional framework, e.g. schizophrenia, borderline personality disorder. Considerable evidence exists that individuals' experiences of distress often do not map neatly onto diagnostic categories, and as such, the "medical model" has been subject to significant critique, with approaches emerging that recognise the range, fluidity, and fluctuating nature of distress (Cromby, Harper, & Reavey, 2013). New digital tools often adopt broad definitions, such as aiming to support "common mental health problems of depression and anxiety" or with specific issues (e.g. hearing voices and virtual reality), rather than mapping directly to existing diagnostic categories (du Sert et al., 2018). In this chapter, we adopt a similar approach and utilise generic terms such as "mental distress" and "mental ill-health" to cover a range of underlying issues. In doing so, we are arguing that experiences of distress cannot be fully understood by focusing only on activity "within" individuals, e.g. bio-chemically. Extending the unit of analysis to include the relations people have with their environments is vital to develop insight regarding experiences of living with distress.

The role of materiality in the experience of distress has become increasingly well-established (McGrath & Reavey, 2015, 2016; Brown & Reavey, 2015; Tucker, 2011, 2017), both in relation to formal and informal spaces of care. Research from human geography began to shift the focus of analysis away from the inner workings of the mind to a place-based approach that sought to highlight the ways that the environment in which care was provided had a significant impact on the way care and support are experienced (Parr, 1997, 2008; Philo, 2005). Considerable insight was gained, from institutional care through to various spaces that constitute community care (e.g. day centres, domestic environments, public spaces). For instance, the role of sound in forensic psychiatric settings (Brown et al., 2019), through to the impact of the organisation of objects in the "making" of domestic settings as spaces of recovery (Tucker, 2011, 2012).

Place-based approaches have been supplemented by work that seeks to emphasise the role of material objects in the production of mental health spaces, which has emerged from areas such as social and medical anthropology (Mol, 2008; Pols, 2012). Materiality can include a focus on individual relations with physical objects and the ways that objects inter-connect in the operation of emergence of particular settings (e.g. a home, clinic, community). In this sense, materialities are said to mediate the relations between individual and environment and therefore play an active role in the modes of experience and emotion that emerge. The digitisation of mental health support presents a new materiality in and through which individuals can access services as well as engage in a range of forms of communication (e.g. peer support). For instance, the use of specialist online forums for peer support provide an immediacy to support that can be valued and beneficial, but the support available is often quite pragmatic and not facilitative of in-depth discussion of issues that underpin individuals' mental ill-heath (Tucker & Lavis, 2019). The immediacy is simultaneously expansive and restrictive in terms of support. Digital platforms make access to other people more immediate, which has the potential to reduce common issues such as isolation. The support one might feel from friends in a community day centre no longer has to stop when the centre closes, but can continue through instant messaging and social media. The power of digital technologies to connect has rightly been viewed as offering much potential in terms of support in mental health communities.

We must not homogenise "the digital" by suggesting that a single device or platform offers a uniform experience. The same device can become part of multiple practices, some of which can be proactively sought, while others are actively resisted. For instance, an individual may be keen to create a WhatsApp group to extend an existing support network, while simultaneously reluctant to use a new mobile app to support their distress, as they see it as a substitute for in-person care. Our analysis concentrates on digitised practices, which are relational and incorporate multiple elements, including connections with other bodies (human and non-human). Digital modes of support manifest as heterogeneous practices, with some involving prescribed forms of activity (e.g. digital CBT), while others involve more self-directed activity, e.g. proactively seeking support in an online forum. Individual bodies in distress come to be experienced in and through digitally mediated practices. For instance, expressing and "projecting" one's distress in an online forum, which does not operate through in-person contact. This is a different mode of seeking support than in the dedicated spaces of mental health services, or other more "informal" spaces, in which practices of peer support are enacted (e.g. community day centres, pubs, clubs, support groups). Translating common experiences and modes of knowledge of support into digital spaces involves learning new skills and ways of being and becoming.

The role of AI in the history and development of digital mental health

Thinking about technologies in terms of health goes back to the early days of AI. Indeed, one of the events that is taken as a seminal moment in the genesis of AI was the early "chatbot", Eliza, developed by MIT professor Weizenbaum as an early natural language processor. Keen to simulate a didactic conversational setting, Weizenbaum modelled Eliza on a patient-psychiatrist interaction, with the "patient" expressing their feelings through written statements on a computer. Eliza was programmed to associate responses with certain keywords and based responses on a Rogerian psychotherapeutic model of responding to patient input with questions. Eliza was designed to "test the limits of a computer's conversation capacity" (Turkle, 1997, p. 105), not to test whether psychotherapy could be administered through a computer programme. And yet, Weizenbaum found that users reported positively about interacting with Eliza and, as such, could be thought to have felt supported. Many did not believe that they were not interacting with a human, leading Weizenbaum to claim that Eliza developed into a useful version of the Turing test (1966).

The fact that people form emotional connections with material objects is well-known (Miller, 2008), for example, objectophilia is understood as literally being in love with an inanimate object, and fetishistic disorder is a diagnostic category in the DSM-5 concerning sexual urges towards non-genital parts of the body and/or inanimate objects. We are not suggesting such strong connections were developed by users of Eliza, but Weizenbaum reported that users emotionally connected with the programme, as its questioning style came to feel like talking with a therapist, even if some of the questions Eliza created did not always follow logically from previous ones. Users started to feel as if the conversations with Eliza should have the same conditions, in terms of privacy and confidentiality, as in-person therapy. Weizenbaum discovered this through the negative responses he received to a suggestion that he was going to collect and analyse all existing user conversations with Eliza. People wanted their interactions to remain private. They shared with Eliza but did not want to share with Weizenbaum. An intimacy developed in the relationships people developed with Eliza, which were generally only based on one-off use rather than several sessions (as per in-person therapy). This led some psychiatrists to suggest that Eliza could be developed into a "nearly completely automatic form of psychotherapy" (Weizenbaum, 1984, p. 5). Weizenbaum was genuinely taken aback by the reception to Eliza, a programme he had set up purely as a language processing experiment. Moreover, he felt the way it came to be seen as a ground-breaking form of computerised psychotherapy reflected a broader societal issue of undue trust and privilege given to computation and technologies. Psychiatrists contacted Weizenbaum about developing and using Eliza in psychiatric practice and other computer scientists, and Weizenbaum's original collaborator on Eliza, Kenneth Colby, advocated its use in psychiatry.

The early interest in Eliza influenced several technological innovations in mental health support. These took two main forms: 1) Creating new technological forms of support; 2) creating technological versions of existing therapies. Kenneth Colby created early versions of each of these. Firstly, the Shrink program, as a follow up computational therapeutic programme (Colby, Watt, & Gilbert, 1966), which he argued had the potential to replicate some of the therapeutic benefits of the patient-therapist relationship, as Shrink had been programmed by a psychiatrist. However, he felt it fell short in not being able to produce meaningful therapeutic content beyond the initial rapport-building part of a patient-therapist conversation (Turkle, 1997). Secondly, he designed the Parry programme, for training purposes (i.e. prior to trainee psychiatrists working with patients). It was modelled on Colby's theory that paranoia was based on structural neurological problem and not a breakdown of mental function. Parry was deemed a success as a training tool and, consequently, informed treatment practice of people suffering with psychosis. It did not become a therapeutic tool directly. Colby also developed the "Overcoming Depression" tool (1989), which utilised an early form of natural language processing for the treatment of depression. This was successful enough for Colby and his son to create a company through which to market it and was subsequently used extensively as a training tool by organisations, including the US Navy and Department of Veteran Affairs (Colby, 1999). Overcoming Depression was also marketed and used by individuals themselves, outside of formal psychiatric practice, which was an important event in the history of mental health support, as it marked the potential for technologies to substitute for human therapists.

The impact of technologies such as Eliza, Shrink, and Parry has been long lasting. They are often used as examples of early successes in the field of AI. The growing interest in digital tools in mental health care and support is often presented as being built on programmes such as Eliza (Bassett, 2019). For Weizenbaum, the "success" of Eliza led him to question the role of computers in society. He felt that advances in technology were often heralded and accepted without enough critique. Dreyfus (1979) shared a similar view, stating that computer science is the least self-critical science. For Weizenbaum, the question was not just whether computers could perform psychological processes, but whether they should. In *Computer Power and Human Reason: From Judgement to Calculation* he argues that some functions should only be undertaken by a human, even if a computer is able to simulate them. He felt science and industry are too easily swayed by the seductive powers of technologies and as such, not sufficiently critical of new developments. For Weizenbaum, the "artificial intelligentsia" hold firm to the view that if a technological capability is identified, then it must be exercised, even if it comes to shape the subsequent practices in ways that can obscure the object under focus in the first instance. This is the point Turkle (1997) makes when discussing the impact of Eliza and other computerised therapies emerging during the second half of the 20th century. Turkle suggests that the impact of close relationships (e.g. family, friends) on mental health was overplayed in psychotherapy (e.g. psychoanalysis) partly because of Eliza and other computerised therapies, despite the fact that close relationships did not feature particularly prominently in the conversations people had with Eliza. The argument was that the demand characteristics of psychoanalysis led to an over emphasis on close relationships. Turkle makes the point that close relationships could, in fact, not have been discussed in detail with Eliza because participants felt they had greater understanding of these issues than Eliza and, as such, did not discuss them. Computer psychotherapy researchers, though, saw this as a limit of psychoanalysis, rather than of computerised therapy. Turkle's claim is that the bias was the researchers, not that of psychoanalysis. This demonstrates the power of technologies to shape psychological theory and practice. In this case, a chatbot designed to test computational capacity to simulate a conversational setting leading to critical debates about the underlying principles of longstanding therapeutic approaches.

The potential role of technologies in mental health care has been a concern at the higher echelons of psychiatry going back to the mid-20th century and, as such, these are not 'new' concerns. The then president of the American Psychiatric Association used his Presidential Address to raise the issue that technological advances could lead to a dehumanising of psychiatric practice through a loss of the therapeutic benefits of the "doctor-patient" relationship (Pickersgill, 2019). The question as to the extent to which technologies could substitute for the "expert" role of the psychiatrist therefore has a longer history than the recent coverage of new digital tools in mental health suggests. This question concerns an expert in terms of whether technology can deliver psychiatric expertise in the place of a therapist (e.g. CBT), so the psychiatric knowledge is delivered by technology, rather than by a professional. It is also the case that new forms of therapy have been claimed to be made possible by technologies. It should be noted that the emerging field of "digital psychiatry" applies to the use of technologies as part of clinical practice, e.g. in the delivery and maintenance of formal therapies. We will expand upon this later in the chapter to consider the impact of digital technologies more broadly in relation to mental health. There is also the question as to the potential for digital technologies to facilitate the collection of data about mental distress on a large scale and for this information to be used to direct decision making about treatments. As such, there are multiple ways that digital technologies have been mentioned in terms of contributing to mental health care, present and future.

The desire of psychiatry and the media to frame Eliza (and later chatbots) as therapeutic technologies presented an understanding of mental ill-health as treatable by interventions without the "warm" touch of human relationships. The "cold" technologies that were not traditionally part of care practices came to be seen as having the capacity to substitute for a patient-therapist relationship, long thought of as the mainstay of the therapeutic environment. This understanding has catalysed an exponential interest and growth in developing digital forms of care and support. The perceived validation of the therapeutic potential of digital technologies has been used as justification for a huge breadth of new digital innovations relating to mental health. Pickersgill (2019) refers to this move as part of the "promissory agenda" of *digital psychiatry*. This is despite there being limited clinical evidence of their efficacy. For individuals living with mental ill-health, there are now a huge range of digital forms of support with which their care and support practices can be enacted daily. Some include contact with mental health professionals and services, some with friends, family, and peers, and some with just the technology itself. The potential to form relations to help manage ongoing mental ill-health is significant, although not in the traditional ways of formal psychiatric practice (e.g. regular meetings with psychiatrists and mental health professionals). This is a move that has not happened as quickly as some people think (i.e. it has been fifty years since Eliza), but is now gaining significant traction in the field of mental health. It is vital to understand more about practices that digital devices and platforms are coming to feature in. Technologies have traditionally been thought of in functional terms, as tools that are designed to deliver specific outcomes regardless of context. And yet, histories of technologies are replete with examples of the *use* of technologies differing to designed-for functions. In the area of mental health, Eliza is a classic example of the need to separate design and use when analysing the impact of technologies. Eliza was designed to demonstrate computational dialogue and ended up being used as a therapist. Technologies are of significant interest to those designing health services; their innovative promise is motivating services to consider how they can be used to provide improved care at a lower cost.

Digital materialities of mental distress

Developing an analytic focus on technologies involves a consideration of the *materialities of care* (Pols, 2012), namely the role that technologies play in formal and informal care practices. Work in medical anthropology has offered a theoretical version of technologies as material agents in the enacting of caring practices. This has emerged in a context in which health technologies have been thought of as functional and "cold" and human relations of care as "warm" and affective (Pols, 2012). The argument being that, for care to be effective, it needs to be warm and consequently, delivered by a human. Cold technologies were seen just as functional tools that can deliver treatments and not as part of the warm, caring relations developed between carer and cared for. Theories of care emerging from science and technology studies and medical anthropology have proposed that framing the role of technologies in care practices through distinctions such as warm vs cold is too simplistic. Instead, theoretical approaches should focus on how care practices are enacted to understand how they perform "in the wild", which is valuable, as it captures care "in situ" (Pols, 2012). This is a theoretical departure from prior understandings of technologies as tools with pre-defined functions that are exercised in a uniform manner whatever the context.

The proposition is that technological forms of care come to shape the specific and localised practices through which individuals' health conditions are experienced and managed. Moreover, technologies can be thought to change the understanding of the problem that requires care. This kind of analysis has emerged in relation to a range of ethnographic studies of physical health problems, including atherosclerosis (e.g. calcification levels of arteries) in a Dutch hospital (Mol, 2002) and remote care for palliative oncology (Pols, 2012) and diabetes (Mol, 2009). Not all this work has included digital technologies, and none, to date, has focused on mental ill-health. This develops existing literature, as it is focused not only on the care delivered by health services, but also "informal" modes of care that emerge in relations with friends, families, and peers. We are concerned to highlight how practices of care and support are enacted with digital technologies and consequently, how digital forms of support come to shape the understanding of mental ill-health that individuals experience. We will discuss the impact of new forms of digital support in mental health, both in relation to the development and use of digital technologies by mental health services and individuals' own digital practices in relation to their mental health (e.g. use of social media).

Emergent themes in the digitisation of mental health

The development of technological therapies that offer new forms of support or that deliver existing therapies is premised on the idea that technologies can deliver in the place of humans. Emotion is at stake in more than one way. It is not just whether the technological intervention has a positive impact on the emotional distress a person is suffering with. It is also whether the technology can *act* in such a way that an individual using it *feels* supported. These elements are inter-connected, and yet, the emotional capacities of these relations are often not included in the evaluation of technological forms of support. Moreover, the criteria by which success is defined are not always clear. Sometimes, the fact that something is in use is taken as evidence that it must be effective. The next section focuses on the emotion of empathy in digital support in mental health. It is a valuable concept through which to explore the impact of new digital platforms designed to provide support within mental health communities. We will draw upon some data from a project exploring the impact of a major digital platform designed to promote and facilitate peer support, www.elefriends.org.uk. The platform was designed and run by the leading UK mental health charity, Mind, and as such, operates outside of mainstream mental health services.

Empathy and digital support

The role of sympathy, compassion and empathy in effective support is well known. They are similar but distinct emotional processes that manifest as different forms of support. Compassion and sympathy can be important parts of the support people feel from friends and family, as well as from formal mental health services. Empathy can constitute support that is created in relations with other people who are (or have) suffered with similar forms of distress and life difficulty. This is the premise of *peer support*, which has become increasingly prominent in mental health support in recent years (Repper & Carter, 2011). The question is, what happens to these emotional relations when the human (therapist or peer) is replaced by a technology? Is the same level of emotional support felt, and is this dependent upon the affective structure and operation of the specific individual-technology relation that emerges? It is important to highlight how a technology is used, e.g. what forms of individuation it comes to operate in and through. The technology is not entirely determining of this, as it is only one of the elements that co-constitute the individuation. Whatever the design of the technology, to understand its impact one must analyse the (multiple) individuations through which it comes to operate. A simple example here is the idea that, whereas one person may find a digital CBT tool useful, as it helps contribute to an improvement in emotional distress, another may not. The emotional impact of new technological forms of support does not exist as a potential "of" the technology, but rather as an unspecified creative realm that is neither technological nor human, but will be followed by the formation of new relations that include technological and human dimensions. Analysing in terms of individuations, which are always relational, helps to capture how preindividual potentials come to be realised in the everyday lives of those suffering with forms of emotional distress.

Digital empathy in practice

In this section, we draw on some online and interview data from a project exploring practices of peer support with Elefriends. The data included below comes from a broader project in which online posts and comments were analysed, along with a smaller set of interviews with Elefriends' users (Tucker & Goodings, 2017, 2018). The project received ethical approval from the University of East London (all names in the interview extracts below are pseudonyms). The project's focus was to understand how peer support operates in a digital space. In this section, we explore the role of empathy in peer support practices enacted in and through use of Elefriends.

In the first extract, empathy operates through Elefriends facilitating communication and connection with other users of the platform who have also experienced mental ill-health. One of the first questions we were interested in was whether feelings of empathy and support could emerge through the digital communication that constitutes Elefriends. What happens to notions of empathy and support in digital, rather than in-person, spaces. Traditional concepts of empathy suggest that it involves an experience of "feeling" the perspective of another, through interpreting the emotional expressions of another (e.g. through their facial expression, body language, speech). This is what is claimed to differentiate empathy from sympathy and compassion, namely that empathy involves feeling another's emotion through having experienced it oneself. Compassion and sympathy do not involve being able to feel another's emotion based on shared experience.

I: Yeah. So, I mean on a day-to-day basis, has it made you feel more supported?
Sue: Yes, it has, yes, because I feel the people who post on there really understand how I feel and I feel I can empathise with them. Whereas if you haven't got mental health issues, I don't know if people really realise what it's like.

Elefriends enacts a feeling of empathy for Sue because it connects her with other users who "really understand" how she feels, and that understanding is only available to those who have also suffered with mental ill-health. Despite not facilitating visual communication between users, empathic practices do emerge.

It appears that descriptions of distress and associated experiences is sufficient to facilitate empathy and feelings of support. The content of posts and comments on the platform provides a feeling of authenticity for users. Sue feels that people on the platform "really understand how I feel and I feel I can empathise with them". Through posts, comments, private messages and the uses of "I hear you", "I'm thinking of you" "buttons" empathic practices are produced that are received as authentic support from others who understand the challenges and difficulties experienced because they have also experienced them. The interpretation of emotion through in-person communication is not required here. Instead, feelings of empathy and support can emanate through a digital materialisation (Tucker & Lavis, 2019) of lived experience. The materiality of the digital device used to access Elefriends, plus the textual materiality of posts and comments facilitate empathic relationships of empathy and support to develop and be maintained.

Sue:　if I want to – if I'm down and I want to speak to someone, I can go to the computer. Whereas before I would – before I joined Elefriends, I would never even have thought a computer could really support like that

In this extract we see that empathy and support come to change the relationship Sue has with the digital device she uses to access Elefriends. The feeling that her computer is now a way to access support is a new feeling, one Sue had not felt prior to using Elefriends. This is not a feeling that changed quickly, but rather, developed through the building of empathic relations through Elefriends over time. The strength of the feeling facilitates its extension to incorporate Sue's relationship with her computer, not just a feeling that happens when she is communicating with other users online. This points to the way that feelings of empathy and support do not only occur when users are communicating, but can extend and endure through the wider network of relations involved in using Elefriends, e.g. with the digital devices used for access. Moreover, feelings of empathy and support do not need to be active to be felt. The knowledge that Elefriends is there, 24/7, can be supportive, users do not have to be using the platform to feel supported:

I:　So it's good to hear that you found Elefriends encouraging for that, as in you were able to get out of the house sometimes if you needed a bit of motivation and stuff.

Clare:　I think the best thing about is, actually, because I access it on my phone, I'll have a – they'll all cheer me on and then I – because even if I don't log in to Elefriends, because I'm carrying that phone with me, it's almost like I'm carrying my cheering squad with me.

I:　(Laughter) Aw, that's lovely.

Clare:　It's like, "Oh. I've got my Eles in my pocket. I'll be fine." Sometimes the internet won't work, so I can't actually log on, but it feels like they live in my phone

The extension of empathy and support to be felt during periods of inactivity is present in Clare's extract. The positivity and motivation other Elefriends' users have provided Clare has developed to the extent that it becomes part of the relationship Clare has with her mobile phone, with which she accesses Elefriends. Even when she is not using the site, or can't, due to the lack of mobile signal, the presence of the phone can still elicit the feelings of empathy and support; "I've got my Eles in my pocket. I'll be fine." This further demonstrates how feelings of empathy and support can emerge through digital communication that does not need to be active to be felt and can extend to the relationship between user and digital device; it does not always need human to human contact. Empathy and support are not of the moment, but come to take temporal form in the way that configure the network of relations that constitute people's use of and experience with Elefriends.

Empathy fatigue

In the preceding extracts empathy and support were co-present in the experiences of using Elefriends. Empathic practices were presented as central to the support that users come to feel. However, over time, empathy can become difficult. One's capacity to provide support to others is shaped by one's own level of distress, and feeling empathic can take a toll on practices of self-care and support.

Rachel: But I've been tempted to leave once or twice, you know, but I have taken advice, you know, and just stepped away for a little while

There is an emotional cost to using Elefriends. The empathic benefits of sharing experiences with others can be significant, and yet, the feeling of other's distress and difficulties can also weigh heavily on users. Being exposed to so many stories of the challenges associated with living with mental distress can lead to feelings that one is not able to "move on" while continuing to use the platform. The need to take a break from Elefriends, or even cease using it permanently, can feature for some users. At these times, feeling empathic can lead to users feeling NOT able to provide support to others. The very feeling that facilitated support originally, and may well do so in the future, at these periods, can result in an incapacity to provide support. Feeling the pain of others can be too painful to oneself.

Rachel: I worry about certain people that have deleted – you know, a couple of the people that were there when I first went on have deleted, and I am sad. You know, I feel real sadness that they're not there, and worry, have they killed themselves, or worry that, you know, they're in a worse place than they used to be, and that sort of thing.

In this extract, a concern is expressed about what it might mean when people delete their Elefriends' account. Absence from the site can be interpreted as a sign that their mental health has deteriorated, potentially in an acute way, to a level of suicidal thoughts. Strong relationships can build through the platform, but they can also be vulnerable in terms of entirely relying on Elefriends to connect. If a user deletes their account, their network of friends online has no other way of contacting them, so cannot confirm whether they are okay or not, e.g. whether the account deletion is cause for concern. This is one of the features of digital support. It can connect individuals to many more fellow sufferers than most in-person forms of support, but is dependent on the digital connection to build and maintain online support networks. Given that people can often use digital platforms such as Elefriends for support when they are feeling particularly distressed, their online behaviour can be interpreted in terms of their level of distress at the time. Deleting one's account can then easily be interpreted as a sign that the user is feeling very distressed and can no longer cope, despite the fact that it could be the opposite, in terms of a user feeling well enough to attempt to cope without the *crutch* of digital support for a period. This is a limit to the support available, unless users are also connected in other ways (some exchange contact details and meet up in person, although this is rare). Analysis of use of Elefriends highlights some of the benefits and challenges to developing online forums to promote and facilitate peer support. In the next section we return to the question of fully automated forms of digital support in the form of chatbots. Online peer support involves connecting individuals through a digital space, whereas chatbots operate through a human-machine relationship. This presents many questions regarding their potential to enact empathy and positive emotional support.

Chatbots

Creating fully automated forms of support is a major part of digital mental health. A variety of technologies utilising AI and machine learning are being developed, often based on digitising an established therapy (e.g. CBT). Developers believe that AI "agents" can deliver psychological therapies through building support-ive relationships with users. Chatbots present new opportunities to explore the emotional content of relationships between bodies and technologies. Their value is dependent on the idea that chatbots can facilitate, through interaction, posi-tive emotional connections, which help individuals manage and cope with their ongoing distress. Chatbots manifest a new agential materialism in terms of digital support. Primarily, this is the text-based conversational form agents take, but it also involves the material relations between bodies and mobile devices, which are constituted through the practices (such as using chatbots) that constitute body-device relations. At the time of writing, the value of chatbots is very much a live issue, with mental health-focused chatbot development moving at pace. To date, limited research has been undertaken as to the challenges and benefits of chatbots. Moreover, the experiences of users have yet to be explored. In this section, we will explore chatbots as part of the emergent materialisation of mental health. This will include a discussion of the limited feedback that exists to date, in the form of reviews of major chatbots.

As noted in the earlier discussion of Eliza, people can develop positive emo-tional relationships with "therapeutic technologies". While the evidence does not yet exist to fully inform the reasons for this, as Weizenbaum noted, the anonymity of interacting with chatbots can feel reassuring. The immediacy of chatbots can facilitate feelings of support being readily available, which differs from the in-person support of mental health services. What is not clear is the extent to which individual-chatbot relationships can facilitate feelings of empathic support, namely that the robot therapist genuinely understands the challenges one faces in respect to mental ill-health. In many ways, technologies developing human capacities to empathise, along with a range of emotions, is the holy grail of AI. AI-technologies have developed certain cognitive abilities on a par with humans (e.g. chess playing), but emotional processes remain out of reach. Creating machines that feel is not necessary to enact positive emotional support in mental health. What is important, though, is that a human-chatbot relationship can enact a feeling of support for the (human) user.

Woebot is one of the leading mental health-focused chatbots currently available. It was developed by psychologists and technology developers and is used to provide CBT-focused therapy. It is available free to download and use on iOS and Android and is marketed as a "self-care expert", helping people to manage challenges of living with "common" mental health problems, such as anxiety and depression. Its CBT focus means the AI is programmed to respond to user requests in ways that help users make sense of and cope with their distress. Moreover, Woebot's AI is designed to learn about users' mental health through identifying patterns in communication and support sought and, as such, to provide tailored support (in a similar way that a human therapist will get to know individuals). Chatbots such as Woebot are the next step in a digitisation of support from online forums and other digital practices that facilitate human relationships (e.g. peer support). Can the emotional dynamics enacted by the relations individuals have with others, facilitated and mediated by digital technologies, translate into human-machine relations? One suspects answers to this question will depend on the specific practices of support made possible through chatbot use. The work with Elefriends (discussed earlier) identified the benefits of the immediacy of digital forms of support, which chatbots also provide, but the limits of the support therein are not (yet) clear. Given chatbots such as Woebot tailor their responses to user requests, we do not know the extent of possible supportive responses available (their database of responses is not available as it is presumably commercially sensitive). Reviewing user feedback provided online (App Store and Play Store reviews), it is clear that a significant proportion is positive (it is hard to know whether any of these reviews were requested and/or incentivised). Positive reviews tend to focus on notions of immediacy, easy access, and anonymity. The idea that Woebot can be used at times when in-person support is not available or sought is a reported benefit. Feeling that support is available can be very important, with support not always needing to be enacted to be felt (Tucker & Goodings, 2017). Users also reported liking the look and feel of Woebot, which encourages use. However, there are several concerns raised in reviews. Despite the learning element of Woebot, designed to ensure appropriate support is provided, users reported receiving unhelpful responses at times. This can significantly impact on users' desire and motivation to use chatbots. If support is deemed to be potentially unhelpful, users can dismiss perceived benefits. Issues of trust are central to individual-technology relationships (Ellis, Tucker, & Harper, 2013). If users do not trust a digital tool, they will not use it. It is particularly important in relation to the use of chatbots for support with mental ill-health. Developing a sense that support suggestions are unhelpful can seriously undermine the potential for therapeutic benefits to be realised.

Chatbots are a significant part of new digital practices of support in mental health. There is major interest in their development in industry and healthcare. As with social media, it may be that much more consideration is needed to help understand the potential parameters of the therapeutic benefit of chatbots and the AI that underpins them. For instance, their emotional power (in a positive sense) may depend upon the severity of distress felt. They may "work" with so-called common mental health problems, such as anxiety and depression, but not with more acute periods and forms of distress (e.g. psychosis). Their benefits may depend on the underlying therapeutic intervention/practice that they digitise, e.g. CBT. It could be that they serve as valuable therapeutic companions between episodes of in-person support, staying with individuals as they negotiate the challenges of everyday life, but not on the premise they are providing the primary therapy individuals need. As a new technology, the impacts of chatbots will continue to come under the analytic gaze, which is necessary to understand the emotional and affective implications of chatbots. They provide potential answers to interesting and longstanding theoretical questions, such as whether they can promote and facilitate human emotion, as well as being at the centre of new initiatives and funding concerns in the delivery of future mental health services. The promises of industry are a significant voice in these debates. We need to ensure a social scientific voice is also clearly heard.

Digitising existing therapies

Digital forms of support, such as specialist platforms like Elefriends, or the use of devices to access existing support, enact new experiences for those suffering with mental ill-health. In some instances, digital platforms and devices mediate existing relationship, such as a WhatsApp group for an existing community support group. In other instances, digital platforms create new relationships and connections which give rise to new practices of support. These come to form part of new digital materialities of mental health support, enacted through practices that are always-already embodied and technical. These elements are not just "tool" and "user" but are co-constitutive of the emergence and unfolding of experiences of mental ill-health. The digital is inter-related with in-person support; an attempt to draw a demarcating line between them would be artificial. They (co-)form the environment in and through which people live with and attempt to manage their mental ill-health. The example of Elefriends provided a valuable discussion of how empathy operates in a digital support forum. It also provided insight regarding the challenge of trying to contextualise and situate digital practices within the broader experiential environment of people's everyday lives. The support in Elefriends primarily stops at the edges of the site. If someone leaves, they are no longer contactable, and questions remain unanswered as to their welfare and whether a cessation in use of the site signals a deterioration of their mental health. When understood as part of the broader set of relations that constitutes their life, a cessation of Elefriends use could be seen as a positive move, a re-engagement with other elements of life that might signal the start of an improvement in mental health. Analysing new digital forms of support in isolation can skew understanding in terms of associating any changes in levels of mental ill-health solely with the digital platform/device. Instead, approaches that situate digital activity with the wider elements and dimensions through which everyday life and experience emerge offers greater potential to understand the impact of the "the digital". Technologies do not operate in a psychological vacuum.

At the time of writing, chatbots acting as substitutes for in-person therapeutic practices is very much a live issue, and this is likely to increase as algorithms become more sophisticated in terms of understanding and guiding responses to data regarding people's mental ill-health. Ensuring that chatbot development is delivered in dialogue with potential users of such technologies and also with insight regarding relevant theories of affective life is necessary to understand any potential benefit in the future of commissioning chatbots. Part of the issue here is whether people trust technologies with data generated about their mental ill-health. This is a question that spans beyond digital mental health to the digitisation of life more broadly. In the next chapter, we explore this issue in relation to notions of *surveillance* and how the datafication involved in mass digitisation facilitates new understandings regarding surveillance. This can help to provide insight as to notions of trust, privacy, and how people feel about using technologies.

References

Bassett, C. (2019). The computational therapeutic: Exploring Weizenbaum's ELIZA as a history of the present. *AI and Society, 34*(4), 803–812.

Brown, S. D., Kanyeredzi, A., McGrath, L., Reavey, P., & Tucker, I. (2019). Organizing the sensory: Ear-work, panauralism and sonic agency on a forensic psychiatric unit. *Human Relations*. Online First.

Brown, S. D., & Reavey, P. (2015). *Vital memory and affect: Living with a difficult past*. New York, NY: Routledge.

Colby, K. M. (1999). Human-computer conversation in a cognitive therapy program. In Y. Wilks (Ed.), *Machine conversations* (pp. 9–19). New York, NY: Springer.

Colby, K. M., Watt, J. B., & Gilbert, J. P. (1966). A computer method of psychotherapy: Preliminary communication. *The Journal of Nervous and Mental Disease, 142*(2), 148–152.

Cromby, J., Harper, D., & Reavey, P. (2013). *Psychology, mental health and distress*. New York, NY: Palgrave Macmillan.

Dreyfus, H. L. (1979). *What computers can't do: The limits of artificial intelligence* (rev. ed.). New York, NY: Harper & Row.

du Sert, O. P., Potvin, S., Lipp, O., Dellazizzo, L., Laurelli, M., Breton, R., … Dumais, A. (2018). Virtual reality therapy for refractory auditory verbal hallucinations in schizophrenia: A pilot clinical trial. *Schizophrenia Research, 197*, 176–181.

Ellis, D., Tucker, I., & Harper, D. (2013). The affective atmospheres of surveillance. *Theory and Psychology, 23*(6), 716–731.

Lupton, D. (2018). *Digital health: Critical and cross-disciplinary perspectives*. London: Routledge.

McGrath, L., & Reavey, P. (2015). Seeking fluid possibility and solid ground: Space and movement in mental health service users' experiences of 'crisis'. *Social Science and Medicine, 128*, 115–125.

McGrath, L., & Reavey, P. (2016). "Zip me up, and cool me down": Molar narratives and molecular intensities in 'helicopter' mental health services. *Health and Place, 38*, 61–69.

Miller, D. (2008). *The comfort of things*. Cambridge, UK: Polity Press.

Mol, A. (2002). *The body multiple: Ontology in medical practice*. Durham: Duke University Press.

Mol, A. (2008). *The logic of care: Health and the problem of patient choice*. London: Routledge.

Mol, A. (2009). Living with diabetes: Care beyond choice and control. *Lancet, 373*(9677), 1756–1757.

Parr, H. (1997). Mental health, public space, and the city: Questions of individual and collective access. *Environment and Planning. D: Society & Space, 15*(4), 435–454.

Parr, H. (2008). *Mental health and social space: Towards inclusionary geographies?* London: Routledge.

Philo, C. (2005). The geography of mental health: An established field? *Current Opinion in Psychiatry, 18*(5), 585–591. (ISI:000231442200022).

Pickersgill, M. (2019). Digitising psychiatry? Sociotechnical expectations, performative nominalism and biomedical virtue in (digital) psychiatric praxis. *Sociology of Health and Illness, 41*(S1), 16–30.

Pols, J. (2012). *Care at a distance: On the closeness of technology*. Amsterdam: Amsterdam University Press.

Repper, J., & Carter, T. (2011). A review of the literature on peer support in mental health services. *Journal of Mental Health, 20*(4), 392–411.

Tucker, I. M. (2011). Somatic concerns of mental health service users: A specific tale of affect. *Distinktion, 12*(1), 26–40.

Tucker, I. M. (2012). Organizing the present in anticipation of a better future: Bergson, whitehead, and the life of a mental health service user. *Theory and Psychology, 22*(4), 499–512.

Tucker, I. M. (2017). Shifting landscapes of care and distress: A topological understanding of rurality. In K. Soldatic & K. Johnson (Eds.), *Disability and rurality: Identity, gender and belonging* (pp. 184–198). New York, NY: Routledge.

Tucker, I. M., & Goodings, L. (2017). Digital atmospheres: Affective practices of care in Elefriends. *Sociology of Health and Illness, 39*(4), 629–642.

Tucker, I. M., & Goodings, L. (2018). Medicated bodies: Mental distress, social media and affect. *New Media and Society, 20*(2), 549–563.

Tucker, I. M., & Lavis, A. (2019). Temporalities of mental distress: Digital immediacy and the meaning of 'crisis' in online support. *Sociology of Health and Illness, 41*(Suppl.1), 132–146.

Turkle, S. (1997). *Life on the screen: Identity in the age of the internet*. New York, NY: Touchstone.

Wang, Y., Kung, L., & Byrd, T. A. (2018). Big data analytics: Understanding its capabilities and potential benefits for healthcare organizations. *Technological Forecasting and Social Change, 126*, 3–13.

Weizenbaum, J. (1966). ELIZA--A computer program for the study of natural language communication between man and machine. *Communications of the ACM, 9*(1), 36–35.

Weizenbaum, J. (1984). *Computer power and human reason: From judgment to calculation*. New York, NY: Penguin.

6   Surveillance and emotion

Do the existence and activity of this body undergoing integration, a body receiving a torrent of landscapes submerging our data banks, now require us to invent a new understanding commensurate with this ever-newly invented body?

(Serres, 2019, p. 114)

The quote above comes from Michel Serres's *Hominescence* (2019), in which he considers the transformations facing bodies entering societies awash with information. Whereas information had traditionally been thought to emanate from the senses (what Serres refers to as the *hard given* of the body), the move into information societies produces an additional layer of data, which has created multiple new forms of knowledge about the body. Serres does not think of this in terms of a singular new form, but as a constantly changing body, moving in concert with an increasing number of data flows. Serres explores whether this constitutes a new age for the body, away from the hard given of sensory experience, to the external processes of databases and their intersections with embodied activity. In this chapter, we explore the emotional impact of increased datafication - framed as facilitating new forms of *digital* surveillance. Not the traditional fixed forms of visual surveillance through closed-circuit television cameras (CCTV), but surveillance of data generated through computers and mobile digital devices. Increased datafication of everyday life is said to have created new forms of *dataveillance* (Clarke, 1988; Van Dijck, 2014), or what we will refer to as *digital surveillance*. The necessity for data about bodies to be created in order to interact with digital technologies means people are faced with new experiences regarding what to consider personal and private data and who and what come to use data that is felt to be *personal*.

This chapter focuses on emotional responses and potential impacts of datafication experienced through everyday interactions with technologies that generate data *about* the body. This includes practices not explicitly targeting emotion (e.g. capture of social media data). Studies of surveillance have tended to focus on the technical and operational capacities of technologies such as CCTV, as well as those whose primary purpose is not explicitly surveillance, for instance, understanding the quantity and quality of data captured by *big tech* companies, along with their use of data (Marshall, 2012). Critical theory has claimed that new digital technologies have facilitated the commodification of information (Thrift, 2005) and that we are increasingly living in *societies of information* (Crang & Graham, 2007). This work has coalesced into the field of surveillance studies, which has broadened its scope beyond the traditional visual forms of CCTV surveillance to the idea that digital technologies have facilitated new forms of surveillance through the capture, storage, and use of data generated from individuals' *private* lives (Ball et al., 2006; Ellis et al., 2016; Lyon, 1994; Marx, 2007). This ranges from governmental and organisational data capture (e.g. big tech companies) through to social media facilitating new ways for individuals to watch each other (so called *peer-to-peer surveillance* (Andrejevic, 2002)).

Affective atmospheres

We have previously written about surveillance and emotion through the spatial lens of the concept of *atmosphere*, which has been used to frame affective life as operating across conscious and non-conscious boundaries (Ellis et al., 2013). The notion of atmosphere has obvious meteorological connotations, but has developed an aesthetic meaning in human and cultural geography through directing analysis to focus on the ways that specific environmental settings can enact certain kinds of feeling. This is a valuable way to consider surveillance because surveillance practices have been claimed to create spaces with specific feelings, e.g. security, safety, risk, privacy (Lyon, 1994, 2007). In relation to emotion, the concept of atmosphere has emerged to try to capture a distributed sense of feeling, which operates in a spatially extended way (Bohme, 1993; Ingold, 2015). What comes to register as feeling and emotion is not reducible to internal psycho-physiological processes, but emanates as a "spatially extended quality of feeling" (Bohme, 1993, p. 118). With atmospheres, feelings exist as part of the physical environments themselves (e.g. a city centre feeling safe due to the presence of multiple CCTV cameras). This *in-betweeness* has been claimed to be what constitutes an atmosphere (Ingold, 2015). Its feeling is a relational emergence; it is not locatable singularly at the level of body or environment. There is an element of setting-specificity about atmospheres, they operate *as* particular space-times, e.g. a work meeting, family meal, train station. These are not reducible to a specific part of the built environment, but do refer to in-person physical interactions. There is commonly a localised proximity to atmospheres.

Atmosphere has become a popular concept, used in areas including democracy (Latour & Weibel, 2005), public transport (Bissell, 2010), health recovery (Duff, 2016), digital support in mental health (Tucker & Goodings, 2017), and in theorising non-human technological agency (Ash, 2013), with all making the argument that the concept valuably draws out a notion of feeling as emerging in a spatially extended way beyond perceived borders of the body. Analysis comes to include objects, memories, imaginations, institutional practices, discourse, and other bodies. In most cases, atmosphere is used in an aesthetic sense, focusing on the sensory qualities of spaces as potentialised feelings for those who enter and occupy them. Rarely does analysis focus on the material constitution of an atmosphere, namely what it is that creates and maintains the relations that come to constitute the atmosphere. The social anthropologist Tim Ingold has sought to (re)claim the meteorological elements of atmospheres. These are commonly missed in the writings of those situated in the aesthetic tradition, but for Ingold, it is qualities of air, sound, and light that constitute atmospheres. They are central to our feeling the sensory qualities of atmospheres; the air we breathe, the lights and sounds we perceive. The two traditions of atmospheres offer what are commonly thought of as mutually exclusive versions; the air-less atmospheres of affect for aesthetic tradition and the affect-less *gas-filled* space for the meteorological tradition. Ingold develops a neo-perceptual account that moves away from an idea that the environment operates as a surface, furnished with objects, which we, as individuals, perceive. Perception is not a passive process of gaining information about an external object, but is an active process through which we engage and *live with* the world (Ingold, 2011). Living is a process of breathing, seeing and hearing – relational activities of bodies, objects, and spaces operating in concert with each other, not as distinct individual entities.

Technologies that facilitate surveillance can create unspecified and non-reductionist feelings that arise in those relating to them, e.g. feelings of safety and security alongside resentment and concern. It is difficult to locate or reduce these emotional processes to one material element of a space (although CCTV cameras obviously play a significant role in potentialising a feeling of being surveilled in a specific space). The perceived indeterminacy of feeling led us to conceptualise surveillance practices as creating and operating as *affective atmospheres* (Ellis et al., 2013). This captures the ways that feelings as wholly internal states are not triggered when entering a surveilled space, but emerge as part of the specific actualisation of feeling in a given setting, which is not prescribed or predetermined. Furthermore, experiences of surveillance can be shaped by individuals' perceptions and knowledge regarding the technical scope of surveillance, but also by a less specific non-conscious *feeling* of the presence of technologies, that can emerge without full awareness of their particular mode of operation (nor their potential for surveillance therein).

The concept of affective atmosphere has become popular across the social sciences to draw attention to the spatial distribution of emotion and affect (Anderson, 2009; Ash, 2013; Bissell, 2010). The datafication of everyday life creates new ways of feeling surveilled, albeit not through technologies that are fixed and setting-specific (e.g. CCTV cameras), but through mobile devices that move with bodies through the landscapes of everyday life. This requires an amended conceptual framing, one that attends to a spatialised sense of experience, but in such a way that captures the almost prosthetic way that digital devices (e.g. smartphones) are commonly a constant bodily companion. The role of data as constituting atmospheres in digital spaces has emerged in the field of mental health (Tucker & Goodings, 2017). The spatial feeling of a digital forum was considered in relation to the feeling of physical spaces. Forums involve the development of relationships in practices of support. Data present a challenge to thinking atmospheres, but they do not operate through, nor rely upon, a closeness of proximity in the formation of local context. Proximity is not important in the role of data. As such, a conceptualisation of data, bodies, and emotion is required to understand feelings associated with living in datafied environments.

From data double to data derivative

The relationship/s between data and bodies have come under considerable conceptual scrutiny, with different views regarding the representative value of data. In surveillance studies, the concept of *data double* (Lyon, 2007) has emerged, framing data as a parallel stream that runs alongside the activity of bodies. This additional layer is taken as operating in direct relation to bodies, and as such, data is seen as a representation of individuals' lives, which facilitates new ways of surveilling lives. Data *and* bodies become means of surveillance (e.g. capturing and categorising individuals' internet search activity). The concept of data double relies on the notion that it is informative as to the activity of an underlying subject. It is data about and related to an individual body. Common understandings of social media are based on this idea of the relation between bodies and data, e.g. that one's Facebook profile is inherently identifiable in relation to an underlying subject. There is a logic to this mode of thinking, and it resonates with the reality of social media activity to an extent. However, it offers a parallelism that frames data as always connected to an underlying subject, and therefore, something that remains bounded by this association. Data always relates to a living being, to be a double *of* an underlying subject. There is limited scope to consider data as untethered from the body, as connecting with other data and producing autonomous data processes that are not reducible to the body. This resonates with Serres's point about data moving away from the senses, but as creating new versions of the body.

The inventive potential of data has been thought of in terms of the use of aggregation of data in databases. Data does not always retain a form that directly relates to an underlying subject, but rather, becomes part of aggregated collectives, melding with data captured from others. Indeed, the idea that data can be clearly separated in terms of a data-subject dualism has been questioned (Goriunova, 2019). The interconnectedness of data into all dimensions of life makes an unravelling that attempts to extrapolate one dimension (i.e. data) difficult. Everyday life becomes a multi-layered experience, operating through the relations between the different elements/dimensions. This moves us away from a focus on data per se, towards an understanding of the psychological individual as operating through experience that is partially constituted through the movement of data and bodies in and through the physical environments and digital devices we inhabit and use. This is a form of *digitally mediated subjecthood* and offers an *expanded* view of the psychological subject, as what we value as constituting *psychology* is not seen to stop at the boundary of the body, or internality, but rather is a broader analytic unit which incorporates body, environment, and technology (Tucker, 2018).

If databases do not operate according to a logic of the data double, then what kind of algorithmic form do they take? One idea is that data collectives emerge as potentialised forms of future action. This has been thought of as a *data deriva-tive*, an association of a set of disaggregated data into a new form. Amoore (2011) names the data derivative in terms of algorithms of security risk, but it can equally apply to new forms of associated data emerging from a broader set of potential-ised data. For instance, an advert for a local event that emerges alongside more generic adverts when using the music streaming service Spotify. Such an event is an association of data, based on the music listened to along with the locational data captured by the app. Derivatives are unpredictable, as their emergence as new associated forms depends on future use of technologies through which data connects. In a sense, this makes them indifferent to the underlying data compo-nents in isolation (e.g. location, music preference), as it is the associations that are meaningful (Amoore, 2011). The concept of the data derivative offers a way of thinking of the specific forms of data that emerge in relation to our interactions with digital technologies. Rather than conceptualising a parallel stream of data relating to a singular bodies, the derivative provides an indication of how data can be collected and collectivised in large databases in which its original refer-ence to an underlying subject is lost. Data derivates are relational, formed through specific aggregations of data, and enacted in relation to individual use of digital devices (e.g. internet, social media). They act to make new forms of future sub-jects possible through generating and aggregating data.

In the remainder of this chapter, we will analyse interview data from a project we conducted with Dave Harper (University of East London) on people's experi-ences and knowledge of surveillance practices (Ellis et al., 2013; Harper et al., 2013; Tucker et al., 2012). Participants discussed their experiences with tradi-tional CCTV and new forms of digital surveillance. We were interested in whether people felt increased datafication *as* surveillance, e.g. whether they related to data in the same way as their bodies, namely as personal, private and *theirs*. And, what feelings emerge in relation to datafication practices. Our analysis demonstrates a conceptual shift from the atmospheres of CCTV surveillance to the derivative operation of data practices.

From atmosphere to derivative

Learning to live with data is something most of the developed world, and increas-ing amounts of the developing world, has had to contemplate in recent times. Technologies that capture and use data are present in almost all areas of life, and as such, bodies operate in environments that are partially constituted by data. An increased datafication of bodies is creating new forms of experience, which involves feelings of being visible to other bodies in new ways, as seen in this extract with Rachel:

> I don't feel comfortable for some reason, it's just feel so weird to (.) not to kind of have a personal sort of communication and you know in a kind of quite formal you know situations I'm all right with it but this seems…this is sort of more you know because you've got this network of people or friends

or whatever and then you know whatever you do you are kind of in a sense exposed to everyone else and sometimes you feel like sharing something with one person. (laughter)

Rachel is referring to her experience with social media and the way its *networked publicness* (Boyd, 2011) leads to her feeling exposed, of being visible to the "network of people or friends" she connects with through social media. She distinguishes this feeling from that of face-to-face interaction or individual communication (e.g. via email). For Rachel, social media operate through a form of network disclosure, in which a body's activity is made available to networks as a whole. This offers a networked visibility that is broader and open, leading to a sense of public exposure. For Rachel, it's too open and uncontained. Not knowing exactly who will see her social media activity is troubling, disconcerting, and out of step with the more contained one-to-one communication of *in-person* friend and family relationships.

Rachel's experience chimes with claims that social media have made possible new forms of lateral, peer surveillance (Albrechtslund, 2008), in addition to traditional top-down models of state and large organisational surveillance that constitute long standing notions of surveillance (e.g. Orwell's "Big Brother"). Digital technologies have helped to facilitate the proliferation of data, re-configuring notions of privacy and individuals' sense of the boundaries of self (Lyon, 2007). The boundaries of the body are no longer thought to contain the personal and private, as the data created and shared moves from the body to technologies and therefore, exist beyond the boundaries of the body. Bucher (2018) argues that social media activity creates a programmed sociality, governed and shaped through software and algorithms. A more expanded sense of psychological individuality is emerging in recognition of the extent of informational activity that co-constitutes everyday lives. For Rachel, this can lead to feeling exposed, while for others (particularly young people growing up in a digital age) it feels more normalised as they have not faced pressure to transition from a less digital time (Boyd, 2014). The experience of transitioning to the datafication of one's body is expressed in relation to data and internet searching. In the following extract Robert, narrates a phase of becoming aware of what the *data cost* is of using search engines such as Google:

you feel safer and in another way it makes you feel quite nervous that you're not really anonymous if someone decides to target you for something erm then you can be tracked erm I think the biggest scary thing watching a documentary recently is the whole Google saga I don't think I had ever really thought about how that works and how Google makes its money and the fact that every search you do is recorded so its a free service for you and you think great! It's this massive search engine its really easy to use erm yet every site you ever hit is recorded and they have huge data banks that record all of that information <mmm> so they can say then they use that for marketing that's how they make their money is companies then go to them and say what percentage of your users are interested in this or they could literally give you a marketing plan and say well to a big corporation you could pay them you know millions of dollars and they could produce a report saying you know 20% of women aged between 25 and 45 are interested in this at the moment and these are the current trends erm so again you know you think now when I'm searching for something and particularly if its something sensitive er I was looking at medical information the other day and I was thinking, oh my God! This is gonna be, everything that I ever put into that system could be traced er but that I don't think is really made clear all of these sites Facebook etc that are about erm making the world a smaller place and making you feel like you're part of some big social network is in a way lots of ways to track you to track trends and watch what people are doing it's like a huge market-ing exercise for huge corporations and I think the majority of people don't think of it like that erm so where that's going to go where that might lead I think until something huge happens peoples' attention won't really be drawn to how it really works and what it means for the little guy.

Something as seemingly innocuous as internet searching becomes weighted with a set of concerns about the potential flow of data elicited. What feels like an iso-lated activity between body and digital device is experienced as a relationship of exchange, in which the data is provided in return for *free* use of the technology. The feeling of being an anonymous body in a personal and private space (e.g. one's home) is reconfigured through a realisation about the role and operation of data provided to the technology. For Robert, this feels personal, with data a pos-session, which must be exchanged to access the search engine. Data becomes a currency, rather than part of a body's identity and sense of individuality. This is not a realisation that everyone will experience. Robert claims that for many peo-ple, such awareness is not a reality, and the simplicity and desire to use the inter-net far outweighs any potential concerns about what the *data cost* might be. Here, the body becomes traceable by data, which forms part of a categorical system (women between 25–45), about which systems of datafication are organised and operate. A concern presents itself regarding the use of data, in terms of becom-ing part of a "huge marketing exercise". The internet is perceived as a singular system of data that comes to *know* bodies through data. Of interest is the power with which data is imbued, with it becoming a way to "track trends and watch what people are doing". Furthermore, data can transform a body's sense of scale and proximity. Distance is one way in which a sense of privacy and individuality is created and maintained, but data can create a feeling of the world shrinking, of being closer to other bodies, and in turn, feeling like one has less *private* space in the world. This feeling also features at the end of the extract in the form of ques-tioning what mass datafication means for "the little guy", who becomes one node in a data network, rather than an individual living body. Data become a means of identification.

Bodies are deemed to be visible to data in a similar way to their visibility to CCTV in traditional notions of surveillance. This involves an expansion of surveillance practices, from the traditional state surveillance through public CCTV to forms of digital surveillance of data activity, often involving industry and large corporations. Mass datafication has facilitated bodies becoming commodities traded through data. This concern can become crystallised around a question as to who or what will use data generated in relation to the body.

Bridget:	perhaps you weren't expecting or you didn't want or even on, I was on a website the other day, and I had loads of emails and I think it was because I was on this website and then I think I must have clicked on something and it got my information and it keeps sending me junk mail
I:	oh right
Bridget:	it's going into my spam but, I'm sort of 'oh no' you feel a bit invaded I didn't give them my information, it like a gambling thing, erm so you always feel like you're being watched so if you apply for a credit card or something you think oh, you know, who's really having my details?
I:	right
Bridget:	erm. There isn't much you can do about it unless you get really paranoid

Bodies becoming tradable through data links to another dimension in terms of creating a pattern of future activity based on the specificity of data previously generated. In this extract, data capture has led to the reception of junk mail based on the initial "clicking on something". A momentary click creates a data stream that elicits junk mail. Here, data is not particularly informative regarding the body. It could have been an accidental *click* that led to the junk mail, rather than a planned search which generated data relating specifically to concerns of the body. However, the data and associated algorithm that respond to the click are still significant; while they may not relate to Bridget's body, instead being aggregated over a large amount of bodies, they are likely to be representative of the gambling body. Perhaps due to the cultural presence of CCTV as a longstanding and widespread surveillance practice, Bridget's concern is with *who* has got access to their data. It remains a sense of another person, or people, *watching* and can only be acted against by becoming "really paranoid". It is as if, to combat what is felt as an invasion, a strong emotional response of paranoia is needed. It is the aggregation of data and related algorithm that leads to the spam mail, which cannot be specifically known in advance. The visibility of the results of aggregation is a major part of digitisation and a new cultural phenomenon. The collectivising of aggregation operates by creating a *distance* between body and data (Goriunova, 2019), with data existing as an agent distinct from the embodied activity from which it was generated. It is the consciousness of the creation of this distance that is central to the emotional and affective impact of data generation. As Amoore notes, in commercial terms, data becomes a derivative. In Chapter Two, we saw how Goriunova (2019) frames this in psychological terms, as creating the *digital subject*. We suggest that both concepts relate to the affective experience of data generation, creating new ways of relating to oneself as a (individual and private) body, as well as relating to an aggregated collective, in which a sense of individuality is much harder (if not impossible) to hold onto. In the extract above, Bridget captures this through a notion of ownership, with data relating to one's own body remaining under ownership, but a sense of losing possession emerging through aggregation. The question of who or what uses data collected can be important for the subsequent feelings about use of digital media.

Paul: If I had to choose I'd definitely rather have people watch me

I: you'd definitely have other people?

Paul: yes, yes, than technology

I: and why is that?

Paul: erm 'cause you have this one to one confrontation, you know, it's, human; it happens at that instance; and whatever happens it's happening in front of you; you are aware and, there's discomfort about you knowing that there's someone watching you, a human watching you from a distance, and whatever happens, I mean if you did anything wrong at the instance you'd get judged right on the spot or maybe told you're wrong if there's a fine to pay you pay the fine and that's sorted. You know. Erm, rather than you have technology monitoring you all the time and when does it stop? When do you get that confrontation about ok 'we've been monitoring you for the last fifteen hours and this is what we think you are, you are the evil' (laughs). I mean but that monitoring can go as long as they desire you know but when you have like a human monitoring you at some point you get this confrontation. Ok, right 'we've been watching you for the last two weeks and this is what we think you are, you are a sad bastard who comes out 6 o'clock in the morning' but then you automatically <u>know</u> about it, and it's dealt with there and then, makes more sense to me though.

In the extract, the experience of datafication is felt as an inversion of the operation of CCTV surveillance. The visibility of the ubiquity of CCTV makes the presence of surveillance very clear, and yet, people do not always register it consciously. With datafication, the practices of capture and use of data are opaquer. The categorisation of data happens in the servers and algorithmic practices of the organisations interacted with online. Paul uses a distinction between human and technological *knowing* to frame his feelings regarding the potential monitoring of his activities. The generation of data by technologies creates a feeling of being *monitored*, which is framed as problematic because it has potential unspecified longevity. *Human surveillance* feels more immediate and visible. The terms of the monitoring are more easily understood and therefore potentially easier to manage. Digital surveillance is presented as problematic because the *watcher* is not visible. It is not known who or what is watching. It is presented as a less equal relationship. The "1–1" operation of human-to-human surveillance is a more equitable proposition. Digital surveillance is felt as obfuscated and lacking clear operational parameters. This creates a shift in terms of the relationship between bodies and technology. A relocation of identity is underway in terms of data moving beyond the boundaries of the body into the digital databases of organisations. The feeling of ownership and agency of one's body is also shifted by the movement of data, beyond the control of individual bodies.

I: so do you feel that our free will as individuals is in a way vanishing? I mean if the fridge decides whether to buy the milk or not.
Paul: exactly! Yeah, yeah.
I: in fact I might not want another one, or I might be broke. I might not have money for the next two weeks.
Paul: yeah. I know it's, it's (.)
I: Everything
Paul: yeah, yeah it's. I mean part of what makes us human is the face to face contact. You know what I mean? You know when like someone smiles at you you re gonna smile back.

Feelings of concern regarding data generation and its relationship to individual bodies extend to a point of predicting potential futures in which daily activity comes to be increasingly shaped by forces outside of personal control. In the extract above, Paul refers to the internet of things and the potential for a fridge to monitor and replenish food, outside the control of the owner. This is not so much a ceding of control as an enforced shift in the control bodies have over everyday life. The idea of living in environments in which domestic decisions are no longer the sole remit of individuals is felt as questioning what it is to be human. This is a noteworthy shift as, in the first instance, it seems an exaggerated response. Why is an intelligent fridge experienced as an existential threat? This could be due to the fundamental (albeit mundane) example of a connected and agential fridge overseeing purchase and replenishment of the basic requirements for survival (i.e. food and drink). Furthermore, the idea of an intelligent fridge is seen as an example of a move towards digitisation that reduces contact and communication between individual bodies. It is as if this is part of a move to digitise life that will render face-to-face contact unnecessary and, moreover, potentially limit the possibilities for it. A move in agency, from human to technology, is felt like a point of no return. Indeed, digitisation can also be felt to be reconfiguring what it is to be a human body.

I: so you feel we are not related as human beings?
Paul: no we're not!
I: By the systems?
Paul: yeah! It's all about numbers, we're catalogued, we're quantified. You know what I learned? It's (.) and you re judged by what you buy (2) you know what I mean? You re seen as (.)

This extract is a good example of what has been conceptualised as *the quantified self* (Lupton, 2016), namely the nature of the data created and captured through digital activity. Instead of individual identity being defined by the body, it is the categorising of quantifiable data that becomes the primary identifier of bodies. For instance, data associated with online activity, such as internet shopping and social media activity. This is a commercialisation of bodies, through an initial commodification (e.g. selling data to marketing companies) and subsequent targeted advertising designed to encourage people to purchase more (and therefore generate further revenue). This is experienced as a tension between what is considered to be internal to the body (one's personal feelings, emotions, etc.) and external processes (which are usually taken as more social/public). A new relationship between inside and outside (the body) emerges, a tension between bodies, hardware, and software (data). Serres talked about hard and soft not in computational terms, but as sensation felt prior to being "anaesthetized by language" (2008, p. 89). Sensation is *hard*, bodily energy that is then subject to the interpretative framework of information in the form of language. Data are coming to take the *soft* place of language, as being that which categorises and renders knowable the *hard*, sensory realm of the body. Data impose on bodies a quantifiable framework of commodification. Sensations and feelings are replaced by data about internet searches and other forms of digital activity. Bodies are no longer constrained by the way institutional forms of knowledge organise the built environment (e.g. schools, workplaces, public spaces), but are subject to the ordering forces of data working through the mobile digital devices that accompany our every move. This was what motivated Deleuze to think of the subject as a *dividual* rather than *individual* (1992), as bodies come to be defined more as nodes of data in a network than by the singularity of their *flesh and blood* body.

A rise in quantification can be experienced as a threat to the *quality* of psychological life. Datafication of emotion often involves a quantification of bodies as part of the categorisation of emotion. For instance, analysing faces through the generation of data points as part of the categorisation of expressions rendered as the manifestation of emotions. This is part of the technologisation of emotion that is underway, which does not allow for inclusion of the *quality* of emotional and affective activity, for instance, the experiential dimensions of emotion – which are not neatly and entirely captured through a focus only on facial (or other physiological) expressions. Emotion and affect have become part of a computational move in relation to psychology, something that was previously primarily concerned with cognition (e.g. artificial intelligence). The *computational gaze* is fast broadening to incorporate affective life, which is introducing new quantified systems of emotional knowledge that are feeding into the cultural consciousness (as seen in the interviews above).

Living in data presents and data futures

The rise of data activity is having significant impacts on the emotional life of individuals and societies. The datafication of bodies has created new patterns of exchange – using free services such as internet search engines in exchange for commodifying data. It appears that many people lack knowledge of the extent of the commodification of the data they create when interacting with digital technologies (Harper et al., 2013). For those who have awareness, there remains considerable uncertainty about what happens when data flows from bodies to the databases of large organisations such as the *big tech* companies who monopolise data capture and use (e.g. Google, Facebook). Data is felt to enter a kind of black box, the inner workings of which remain out of sight of those from whose bodies data are generated. There is, of course, no motivation for companies to disclose their algorithmic activity, and there is limited evidence that people want to know more (Ellis, 2019). Many are content to keep using valuable services without financial cost and may well continue to do so even if they know more about the commodifying logic of *free* use of digital services, such as social media and internet search.

As it stands, bodies are leaking and creating higher amounts of data as they move through increasingly *datafied* environments (McCormack, 2018). The previous chapters have demonstrated multiple ways in which digital technologies are generating data related to emotion, often based on physiological models of emotion. The current chapter has demonstrated some of the concerns that are created when the commodification of data originating from individual bodies becomes apparent (e.g. through tailored advertising). These come to be experienced as practices of surveillance and associated with understandings and experiences of traditional forms of visual surveillance such as CCTV. This can create a tension of the separation of bodies and data. The collectivising aggregation of data generated through bodily activity produces new feelings regarding ownership and agency. Individuals can feel that data remains *theirs*, even when it is aggregated through the *distancing* of bodies and data. In the interviews analysed in this chapter, individuals struggled to disconnect body and data and retained a sense that bodies remain surveilled through the generation of data, rather than the technical reality that it is not bodies that are surveilled, but data. In our interviews, the operation of surveillance is not felt as immediately as CCTV surveillance. Surveillance through data is opaquer, although a similar frame of reference of *the watcher* and *the watched* is used when reflecting on datafication. Participants in our study had a concern about who or what is *watching* and what their intentions are. People's frame of reference regarding surveillance commonly comes from experiences with CCTV, which is seen largely to be operated by the state to reduce and/or prevent crime. Even if it is not clear who is *behind* the camera, its role and impact is generally understood. What happens to data once it leaves the body has a less immediate frame of reference for understanding. The role of technology itself can be felt to be agential in terms of the idea that the *machine* is watching bodies through data. Vannini goes as far to suggest that algorithms "are no mere props for performance but parts and parcel of hybrid assemblages endowed with diffused personhood and relational agency" (2015, p. 5).

Our previous conception of surveillance as operating as affective atmospheres captured the non-conscious dimensions of living in environments populated by surveillance practices. The ubiquity of surveillance technologies (i.e. CCTV) meant that they were not always registering consciously as active forms of surveillance, and yet, they operated as potentialised forms of affect. They can operate as actors in the constitution of the feeling of a space, without being captured entirely in conscious processes. We concluded that their affective impact and operation could not be thought of entirely in terms of the psychological individual as an experiencing entity, because the operation of affective atmospheres cannot be entirely understood in terms of relationships between separate entities (e.g. bodies and technologies). Moreover, registering at the individual psychological level tends to operate as a form of apathy, or indifference. Strong emotional responses were not forthcoming, produced by the reality of inevitability of the datafication of our environments. Trying to avoid it may be thought to be futile, and as such, apathy develops. Similarly, Ellis (2019) coined the term surveillance-apatheia, denoting an attitude that individuals learn which decreases the agitation and anxiety produced by surveillance systems and their associated practices.

Affective atmospheres of surveillance operating through mass use of fixed CCTV surveillance are shifting into mobile atmospheres produced through the continual exchange and movement of data between bodies and (often mobile) technologies. In a sense, bodies and technologies are becoming manifestations of two ends of continuums constituted by data. Rather than the contemporary social issue being the debate about the power balance between bodies and machines, data has come to operate as the key agent in shaping bodily and technological activity. Analysis comes to focus on the movement of data and how they act as co-constituents of atmospheres whose operation is not a product of the actions of a set of interacting singular entities, but a multi-dimensional configuration of the processes of a set of *patterned stabilities* (McCormack, 2018). In relation to digital life, this primarily involves the creation, sharing, and monitoring of data that modulates bodies and technologies and atmospheres of affect and potentialised emotion. Data are not static representations of bodies, but are sets of intensive processes that take form *in the making*, and as such, should not be thought as referring straightforwardly to specific objects. Instead, data are milieus that accompany bodies and co-constitute what comes to be felt as individual life. The concept of milieu takes a more temporal form than the spatial connotation of atmospheres and can facilitate the forms of metastability that bodies take.

We propose that living with data is experienced as a temporal form of anticipatory potential, in which it is not clear when or how data previously associated with an individual body may emerge and *act back* upon a body. Mass data generation from bodily activity creates a *derivative* dimension, as data is something that creates future value (commercially and socially). This value is not always predictable however, but its presence requires new responses in terms of what *feels* personal and private. Living in environments mediated by data involves a conceptual shift away from the spatial connotations of the physical environment, towards a mobile reality in which bodies exist in concert with a potential range of personal digital devices in and through which bodies can feel surveilled. Bodies and devices are the product of, as well as being productive of, multi-dimensional systems. These systems of reality operate in terms of what Gilbert Simondon called *milieus*. These have a more temporal constitution than atmospheres and capture the emergence of a system of reality constituted by the formation of new relations between bodies and technologies. Milieus are multi-levelled and novel. Their existence is not reducible through the notion of bodies and technologies being distinct entities, but as creating a new relationship between previously unrelated elements. For instance, being subject to an advert for a brand of shoes because of previously browsing them is the novel relationship between data and an individual. The nature of the milieu changes with time, with adverts modifying as new data are collected and algorithms subsequently alter. Living in *data milieus* captures the multi-dimensional reality of continually creating and receiving data in all parts of life. In essence, milieus come to act as the systems of reality in and through which individual bodies exist and operate, subject to and being active in the ongoing production of novel relationships that (re)configure the temporality of data milieus.

As the preceding chapters have shown, there is considerable scope to the use of digital technologies designed to collect information relating to emotion. Data is generated from individual bodies and subsequently used by organisations in diverse ways. It is not always clear how data collected from people directly feeds back into their lives at a later stage, although there are instances in which this is clearer, e.g. online tailored advertising. In this chapter, we argue that digital technological claims regarding emotional life are making new practices of surveillance relating to emotion possible. In doing so, we argue that data is not just the passive mechanism that links bodies and technology, but is an agential element that co-constitutes life in a digital age. Furthermore, it is a growing awareness that technologies *know* us better than ever before that can create feelings relating to digital surveillance. This is not always a sense of knowing *the watcher* (e.g. the police through CCTV), but awareness that information we have created exists in a technological realm, without transparency about how it is being used and who has access and control over it. For many people, such awareness does not exist, which is of interest and suggests that a lot of informational activity is at work outside of consciousness (Ellis et al., 2013).

For some, surveillance has become a lens through which to understand the operation of digital life in entirety. This is based on the reality of several behemothic companies controlling a large proportion of digital activity – particularly in relation to the internet (e.g. Facebook, Google, Twitter, Amazon, Microsoft, Apple), the commodifying drive that makes possible perceived *free* access to much digital activity has led to surveillance being used as the defining concept of our times (e.g. the high sales and popularity of Zuboff's (2019) *Surveillance Capitalism* book). We agree with much of the rationale of understanding modern digital life as operating through a variety of surveillance practices. However, we decided to include a specific focus on surveillance towards the end of the book to avoid it becoming a defining concept in our analysis and discussion of emotion and affect in a digital age. Generating data on a huge scale for commercial ends clearly resonates with surveillance – the industrial gaze to generate data from all parts of life can only operate through having a technological means through which to make life *visible*. However, we were keen to draw attention to a range of other issues in relation to emotion, affect, and digital life. For instance, the models of emotion underlying the fast-growing emotional AI field and the changed notions of what is *personal* about data in relation to social media. As we have seen, other concepts are valuable to draw attention to the emotional and affective dimensions of new digital practices. This is particularly important given our view that emotion and affect are core ways through which we relate to ourselves as individual bodies and to the world. With *the world* becoming increasingly digitised, it is important to see how relations – as emotion and affect – are changing as the world transforms. We will continue this discussion in the final chapter, as part of our drawing together of the various threads followed through the chapters of the book.

References

Albrechtslund, A. (2008, March 3). Online social networking as participatory surveillance. *First Monday, 13*(3).

Amoore, L. (2011). Data derivatives: On the emergence of a security risk calculus for our times. *Theory, Culture and Society, 28*(6), 24–43.

Anderson, B. (2009). Affective atmospheres. *Emotion, Space and Society, 2*(2), 77–81.

Andrejevic, M. (2002). The work of watching one another: Lateral surveillance, risk, and governance. *Surveillance and Society, 2*(4), 479–497.

Ash, J. (2013). Rethinking affective atmospheres: Technology, perturbation and space times of the non-human. *Geoforum, 49*, 20–28.

Ball, K., Lyon, D., Murakami Wood, D., Norris, C., & Raab, C. (2006). *A report on the surveillance society* (A report for the information commissioner). Retrieved from https://ico.org.uk/media/about-the-ico/documents/1042390/surveillance-society-full-report-2006.pdf.

Bissell, D. (2010). Passenger mobilities: Affective atmospheres and the sociality of public transport. *Environment and Planning D: Society and Space, 28*(2), 270–289.

Bohme, G. (1993). Atmosphere as the fundamental concept of a new aesthetics. *Thesis Eleven, 36*(1), 113–126.

Boyd, D. (2014). *It's complicated: The social lives of networked teens.* New Haven, CT: Yale University Press.

Boyd, Danah (2011). Social network sites as networked publics: Affordances, dynamics, and implications. In Z. Papacharissi (Ed.), *A networked self identity, community, and culture on social network sites* (pp. 39–58). New York: Routledge.

Bucher, T. (2018). *If...then: Algorithmic power and politics.* Oxford: Oxford University Press.

Clarke, R. (1988). Information Technology and dataveillance. *Communications of the ACM, 31*(5), 498–512.

Crang, M., & Graham, S. (2007). Sentient cities: Ambient intelligence and the politics of urban space. *Information, Communication and Society, 10*(6), 789–817.

Deleuze, G. (1992). Postscript on societies of control. *October, 50*, 3–7.

Duff, C. (2016). Atmospheres of recovery: Assemblages of health. *Environment & Planning A: Economy and Space, 48*(1), 58–74.

Ellis, D. (2019). Techno-securitisation of everyday life and cultures of surveillance-apatheia. *Science as Culture.* Online First.

Ellis, D., Harper, D., & Tucker, I. (2016). Experiencing the 'surveillance society'. *Psychologist, 29*(9), 682–685.

Ellis, D., Tucker, I., & Harper, D. (2013). The affective atmospheres of surveillance. *Theory and Psychology*, *23*(6), 716–731.

Goriunova, O. (2019). The digital subject: People as data as persons. *Theory, Culture and Society*, *36*(6), 125–145.

Harper, D., Tucker, I., & Ellis, D. (2013). Surveillance and subjectivity: Everyday experiences of surveillance practices. In K. Ball & L. Snider (Eds.), *The surveillance-industrial complex: A political economy of surveillance*. London: Routledge.

Ingold, T. (2011). *Being alive: Essays on movement, knowledge and description*. London: Routledge.

Ingold, T. (2015). *The life of lines*. London: Routledge.

Latour, B., & Weibel, P. (2005). *Making things public: Atmospheres of democracy*. Massachussetts: MIT Press

Lupton, D. (2016). *The quantified self: A sociology of self-tracking*. Cambridge: Polity Press.

Lyon, D. (1994). *The electronic eye: The rise of surveillance society*. Minneapolis: University of Minnesota Press.

Lyon, D. (2007). *Surveillance studies: An overview*. Cambridge: Polity Press.

Marshall, T. C. (2012). Facebook surveillance of Former Romantic Partners: Associations with PostBreakup recovery and personal growth. *Cyberpsychology, Behavior, and Social Networking*, *15*(10), 521–526.

Marx, G. (2007). What's new about the 'new surveillance'? In S. P. Hier & J. Greenberg (Eds.), *The surveillance studies reader*. Maidenhead, UK: Open University Press.

McCormack, D. P. (2018). *Atmospheric things: On the allure of elemental envelopment*. Durham: Duke University Press.

Serres, M. (2008). *The five senses: A philosophy of mingled bodies*. London: Continuum.

Serres, M. (2019). *Hominescence*. London: Bloomsbury Publishing.

Thrift, N. (2005). *Knowing capitalism*. London: Sage Publications.

Tucker, I. M. (2018). Deleuze, Simondon and the problem of psychological life. *Annual Review of Critical Psychology Special Issue*, *14*, 127–144.

Tucker, I. M., Ellis, D., & Harper, D. (2012). Transformative processes of agency: Information technologies and the production of digitally mediated selves. *Culture and Society: Journal of Social Research*, *3*(1), 9–24.

Tucker, I. M., & Goodings, L. (2017). Digital atmospheres: Affective practices of care in Elefriends. *Sociology of Health and Illness*, *39*(4), 629–642.

Van Dijck, J. (2014). Datafication, dataism and dataveillance: Big Data between scientific paradigm and ideology. *Surveillance and Society*, *12*(2), 197–208.

Vannini, P. (2015). *Non-representational methodologies : Re-envisioning research*. London: Routledge.

Zuboff, S. (2019). *The age of surveillance capitalism: The fight for a human future at the new frontier of power*. New York, NY: Public Affairs.

7 Digital futures and emotion

Problematising emotional, affective, and digital life

This book has sought to draw attention to emotional and affective life in relation to the increasing digitisation of everyday life. This is a broad remit, and is one we approached through key areas in which questions as to the emotional and affective implications of digitisation are particularly prominent and requiring of social scientific analysis. Our aims have not been definitional nor singular. The processes that are labelled as emotion and affect are multiple, from non-conscious psychophysiological activity to social and cultural meaning-making through language. These processes operate as dimensions that span the contents and boundaries of individual bodies. Moreover, many disciplines have directed their explanatory power to attempt to capture, define, and categorise the multiplicity of emotional and affective life. Making sense of the entirety of this complex terrain is no insubstantial task, and it is one beyond the capacities of the current book. Our approach has been to articulate a philosophical orientation that remains *open* to notions of multiplicity in relation to emotional and affective life, which we think befits a social scientific approach that has been largely missing to date. This required resources from the philosophy of science in terms of highlighting notions of multiplicity in relation to forms of knowledge (e.g. Vinciane Despret) and philosophy and theory in relation to highlighting how mass datafication is creating new forms of psychosocial life (e.g. Gilbert Simondon).

Our *selective* approach to illuminate key areas of digitisation in relation to emotional and affective life sought to avoid essentialism and determinism. While discussing multiple categories of emotion, many of which relied on notions of universality, it was important for our analysis to frame *all* the models and categories reviewed as *versions* of emotion and/or affect, past or present. The concept of *version* operates as a form of critique, without demanding an alternative (i.e. better) model/theory/category to be offered. This was valuable, because while we did not set out to produce a descriptive *review* book, we did want to cover a range of areas (and the categories of emotion and affect therein) to map *a* terrain of current theory and practice. Having said that, our argument for a social scientific analysis is partially motivated by a need to provide a counter perspective to the increasingly dominant voice of the physical sciences in digital research and emotional and affective life. As highlighted in the introduction, the *shiny-ness* of new technologies can often blind the analytic gaze to underpinning theories and models. This book is one attempt to shine a light under the *theoretical bonnet* of contemporary emotion-related digital technologies.

The mass generation of data relating to emotion and affective processes (and beyond) operates in and through multiple speeds, rhythms, and flows. This makes an approach (or *version* of emotion) prioritising process over stasis valuable. Neither data, nor the bodies they are claimed to refer to, remain static. Motion is of prime concern. Moreover, data and bodies do not operate as distinct entities with pre-existing properties that determine their mode of operation in the world. Both transform through the movement and interaction that constitutes psychological and social life. Process philosophies (e.g. Simondon) have become an increasingly valuable resource for the social sciences to address the complexity and transformative operation of contemporary social worlds (Brown & Stenner, 2009; Stenner, 2017; Tucker, 2010). We are indebted to a philosophical orientation that emphasises the processes through which objects and subjects come to be. This is an alternative to setting out our analytic journey with a set of distinct objects and subjects whose operation in the world is understood as being reducible to properties inherent to them as individuals. Our approach has not been to piece together an analysis of emotional and affective life in a digital age through an ontology of forms with fixed properties, akin to pieces on a chess board. Instead, we have sought to interrogate the stakes for emotional and affective life in relation to the increased digitisation of life *with* notions of process and relationality and to recognise and embrace the provisionality and context-dependency that comes with such an approach.

As with many social scientific offerings, this book does not offer definitive solutions to the questions posed in the introduction, but does (hopefully) offer more informed problems than those set out at the beginning of the book. The pace of development of emotion-related digital technologies makes it difficult for research to keep up. This is a recognised problem in terms of the validation of new technologies, particularly in fields subject to regulatory systems, such as mental health care (Pickersgill, 2019). In this concluding chapter, we aim to offer some thoughts and reflections regarding digitisation and datafication in relation to emotional and affective life. The starting point is to highlight the breadth of technological focus on emotion. This is a relatively recent phenomenon, and one that appears likely to increase substantially in the years to come. Commercial interests are largely driving these moves, supported by a growing confidence (in industry particularly) that technologies can now recognise, interpret and potentially mimic emotional processes. Emotion remained on the periphery of computation for a long time, with the latter concerned to elevate itself to (or beyond) the level of human cognition and intelligence. While work on intelligence (in a traditional sense) continues, the idea that technologies can reliably inform as to how people feel has become the holy grail for industry. The advertising industry has been quick to try to capitalise this and has heavily invested in developing technologies wherein emotional data are promised to be of significant commercial value. For example, we have discussed examples of academic research institutes spinning off their work into tools for commercial use (e.g. Affectiva). One of the aims of this book was to address this point as part of the multiple ways in which emotion and affect are at stake in digitisation. It is not just the validity of the models of emotion underpinning emotion-focused technologies, it is also the emotional-affective impacts for bodies living in digitised environments. It may seem relatively harmless for advertisers to get data that do not always correctly identify whether an individual wants to purchase a product, but using data regarding micro-expressions to socially sort individuals at border control (i.e. iBorderCtrl) can have very serious ramifications for the freedom of movement for those individuals. This is a layer of reality that requires significant social scientific analysis, as it does not always feature in the physical science gaze on technologies.

Re-psychologising emotion and affect

The commodifying practices of digitisation place significant value on generating data regarding people's emotions. The advertising industry is unremittingly interested in knowing more about how people feel, to provide evermore personalised adverts (so-called digital capitalism at work), but government agencies, such as the security services, are also interested in how people feel and are being sold a story that affective technologies can offer objective *truths* in relation to how bodies are *really* feeling. In Chapter Three, we discussed the proliferation of emotional-AI technologies, which to date, have focused primarily on reducing emotion and affect to an expressive physiological level, e.g. generating data regarding micro-facial expressions. Such efforts amount to a de-psychologisation of emotion and affect, as only physiological data is deemed necessary to understand emotional and affective life. This is a simplified approach, but one that is coming to dominate digital approaches to emotion and affect. Throughout the book, we have sought to emphasise the need to (re)psychologise research and understanding regarding emotion and affect in a digital age. This involves (at least) two elements. Firstly, to interrogate the models and theories of emotion that underpin emotion-related technologies such as emotional AI. Secondly, to shine an analytic gaze on the psychological and social implications of living in data-saturated environments.

In Chapter Four, we focused on what we see as relatively impoverished psychological models of mind that are informing various industries and government agencies. In the social media context, *motivations* are usually researched as categories that are relatively internally-fixed cognitive psychological constructs. This has enabled computer scientists to develop social media landscapes that capitalise on capturing affective data pertaining to these categories. In this way, motivations are likely to be manufactured at the platforms' behest, rather than them denoting some inner need that social media has been developed to fulfil. What may have begun as a philanthropic endeavour is now aimed toward monetisation, potentially creating alienation, anxiety, and decreased mental health. Additionally, we have seen impoverished versions of *personality* put forward by computer scientists and companies (particularly Cambridge Analytica) who claim to be able to predict our personality type based upon social media activity. Social scientists and critical psychologists have, for over 50 years, contested trait theories of personality as being limiting and limited versions of human potentiality. However, trait theories have been *successful* because they offer seemingly eloquent versions of human psychology that are neatly packaged and easily configured by both humans and machine-learning algorithms. Additionally, emoticons, emojis and emotion-based text are commodifiable through such practices as sentiment analysis. Again, we have seen extremely poor models and conceptualisations of human affect and emotion-based activity derive from research in this area, wherein it is reduced to being either positive, negative, or neutral in most cases. This offers companies a dirty and quick insight into how products, for example, are being publicly experienced. No doubt this information is useful for brief and non-complex insights, but we must be very wary of using such technology in other contexts, such as wherein sentiment analysis informs policy, political decisions, and in more specific research domains, for example, obtaining insight into affective life online.

Chapter Five looked at ways that technology is being used in the mental health context, where peer-to-peer or robot-to-client support occurs. The mental and affective lives of individuals in these contexts face growing pressure to utilise digital technologies. When traditional psychotherapy is underfunded and unaffordable for individuals, reliance is turning to technology. We can have *a therapist in our pocket* in the form of a mobile phone app. Quite often, cognitive-behavioural approaches are offered through digitised therapy instead of human-to-human relational therapies. In-person therapy involves the sharing of experiences and intimate information, which has long been known in the psychotherapy context to facilitate healing processes. For example, psychoanalysts put forward the well-established and practiced use of psychical transference and countertransference – a phenomenon that occurs through the patient and client's relationship, which comes about through the psychophysicality of bodies in collision within the clinical space and context of the analyst's room. The precise working of the psychological and social dimensions of the therapeutic context are not fully known and as such trying to programme *therapy* into digital technologies remains at a provisional stage.

Chapter Six discussed how surveillance is increasingly attempting to obtain data on emotion, with psychological models still drawing on models of emotion as identifiable through microfacial expressions. Sociologists, developmental psychologists, and lay people are very aware of how versed humans are at hiding what we are feeling. We are taught from a very young age, in many cultures, to hide and dramatize emotion phenomena. Feelings are personal, and some would argue they should remain so. Even if technologies did exist that were able to relay insight into internal feelings, are these not some of the most private aspects of personal information? What right does anybody have of attempting to find out about your inner feelings and emotions (even if it were possible)? If Manfred Clynes was right (which we doubt) that a variety of human emotions (essentic forms), have unique signatures that can be garnered from a variety of parts of the body (such as the middle finger), should these be available for capture by those who have the means to do so? How do we consciously and cognitively give consent to such practices? Will we be caught out through a click-wrap at the end of a long contract stating that we will not have access to the technology unless we are prepared to click and consent to the capture and use of our emotional data? Presently, people are quite confused, it seems, as to what aspects of their selves can be captured, datafied, and processed for capitalisation or securitisation. We have argued that the techno-securitisation of everyday life has led to affective atmospheres of surveillance that give way to feelings and cultures of suspicion, anxiety, and paranoia. Others have decided that it is too complex and taxing to cognise the technological and moral complexity of everyday surveillance systems and the psychosocial impacts they have; therefore, it is psychologically beneficial to normalise and suppress their affectivities and psychically institute what we term *surveillance-apatheia.*

Re-psychologising the digitised community

Analysing experience involves understanding the relationships people have with themselves as subjects, as well as objects in others' worlds. A psychosocial approach constituted through dimensions of *relationality* and *processurality* renders psychological life as most fully understood by a study of the relations in and through which it emerges. This is a different perspective on emotion and affect than much psychophysiological emotion theory in relation to technologies. It is a more *expanded* view of emotion and affect as core to the way we relate to ourselves as bodies, as well as relate to social and collective life. It is this dual-relationality (of experience as a tension) that is central to Simondon's concept of affectivity. Much of the technological work discussed throughout the book has yet to enter the wider cultural consciousness in the form of public awareness. As noted in Chapter Six's focus on surveillance, people often are not aware of surveillance of data for the commercial ends of *big tech*. We continue to use search engines, communicate with social media, and use health trackers because they bring perceived benefits, but we rarely do so with the extent of data generation about our activities at the forefront of conscious awareness. This will no doubt change as people gain knowledge as to data generation practices. Increased knowledge and awareness will create new emotional and affective responses, which, in turn, will require new analysis.

Digitisation is creating new psychosocial ways of being through a huge rise in the connectedness of our social worlds. Notions of the social and collective are modified by datafication, which is changing traditional notions of the group as commonly defining the social. Data generated through interactions of bodies and technologies is creating new forms of collectivity, which are not formed though the coming together of multiple individual bodies. Data collectives emerge in relation to bodies, but take a digital form through aggregation. Data are becoming new mediators of the relationships between bodies and technologies through mass generation which comes *from* bodily activity as well as *shaping* subsequent experience. Data generation is increasingly focused on categorising physiological processes as relating to emotions as well as data having emotional and affective impacts on psychological and social life more broadly (i.e. when generation of data is not emotion focused). The emotional and affective stakes of digitisation are multi-dimensional and not only about data practices that are explicit in their focus on emotion. As technologies develop that can *read* more physiological data regarding bodily processes, the claims of scientists and industry regarding the emotional intelligence of technologies will grow. Pressure to accept, as veridical, the explanations and interpretations of industry-led developments will continue to increase. The social sciences need to retain a position of critique regarding the neo-behavioural tendencies of developments in emotional AI. Furthermore, claims that technologies can replicate and mimic emotional processes need to be analysed through a critical lens. Much of the work on digital forms of support in mental health operates on the premise that emotions, such as empathy and compassion, can either be programmed into technologies (e.g. chatbots) or enacted when communicating digitally (e.g. online forums). These raise questions as to the emotional and affective potential of human-technology relations.

Anticipating future emotional and digital lives

Practices of digitisation and datafication are too diverse and potentially far-reaching to offer a pithy summary end comment for this book. As already stated, we do know considerable (largely commercial) efforts are underway and planned to develop digital and technological versions of psychological processes, such as emotion recognition and personal relationships. We do not subscribe to a dystopian reading of these developments as signalling a line in the sand for human life, but do acknowledge that data generation from and relating to human, embodied activity is on an upward trajectory in terms of quantity and potentially quality. Not all data is of good quality – data scientists will attest to this – but improvements in quality will be sought. Part of the problem in relation to emotion is the sophistication of the algorithms designed to be emotionally skilled. Chapter Three demonstrated how much emotional-AI is based on problematic and overly-simplistic models of emotion. For so long as the underpinning models remain, any increased sophistication in digital recognition and categorisation will be hamstrung. In other areas, the emotional potential of digitisation will need to be tracked and analysed as developments progress. Digital technologies and data come to constitute relations we have with ourselves and with others. Chapters Four and Five demonstrated this in relation to social media (practices of emotional communication) and mental health (digital peer support and interacting with chatbots). Chapter Six considered datafication in terms of individuals' experiences in relation to digital practices of surveillance.

Throughout the book, we hope to have pointed to ways (past, present, and potentially future) that emotion and affective events and processes are central dimensions of psychological AND social life, which are intrinsically linked, rather than being two ontologically distinct entities. The thrust of the book is that digitisation is increasingly present in the everyday environments in which psychological and social life operates, and as such, is becoming ever more implicated in emotional and affective processes. In places, this is very explicit, e.g. emotional AI clearly stating it can accurately interpret emotional expressions. Elsewhere, it is more implicit, e.g. emotional responses to data generation. Some of the technologies we discussed are in early stages of development (e.g. mental health chatbots) and have not yet entered the mainstream. In such cases, our analysis is *anticipatory* in terms of considering their implications for future psychosocial life. Indeed, this book has only scratched the surface of understanding emotion in a digital age. We do though have some recommendations for future research in the area:

- Social scientific research is vitally important for insight regarding emotional and affective implications of digital life. The physical sciences have a strong position in the area due to their technological expertise, but it is pivotal that social scientific analysis retains a strong analytic voice. There are several reasons for this: Ensuring the appropriateness of models of emotion and affect recruited from the social sciences by physical sciences; the need to highlight how new digital (and data) practices intersect with existing psychological and social processes (and potentially disrupt them); and analysing digitisation and datafication as social artefacts and practices
- Empirically-grounded theory development is important. Affect studies has proven very successful in terms of the breadth and depth of use of theories of affect in the social sciences, cultural studies, and critical theory. Considerable insight has emerged pertaining to intensities, feelings, and pre-emotional states without propagating essentialist or reductionist modes of thought. However, a focus on *experience* is absent in much affect theory, particularly in terms of including empirical studies (qualitative or quantitative). We argue for more empirical focus on the experiences of living in digitised and datafied environments, which can inform existing and future theory development (e.g. in affect studies and the broader emotion literature).
- Although funding often determines the direction of research, it is important that it is not dominated by industry-led concerns, but should equally, if not chiefly, concern the psychosocial wellbeing of humans and other animals.
- Finally, it is important to avoid becoming caught up in the digital determinism doctrine, namely that digitisation is inevitable and progressive and will lead to better lives. As we saw, highlighting the impact of technologies on emotion is not new, and therefore, the increased digital presence in life is not, by definition, a new concern. Societal concerns have emerged in relation to all mass media developments (e.g. cinema).

Keeping these recommendations in mind, as we anticipate future emotional and affective life as emerging in concert with digital practices, is a valuable way to retain a critical lens through which to gain theoretical and empirical insight regarding the diversity of emotional and affect experience enacted in a digital age. Our final word is about our title. *Emotion in the Digital Age* works because it is marketable (and was the preferred title of the publisher, although we also use *a digital age* in places). However, we are aware of the danger of referring to an *age*, namely that it opens up the (likely) possibility of a *ready-made* critique in the form of suggesting a *post-digital age*. This is already happening (albeit without explicit focus on emotion and/or affect). The underlying practices and processes do not cease, and as mentioned, it is the focus on practices, as opposed to defining an age, that remains important.

References

Brown, S. D., & Stenner, P. (2009). *Psychology without foundations: History, philosophy and psychosocial theory.* London: Sage.

Pickersgill, M. (2019). Digitising psychiatry? Sociotechnical expectations, performative nominalism and biomedical virtue in (digital) psychiatric praxis. *Sociology of Health and Illness, 41*(S1), 16–30.

Stenner, P. (2017). *Liminality and experience: A transdisciplinary approach to the psychosocial.* London: Palgrave Macmillan.

Tucker, I. (2010). Space, process philosophy and mental distress. *The International Journal of Interdisciplinary Social Sciences, 4*(11), 165–174.

Index

For Product Safety Concerns and Information please contact our EU
representative GPSR@taylorandfrancis.com
Taylor & Francis Verlag GmbH, Kaufingerstraße 24, 80331 München, Germany